Thomas Wright, William Langland

The Vision and Creed of Piers Ploughman

Volume 1

Thomas Wright, William Langland

The Vision and Creed of Piers Ploughman
Volume 1

ISBN/EAN: 9783337117290

Printed in Europe, USA, Canada, Australia, Japan

Cover: Foto ©Raphael Reischuk / pixelio.de

More available books at **www.hansebooks.com**

THE VISION AND CREED

OF

PIERS PLOUGHMAN.

EDITED,

FROM A CONTEMPORARY MANUSCRIPT,

WITH A HISTORICAL INTRODUCTION,

NOTES, AND A GLOSSARY,

BY THOMAS WRIGHT, M.A. F.S.A. &c.

Corresponding Member of the Imperial Institute of France,
Académie des Inscriptions et Belles-Lettres.

IN TWO VOLUMES.

VOL. I.

SECOND AND REVISED EDITION.

LONDON:
REEVES AND TURNER, 196 STRAND.
1887.

PREFACE TO THE SECOND EDITION.

IT is now thirteen years since the first edition of the following text of this important poem was published by the late Mr. Pickering, during which time the study of our old literature and history has undergone considerable development, and it is believed that a reprint at a more moderate price would be acceptable to the public. Holding still the same opinion which he has always held with regard to the superior character of the manuscript from which this text was taken, the editor has done no more than carefully reprint it, but, in order to make it as useful as he could, he has revised and made additions to both the Notes and the Glossary.

The remarkable poem of The Vision of Piers Ploughman is not only so interesting a monument of the English language and literature, but it is also so important an illustration of the political history of our country during the fourteenth century, that it deserves to be read far more generally than it has been, and the editor will rejoice sincerely if he should have contributed by this new edition to render it more popular, and place it within the reach of a greater number of readers. Independent of its historical and literary importance, it contains many beauties which will fully repay the slight labour required to master its partially obsolete language, and, as one of the purest works in the English tongue as it existed during the century in which it was composed, it is to be hoped that, when the time shall at length arrive when English antiquities and English philology and literary history are at length to be made a part of the studies in our universities and in the higher classes of our schools, the work of the Monk of Malvern, as a link between the poetry and language of the Anglo-Saxon and those of modern England, will be made a prominent text-book.

THOMAS WRIGHT.

14, SYDNEY STREET, BROMPTON,
Nov. 1855.

THE History of the Middle Ages in England, as in other countries, represents to us a series of great consecutive political movements, co-existent with a similar series of intellectual revolutions in the mass of the people. The vast mental development caused by the universities in the twelfth century led the way for the struggle to obtain religious and political liberty in the thirteenth. The numerous political songs of that period which have escaped the hand of time, and above all the mass of satirical ballads against the Church of Rome, which commonly go under the name of Walter Mapes, are remarkable monuments of the intellectual history of our forefathers. Those ballads are written in Latin; for it was the most learned class of the community which made the first great stand against the encroachments and corruptions of the papacy and the increasing influence of the monks. We know that the struggle alluded to was historically unsuccessful. The baronial wars ended in the entire destruction of the popular leaders; but their cause did not expire at Evesham; they had laid foundations which no storm could overthrow, not placed hastily on the uncertain surface of popular favour, but fixed deeply in the public mind. The barons, who had fought so often and so staunchly for the great charter, had lost their power; even the learning of the universities had faded under the withering grasp of monachism; but the remembrance of the old contest remained, and what was more, its literature was left, the songs which had spread abroad the principles for which, or against which, Englishmen had fought, carried them down (a precious legacy) to their posterity. Society itself had undergone an important change; it was no longer a feudal aristocracy which held the destinies of the country in its iron hand. The plant which had been cut off took root again in another (a healthier) soil; and the intelligence which had lost its force in the higher ranks of society began to spread itself among the commons. Even in the thirteenth century, before the close of the baronial wars, the complaints so vigorously expressed in the Latin songs, had begun, both in England and France, to appear in the language of the people. Many of the satirical poems of Rutebeuf and other contemporary writers against the monks, are little more than translations of the Latin poems which go under the name of Walter Mapes.

During the successive reigns of the first three Edwards, the public mind in England was in a state of constant fermentation. On the one hand, the monks, supported by the popish church, had become an incubus upon the country. Their corruptness and immorality were notorious: the description of their vices given in the satirical writings of the thirteenth and fourteenth centuries exceeds even the bitterest calumnies of the age of Rabelais or the reports of the commissioners of Henry the Eighth.[1] The populace, held in awe by the imposing appearance of the popish church, and by the religious belief which had been instilled into them from their infancy, were opposed to the monks and clergy by a multitude of personal griefs and jealousies : these frequently led to open hostility, and in the chronicles of those days we read of the slaughter of monks, and the burning of abbeys, by the insurgent towns-people or peasantry. At the same time, while the monks in revenge treated the commons with contempt, there were numerous people who, under the name of Lollards and other such appellations,—led sometimes by the love of mischief and disorder, but more frequently by religious enthusiasm,—whose doctrines were simple and reasonable (although the church would fain have branded them all with the title of heretics),—went abroad among the people preaching not only against the corruptions of the monks, but against the most vital doctrines of the church of Rome, and, as might be expected, they found abundance of listeners. On the other hand, a new political system, and the embarrassments of a continued series of foreign wars, were adding to the general ferment. Instead of merely calling together the great feudal barons to lead their retainers to battle, the king was now obliged to appeal more directly to the people ; and at the same time the latter began to feel the weight of taxation, and conse-

---

[1] See the "Apocalypsis Goliæ" and other pieces in the poems of Walter Mapes; the Order of Fair Ease in the Political Songs, and the Poems of Rutebeuf; and, in English, the remarkable "Poem on the Evil Times of Edward II." in the appendix to the Political Songs. The Poem entitled the Order of Fair Ease bears some resemblance to the *Abbaye de Thélème* of Rabelais.

quently they began to talk of the defects and the corruptions of the government, and to raise the cries, which have since so often been heard, against the king's "evil advisers." These cries were justified by many real and great oppressions under which the commons, and more particularly the peasantry, suffered ; and (as the king and aristocracy were too much interested in the continuance of the abuses complained of to be easily induced to agree to an effective remedy), the commons began to feel that their own interests were equally opposed to those of the church, of the aristocracy, and of the crown, and amidst the other popular doctrines none were more loudly or more violently espoused than those of levellers and democrats. These, though comparatively few, aggravated the evil, by affording a pretence for persecution. The history of England during the fourteenth century is a stirring picture ; its dark side is the increasing corruption of the popish church ; its bright side, the general spread of popular intelligence, and the firm stand made by the commons in the defence of their liberties, and in the determination to obtain a redress of grievances.

Under these circumstances appeared PIERS PLOUGHMAN. It is not to be supposed that all the other classes of society were hostile to the commons. The people, with the characteristic attachment of the Anglo-Saxons to the family of their princes, wished to believe that their king was always their friend, when not actuated by the counsels of his " evil advisers ; " [2] several of the most powerful barons

---

[2] This sentiment was perpetuated in a numerous class of ballads, in which the monarch is represented as thrown incognito among the lower classes, as

stood forward as the champions of popular liberty; and many of the monks quitted their monasteries to advocate the cause of the reformation. It appears to be generally agreed that a monk was the author of the poem of Piers Ploughman; but the question, one perhaps but of secondary importance, as to its true writer, is involved in much obscurity.[3] Several local allusions and other circumstances

---

listening to their expressions of loyalty and to the tale of their sufferings. See the "Tale of King Edward and the Shepherd" in Hartshorne's *Ancient Metrical Tales;* "The King and the Barker," in Ritson's *Pieces of Ancient Popular Poetry;* "The King and the Miller," and "King Edward IV. and the Tanner of Tamworth," in *Percy's Reliques;* &c. The earliest known form of this tale is the story of "Henry II. and the Cistercian Abbot," printed from Giraldus Cambrensis in the *Reliquiæ Antiquæ*, vol. ii. p. 147.

3 It was at least a tradition early in the sixteenth century (for we have no means now of ascertaining whether there were any substantial grounds for the statement), that the author was named Robert Longlande (or Langlande), that he was born at Cleobury Mortimer in Shropshire, and that (after receiving his education at Oxford) he became a monk of Malvern. I do not think, with Tyrwhitt and Price, that the name *Wil*, given in the poem to the dreamer, necessarily shows that the writer's name was *William;* and still less that the mention of "Kytte my wif" and "Calote my doghter" (p. 395 of the present volume), and of the dreamer's having resided at Cornhill, refer to the family and residence of the author of the poem. If he were a monk (as appears probable by his intimate acquaintance with the Scriptures and the Fathers), he would not be married. Sir Frederick Madden discovered a very important entry in a hand of the fifteenth century on the fly-leaf of a manuscript of Piers Ploughman in the library of Trinity College, Dublin, to the following effect—" Memorandum, quod Stacy de Rokayle, pater Willielmi de Langlond, qui Stacius fuit generosus, et morabatur in Schiptone under Whicwode, teneus domini Le Spenser in comitatu Oxon., qui prædictus Willielmus fecit librum qui vocatur Perys Ploughman."—It would perhaps be not impossible to trace the name and history of this Stacy de Rokayle; but till that be done, I do not think this memorandum ought to be considered as overthrowing the old tradition relating to Robert Longlande. It may be mentioned as a remarkable specimen of the patriotism of David Buchanan, that he lays claim to the author of Piers Ploughman as a Scotchman:—"Robertus Langland, natione Scotus, professione sacerdos, vir ex obscuris ortus parentibus, pius admodum et ingeniosus et zelo divinæ gloriæ plenus; inter monachos Benedictinos educatus in civitate Aberdonensi, vir æque erat in omni humaniore literatura insigniter doctus, et in medicina admodum

seem to prove that it was composed on the borders of
Wales, where had originated most of the great political
struggles, and we can hardly doubt that its author resided
in the neighbourhood of "Malverne hilles." We have
less difficulty in ascertaining its date. At ll. 1735–1782,
we have, without doubt, an allusion to the treaty of
Bretigny, in 1360, and to the events which preceded it:
in the earlier part of this passage there is an allusion to
the sufferings of the English army in the previous winter
campaign, to the retreat which followed, and the want
of provisions which accompanied it, and to the tempest
which they encountered near Chartres (the "dym cloude"
of the poem). The "pestilences" mentioned at l. 2497
were the great plague which happened in 1348–9 (and
which had previously been alluded to in the opening of
the poem, l. 168), and that of 1361–2,—the first two of
the three great pestilences which devastated our island
in the fourteenth century. The south-western wind,
mentioned in l. 2500, occurred on the fifteenth day of
January 1362. It is probable that the poem of Piers
Ploughman was composed in the latter part of this
year, when the effects of the great wind were fresh in
people's memory, and when the treaty of Bretigny had
become a subject of popular discontent.[4]

clarus, plum opus sermone vulgare scripsit cui imposuit, ǁ Visionem Petri Aratoris,
lib. 1. ǁ Pro conjugio sacerdotum, lib. 1. | Claruit anno Christi Redemptoris, 1369.
Regnante Davide Secundo in Scotia."—Dav. Buchanan, *de Scriptoribus Scotis. MS.
Bibl. Univ. Edin.*

[4] We may mention another historical allusion in Piers Ploughman, which
seems to involve a chronological difficulty; the dry April in the mayoralty of
John Chichester, l. 8567. It appears clear that this is an allusion to a remarkable drought in the year 1351, which answers precisely to a calculation of the

The poem was given to the world under a name which could not fail to draw the attention of the people. Amid the oppressive injustice of the great and the vices of their idle retainers, the corruptions of the clergy, and the dishonesty which too frequently characterised the dealings of merchants and traders, the simple unsophisticated heart of the ploughman is held forth as the dwelling of virtue and truth. It was the ploughman, and not the pope with his proud hierarchy, who represented on earth the Saviour who had descended into this world as the son of the carpenter, who had lived a life of humility, who had wandered on foot or ridden on an ass. "While God wandered on earth," says one of the political songs of the beginning of the fourteenth century,[5] "what was the reason that he would not ride?" The answer expresses the whole force of the popular sentiment of the age: "because he would not have a retinue of greedy attendants by his side, in the shape of grooms and servants, to insult and oppress the peasantry."

At the period when this poem was first published, England, in common with the rest of Europe, had been struck with a succession of calamities. Little more than twelve years had passed since a terrible pestilence had swept away perhaps not less than one-half of the popula-

---

date given in the text, in which all the manuscripts that I have consulted agree But the only year in which Chichester is said to have been mayor was 1368-0 according to some, or 1369-70 according to others. Stowe (as quoted in the note on this passage) has altered the text of Piers Ploughman to suit the year in which Chichester is known to have been mayor: yet there can be little doubt (even from the allusion to the treaty of Bretigny) that the poem itself was composed before that date, and therefore the same or another Chichester had probably been mayor before.

[5] Political Songs, p. 240.

tion.[6] The lower classes, ill fed and neglected, perished by thousands, while the higher ranks—the proud and pampered nobility—escaped ; "he who was ill nourished with unsubstantial food," says a contemporary writer, "fell before the slightest breath of the destroyer ; to the poor, death was welcome, for life is to them more cruel than death. But death respected princes, nobles, knights, judges, gentlemen ; of these few die, because their life is one of enjoyment."[7] It was the general belief that this fearful visitation had been sent by God as a punishment

---

6 This terrible calamity was said by the astrologers to have been brought about by an extraordinary conjunction of Saturn with the other planets, which happened scarcely once in a thousand years. An astrologer and physician, who witnessed its effects, Symon de Covino, has left a Latin poem on the subject under the title *De Judicio Solis in Conviviis Saturni*, in which he describes Saturn as indulging his malevolence towards the human race by obtaining a judgment against men for their sins. This opinion is alluded to in Piers Ploughman, l. 4453,

> "And so seide Saturne,
> And sente yow to warne."

The influence of this planet was represented by astrologers as being peculiarly noxious, as is expressed in the following old distich:—

> " Jupiter atque Venus boni, Saturnusque malignus,
> Sol et Mercurius cum Luna sunt mediocres."

7 " Qui male pastus erat fragili virtute ciborum,
> Labitur exiguo percussus flamine cladis ;
> Indeque Saturni vulgus, pauperrima turba,
> Grata morte cadunt, quia vivere talibus est mors.
> Post quos lunares pereunt et mercuriales,
> Et sic debilior succumbit in ordine primo ;
> Post alii tandem pestem secuntur eamdem.
> Sed dea principibus et nobilibus, generosis,
> Militibus, seu judicibus fera Parca pepercit.
> Raro cadunt tales, quia talibus est data vita
> Dulcis in hoc mundo, quam gloria laudat inanis."
>> *Symon de Covino*, in the *Bibliothèque de l'Ecole des Chartes*, tom. ii. p. 236.

for the sins which had more particularly characterised the higher orders of society ; yet instead of profiting by the warning, they became, during the years which followed, prouder, more cruel and oppressive, and more licentious, than before. Another pestilence came, which visited the classes that had before escaped, and at the same time a tempest such as had seldom been witnessed seemed to announce the vengeance of heaven. The streets and roads were filled with zealots who preached and prophesied of other misfortunes, to people who had scarcely recovered from the terror of those which were past. At this moment the satirist stepped forth, and laid open with unsparing knife the sins and corruptions which provoked them.

From what has been said, it will be seen that the Latin poems attributed to Walter Mapes, and the Collection of Political Songs, form an introduction to the Vision of Piers Ploughman. It seems clear that the writer was well acquainted with the former, and that he not unfrequently imitates them. The Poem on the Evil Times of Edward II. already alluded to (in the Political Songs) contains within a small compass all his chief points of accusation against the different orders of society. But a new mode of composition had been brought into fashion since the appearance of the famous " Roman de la Rose," and the author makes his attacks less directly, under an allegorical clothing. The condition of society is revealed to the writer in a dream, as in the singular poem just mentioned, and as in the still older satire, the *Apocalypsis Goliæ;* but in Piers Ploughman the allegory follows no systematic plot, it is rather a succession of pictures in which the allegorical painting sometimes disappears altogether, than a whole like the Roman de la Rose, and it is on that account less tedious to the modern reader, while the vigorous descriptions, the picturesque ideas, and numerous other beauties of different kinds, cause us to lose sight of the general defects of this class of writings.

Piers Ploughman is, in fact, rather a succession of dreams, than one simple vision. The dreamer, weary of the world, falls asleep beside a stream amid the beautiful scenery of Malvern Hills. In his vision, the people of the world are represented to him by a vast multitude assembled in a fair meadow ; on one side stands the tower of Truth, elevated on a mountain, the right aim of man's pilgrimage, while on the other side is the dungeon of Care, the dwelling place of Wrong. In the first sections (*passus*) of the poem are pictured the origin of society, the foundation and dignity of kingly power, and the separation into different classes and orders. In the midst of his astonishment at what he sees, a fair lady, the personification of "holy church," approaches, to instruct the dreamer. She explains to him the meaning of the different objects which had presented themselves to his view, and shows by exhortations and examples the merit of content and moderation, the danger of disobedience (exemplified in the story of Lucifer's fall), and the efficacy of love and charity. In the midst of his conversation with his instructor, a lady makes her appearance on the scene. This is lady Mede, the personification of that mistaken object at which so large a portion of mankind direct their aim—the origin of most of the corruptions and evil deeds in the world—not the just remuneration of our actions which we look forward to in a future life, but the reward which is sought by those who set all their hopes on the present. Holy Church now quits the dreamer, who is left to observe what is taking place amid the crowd in the field. (*Passus II.*) They all pay their court to lady Mede, who, by the intermediation of Cyvyle, or the law, is betrothed in marriage to Falsehood. The marriage is forbidden by Theology, and Cyvyle agrees to carry the cause to London for judgment, contrary to the desire of Simony. Falsehood and Flattery bribe the lawyers to aid the former in his suit, but their designs are baffled by Conscience, at whose suggestion the king takes the lady into his own custody, and drives away Falsehood and his greedy followers. Mede soon finds favour at court (*Passus III.*), and especially with the friars, who are ready to absolve her of all her sins for a proper consideration. The king proposes to marry her to Conscience; who, however, declines the match, and as a reason for his refusal gives a very unfavourable picture of the lady's previous life and private character. Mede defends herself, and accuses Conscience of thwarting and opposing the will and designs of kings and great people. The dispute becoming hot, the king interferes and orders Mede and Conscience to be reconciled and kiss each other. (*Passus IV.*) This Conscience refuses to do, unless by the advice of Reason; on whose arrival, Peace comes into the parliament to make his complaint against the cruel oppressions of Wrong. Wrong is condemned, but Mede and the lawyers attempt to get him off with the payment of a sum of money. The king, however, allows himself to be guided by Reason and Conscience, expresses his dissatisfaction that law is influ-

enced by Mede, and his determination to govern his
realm by the counsel of Reason.

In a second vision (*Passus V.*), the dreamer is again
carried to the "field full of folk," where Reason has taken
upon himself the character of a preacher, and, fortified with
the king's authority, induces the various classes of sinners
to confess and repent.   The personification of the different
sins forms perhaps the most remarkable part of the whole
poem.   The multitude being thus converted from their
evil courses, are persuaded by Repentance and Hope to set
out on a pilgrimage in search of Truth.   In their ignorance
of the path which they must follow in this search, they
apply to a palmer who had wandered over a large portion
of the world in search of different saints; but they find
him as little acquainted with the way as themselves.
They are helped out of this dilemma by Piers the Ploughman, who, seeing them terrified by the difficulties of the
road, offers to be their guide, if they will wait till he has
sown his half acre. (*Passus VI.*) In the mean time all
the pilgrims who have strength and skill, are employed on
some useful works, except the knight, who undertakes,
in return for the support which he is to derive from the
ploughman's labours, to watch and protect him against
plunderers and foreign enemies. The peace of the labourers
is first disturbed by Waster, who refuses to perform the
conditions by which the others are bound : the aid of the
knight being found inefficient against this turbulent gen-
tleman, the Ploughman is obliged to send for Hunger, who
effectually humbles him.   This section of the poem is a
continued allusion to the effects of the famine and pestilence, and a satire upon the luxurious and extravagant life

of our forefathers in the fourteenth century. (*Passus VII.*) Truth, hearing of the intentions of Piers the Ploughman to leave his labours in order to serve as a guide to the pilgrims in their journey, sends him a messenger, exhorting him to remain at home and continue his labours, and giving him a " pardon " which was to embrace all those who aided him honestly, by their works, and who should carry on their various avocations in purity of heart. The writer here takes occasion to sneer at the " pardons " of the pope, then so much in vogue ; a priest questions the legitimacy of Piers' bull of pardon, and the altercation between them becomes so loud that the dreamer awakes. The pardon of Piers Ploughman is granted to those who do good works : the dreamer is lost in the speculation on the question as to what the good works are, and he becomes engaged in a new pilgrimage, in search of a person who has not appeared before,—Do-well.

(*Passus VIII.*) All his inquiries after Do-well are fruitless : even the friars, to whom he addresses himself, give but a confused account ; and, weary with wandering about, the dreamer is again overtaken by slumber. Thought now appears to him, and recommends him to Wit, who describes to him the residence of Do-well, Do-better, and Do-best, and enumerates their companions and attendants. (*Passus IX.*) The Castle of Do-well is an allegorical representation of man (the individual), in which lady Anima (the soul) is placed for safety, and guarded by a keeper named Kynde (nature). With Do-well, the representative of those who live according to truth in honest wedlock, are contrasted the people who live in lust and wickedness, the descendants of the murderer Cain, who

was begotten by Adam in an evil hour. (*Passus X.*) Wit
has a wife named lady Study, who is angry that her spouse
should lay open his high truths to those who are unini-
tiated—it is no better than "throwing pearls to swine,
which would rather have hawes." Wit is daunted by his
wife's long lecture, and leaves the dreamer to pursue his
own suit. This he does with so much meekness and
humility, that the wrath of dame Study is appeased, and
she sends him to Clergy, with a token of recommendation
from herself. Clergy receives the pilgrim, and entertains
him with a long declamation on the character of Do-well,
Do-better, and Do-best, and on the corruptions of the
church and the monkish orders, in the course of which is
uttered the remarkable prophecy of the king who was to
" confess and beat " the monks, and give them an " incurable knock," which was after less than two centuries so
exactly fulfilled in the dissolution of the monasteries.
The wanderer confesses himself "little the wiser" for
Clergy's lecture, and by his pertness of reply merits a
reproof from Scripture. (*Passus XI.*) In another vision
the dreamer is exposed to the seductions of Fortune,
whose two fair damsels, Concupiscentiacarnis and Co-
vetousness-of-the Eyes, persuade him to enjoy the present
moment, and lead him entirely from his previous pursuit.
He is only recalled from his error by the approach of Old
Age, and then he falls into the contemplation of a series of
subjects, the covetousness of the friars who gave absolu-
tion from motives of personal interest, predestination, &c.
Then Kynde, or Nature, came and carried him to a mountain, which represented the world, and there showed him
how all other animals but man followed Reason ; and

Imaginative came after, and told him that all his present doubt and anxiety had been brought upon him for contending with Reason and suffering himself to be led astray by Fortune. (*Passus XII.*) The whole of the next section of the poem is occupied with a long exhortation by Imaginative, concerning God's chastisements, the merits of Charity and Mercy, the greater responsibility before God of those who are learned and cannot sin ignorantly, the difficulty for the rich man to enter heaven.

(*Passus XIII.*) In another vision, Conscience meets with the dreamer, and takes him to dine with Clergy. Patience comes to the feast in beggar's weeds, but is seated in the most honourable place at the table. A doctor of the church is of the party, and distinguishes himself by his gluttony; and by discussing theological questions after dinner. At length Conscience and Patience go on a pilgrimage. In their way they meet with a minstrel, named Activa Vita, or Haukyn the Active-man, with a coat covered with spots of dirt, whom they question on his mode of life. (*Passus XIV.*) Haukyn the Active-man, the representative of that class of people who neglect their souls for their worldly affairs, excuses the dirtiness of his apparel on the ground that he has none to change, and that he has too many occupations to allow him time to have it cleaned. Conscience and Patience teach him a method to clean his coat, inform him where charity is to be found, and recommend patient poverty to him, showing him the advantage of poverty over riches. Haukyn's repentance and lamentation for the neglect of his duties awake the dreamer.

(*Passus XV.*) Amid his anxiety to know something

more certain of Do-well, the dreamer has another vision, in which Soul appears to him, and enters into a long relation of the corruptions and negligence of the clergy. (*Passus XVI.*) Soul finally sends him to Piers the Ploughman, who possesses the garden in which the tree of Charity grows, and which is rented under him by Free-will. Piers explains to him the nature of the tree, and of the props which support it ; and shakes down some of the fruit for him. The allegory then changes, and we are introduced to the birth and passion of the Saviour, as arising out of the fruit of Charity. At this moment the dreamer awakes, and therewith loses sight of Piers the Ploughman; in his anxiety to find Piers, he meets with Faith, in the garb of Abraham, who was in search of God, now incarnate, and who waited for his passion in order to be delivered from hell. (*Passus XVII.*) Then comes Spes, or Hope, who also was in search of the knight that was to vanquish the evil one. As they go along the way towards Jerusalem to the "justes," discoursing on the obligations of the old and new law and the abrogation of the former, they meet with a man who had been left helpless by thieves, wounded and naked : Faith and Hope passed by without helping him, but the Samaritan, who was also riding to the "justes," descended from his horse, bound his wounds, and deposited him in an inn at the grange named *Lex Christi.* The Samaritan gives the dreamer a singular explanation of the mysteries of the Trinity ; and, after having represented to him the heinousness of sins against the different persons, and the necessity of making reparation, he pursues his way to Jerusalem.

(*Passus XVIII.*) The vision which forms the eighteenth

section or *passus*, and in which the character of Piers the Ploughman is identified with that of the Saviour, is entirely occupied with an allegorical description of Christ's Passion, and his descent into Hell. (*Passus XIX.*) In the next section the history of Christ's passion and victory, and his figurative representative Piers the Ploughman, is continued. Grace, through Piers the Ploughman, descends upon the people, and lays the foundation of the Church, which is cultivated by Piers with his four oxen (the four Evangelists). Piers is attacked by Pride, who gathers a great host to assail the Church. Conscience advises the people who follow Piers (the Church), to take shelter in the stronghold of Unity, and make preparations for their defence. By the counsel of Kind-wit and Conscience they dig a great ditch around Unity. The measures of Surety are embarrassed by the unreasonable opposition of some members or parts of the community, who oppose Pier's doctrine of restitution—the brewer will not repent of the tricks which he puts on his customers, the vicar adheres to his simony, the lord will continue to oppress his tenants, and the king will not be restrained by his laws. (*Passus XX.*) In the last section of the poem, the dreamer, after having been accosted by Need, who preaches on the virtues of temperance, has a vision of Antichrist, who comes to attack the Castle of Unity. It must be remembered that at this period many people supposed that Antichrist was already on the earth, and that he was the cause of all the evils with which mankind was then visited, so that this last notion brought the allegory home to people's feelings. The standard-bearer of Antichrist was Pride. Conscience called Kynde, or Nature, to his aid, who brought an army

of diseases and pestilences.   Death, one of his chief sol-
diers, made terrible havoc.   At length Kynde ceased his
ravages; and a horde of enemies immediately arose against
Conscience, such as Fortune, Lechery, Covetousness,
Simony.   Life, with his mistress Fortune, indulged in all
kinds of excess, until he was visited by Age and Despair,
who treated him very roughly.   The dreamer, forsaken
by Fortune, and participating in the misfortunes of Life,
by the advice of Kynde takes shelter with Conscience in
the castle of Unity, which is threatened by an army of
priests and monks.   At length this stronghold is endan-
gered by the entrance of Flattery, who is admitted in the
disguise of a Physician.   Conscience, unable to retain
possession, embarks upon another pilgrimage in search of
Piers the Ploughman, and the dreamer awakes.   This is
the conclusion of the poem.   Whitaker thought that it
should have had a more consoling end; but it must be
remembered that the writer of Piers Ploughman designed
to paint the world as it was, and to describe the numerous
obstacles which lay in the way of the improvement and
amelioration of mankind when he wrote.

While one member of the monastic order was thus
contributing by his satirical pen towards producing a re-
form among his countrymen, another monk was beginning
to preach in a still bolder manner against the popish
system.   This was John Wycliffe, under whom the despised
lollards became an important sect.   This attempt at religious reformation only formed part of the great movement
of the fourteenth century, which soon afterwards broke
out in the popular commotions of the reign of Richard II.
The writer of Piers Ploughman was neither a sower of

sedition, nor one who would be characterised by his contemporaries as a heretic. The doctrines inculcated throughout the book are so far from democratic, that he constantly preaches the Christian doctrine of obedience to rulers. Yet its tendency to debase the great, and to raise the commons in public consideration, must have rendered it popular among the latter: and, although no single important doctrine of the popish religion is attacked, yet the unsparing manner in which the vices and corruptions of the church are laid open, must have helped in no small degree the cause of the Reformation. Of the ancient popularity of Piers Ploughman we have a proof in the great number of copies which still exist, most of them written in the latter part of the fourteenth century; and the circumstance that the manuscripts are seldom executed in a superior style of writing, and scarcely ever ornamented with painted .initial letters, may perhaps be taken as a proof that they were not written for the higher classes of society. From the time when it was published, the name of Piers Ploughman became a favourite among the popular reformers.[8] The earliest instance of the adoption of that

---

[8] We have a very remarkable proof of the popularity of Piers Ploughman with the lower orders (among whom probably parts of it were repeated by memory), and of its influence on the insurrections of the peasantry in the reign of Richard II., in the seditious letter of John Ball to the commons of Essex, preserved by Thomas Walsingham (*Hist. Angl.* p. 275). I am not sure if "John *Schep*" may not contain an allusion to the opening of the poem; but the second passage, here printed in Italics, refers evidently to Passus VI. and VII., and the third is an allusion to the characters of Do-well and Do-best.

"John *Schep* sometime Seint Mary priest of Yorke, and now of Colchester, graeteth well John Namelesse, and John the Miller, and John Carter, and biddeth them that they beware of guyle in borough, and stand together in Gods name, and biddeth *Piers Plowman goe to his werke*, and chastise well Hob the robber, and take with you John Trewman, and all his fellows, and no moe.

name for another satirical work is found in the Creed of
Piers Ploughman, printed also in the present volume, and
in which even the form of verse of the Vision is imitated.

In this latter poem, which was undoubtedly written by
a Wycliffite, Piers Ploughman is no longer an allegorical
personage—he is the simple representative of the peasant
rising up to judge and act for himself—the English *sans-
culotte* of the fourteenth century, if we may be allowed
the comparison. When it was written, a period of great
excitement had passed since the age of Langlande, the
reputed author of the Vision—a period characterised by
the turbulence of the peasantry—which had witnessed
in France the fearful insurrection of the *Jacquerie*, and
in England the rebellion of Wat Tyler and Jack Straw.[9]

In Piers Ploughman's Creed it is the church simply, and
not the state, which is the object of attack. The clergy—
and more particularly the monks—are accused of having
falsified religion, and of being actuated solely by worldly
passions—pride, covetousness, self-love. The writer,
placing himself in the position of one who has just learnt
the first grounds of religious knowledge, is anxious to find
a person capable of instructing him in his creed, and with
this object he addresses himself to the different orders of

John the Miller hath y-ground, smal, small, small. The kings sonne of heaven
shal pay for all. Beware or ye be woe, know your frende fro your foe, Have
ynough, and say hoe: And *do well and better*, and flee sinne, and seeke peace and
holde you therin, and so biddeth John Trewman and all his fellowes."

9 The mention of Wycliffe and of Walter Brute and other circumstances, fix the
date of Piers Ploughman's Creed with tolerable certainty in the latter years of
the reign of Richard II. It was probably written very soon after the year 1393,
the date of the persecution of Walter Brute at Hereford; and from the particular
allusion to that person we may perhaps suppose that like the Vision it was written
on the Borders of Wales.

friars. He applies first to the Minorites, who abuse the
Carmelites, and pride themselves in their own holiness.
Disgusted with their jealousies and self-sufficiency, the
inquirer seeks the Preachers, or Dominicans; amid their
stately buildings, and under their sleek and well filled
skins, he finds the same want of Christian charity : their
pride drives him to the order of St. Austin. The Austin
Friars, as well as the Carmelites, will only instruct him for
money, and, shocked at their covetousness, he continues
his wanderings, until at last he meets with a poor Ploughman, in whom he finds the charity and knowledge after
which he has been seeking. The Ploughman enters into
a bitter attack on the vices of all the four orders of friars :
he describes their spirit of persecution, exemplified in the
case of Wycliffe and others, and their simony; speaks
of Wycliffe and Walter Brute as preachers of the truth;
and finishes by teaching the inquirer his simple creed.

The Creed of Piers Ploughman was written by one who
approved the opinions of Wycliffe, and it seems to have
been carefully proscribed. There does not appear to exist
any manuscript older than the first printed edition.

The great popularity of the Vision of Piers Ploughman
in the fourteenth century, and its political influence, are
proved by another close imitation, which was composed
immediately after the capture, and previous to the depo-
sition, of king Richard II. This poem also appears to
have been proscribed, and we have only a fragment left,
which was printed from an unique manuscript for the
Camden Society. It also is composed in alliterative verse,
and its meaning is rendered obscure by a confused allegorical style. It was evidently written towards the Welsh

Border, perhaps at Bristol, which is mentioned in the opening lines; and it appears to have been intended as a continuation of, or as a sequel to, Piers Ploughman, which it immediately follows in the only manuscript in which it is preserved.

Another early poem, of which the Ploughman is the hero, was inserted in the works of Chaucer under the title of the Ploughman's Tale. This, like the Creed, is free from allegory; and it differs from the others also in being written in rhyme, and not in alliterative verse. The Ploughman's Tale was probably written in the earlier half of the fifteenth century.[10] It is a coarse attack on the

---

[10] Different circumstances connected with this poem (which also appears to have been proscribed, for we have no early manuscript of it) lead me to suppose that it was written in the reign of Henry IV., when the *burning* of heretics came into fashion, which is alluded to in the following stanza :—

> " Were Christ on earth here, eftsoone
> These would damne him to die :
> All his hestes they han for-done,
> And saine his sawes ben heresie :
> And ayenst his commaundements they crie,
> And *damne all his to be brende ;*
> For it liketh not hem such losengerie,
> God almighty hem amend ! "

In another passage, the writer of this poem alludes to the Creed of Piers Ploughman as though he were the author of it, and as a piece then known to everybody.

> " And all such other counterfaitours,
> Chanons, canons, and such disguised,
> Been Gods enemies and traitours,
> His true religion han foule despised.
> Of *freres* I have told before,
> In a *making of a Crede ;*
> And yet I could tell worse and more,
> But men would werien it to rede."

Perhaps, however, the writer only claims the authorship of the Creed in his allegorical character, as the representative of that class of satirical writers who were then attacking the monastic orders.

different orders of the clergy, for their pride, covetousness, and other vices. Its versification has little merit; and there appears to be no good reason for inserting it among the Canterbury Tales.

The vision of Piers Ploughman appears to have continued to enjoy a wide popularity down to the middle of the fifteenth century. We hear nothing of it from that period to the middle of the sixteenth, when it was printed by the reformers, and received with so much favour, that no less than three editions, or rather three impressions, are said to have been sold in the course of one year. Another edition was printed at the beginning of the reign of Queen Elizabeth; and it appears to have been much read in the latter part of the sixteenth century, and even at the beginning of the seventeenth. The name of Piers Ploughman is not uncommon in the political tracts of that period.[11]

The Poem of Piers Ploughman is peculiarly a national work. It is the most remarkable monument of the public spirit of our forefathers in the middle, or, as they are often termed, dark ages. It is a pure specimen of the

---

[11] We may enumerate the following as specimens of such works published in the sixteenth century. Several similar publications appeared in the century following.

"Pyers Plowmans Exortation vnto the lordes, knights, and burgoysses of the parlyament house." 8vo. printed by Anthony Scholoker, in the reign of Edward VI.

"Newes from the North, Otherwise called the Conference between Simon Certain, and Pierce Plowman, faithfully collected and gathered by T. F. Student." 4to. London, John Allde, 1570.

"The Plowmans complaint of sundry wicked livers, and especially of the bad bringing vp of children; written in verse by R. B. printed for Hugh Corne, 1580." 8vo.

" A goodlye Dialogue and dysputacion between Pyers Ploweman and a Popish Preest, cōcernynge the Supper of the Lorde." 8vo, without date.

English language at a period when it had sustained few of the corruptions which have disfigured it since we have had writers of " Grammars ; " and in it we may study with advantage many of the difficulties of the language which these writers have misunderstood. It is, moreover, the finest example left of the kind of versification which was purely English, inasmuch as it had been the only one in use among our Anglo-Saxon progenitors, in common with the other people of the North. To many readers it will be perhaps necessary to explain that rhyming verse was not in use among the Anglo-Saxons. In place of rhyme, they had a system of verse of which the characteristic was a very regular *alliteration*, so arranged that, in every couplet, there should be two principal words in the first line beginning with the same letter, which letter must also be the initial of the first word on which the stress of the voice falls in the second line. There has, as yet, been discovered no system of foot-measure in Anglo-Saxon verse, but the common metre consists apparently in having two rises and two falls of the voice in each line. These characteristics are accurately preserved in the verse of Piers Ploughman ; and the measure appears to be the same, if we make allowance for the change of the slow and impressive pronunciation of the Anglo-Saxon for the quicker pronunciation of Middle English, which therefore required a greater number of syllables to fill up the same space of time.

We can trace the history of alliterative verse in England with tolerable certainty. The Anglo-Normans first brought in rhymes, which they employed in their own poetry. The adoption of this new system into the English language was gradual, but it appears to have commenced in the first half of the twelfth century. It was, at first, mixed with alliterative couplets: that is, in the same poem were used sometimes rhyming couplets, which were suddenly changed for alliterative couplets, and then, after awhile, rhyme was again brought in, and so on. Of this kind of poetry we have four very remarkable examples, the *Proverbs of King Alfred*, a poem which was certainly in existence in the first half of the twelfth century;[12] the *Early English Bestiary;*[13] the Poem on the *Debate between the Body and the Soul;*[14] and the grand work of Layamon.[15] The following lines from the Bestiary may serve as a specimen of the manner in which the two systems are intermixed; they form part of the account of the spider :—

> "ðanne renneð ge rapelike,
> for ge is ai redi,
> nimeð anon to ðe net,
> and nimeð hem ðere,
> bitterlike ge hem bit
> and here bane wurðeð,
> dropeð and drinkeð hire *blod*,
> doð ge hire non oðer *god*,
> bute fret hire *fille*,
> and dareð siðen *stille*."
> *   *   *

---

12 Printed in the *Reliquiæ Antiquæ*, vol i. pp. 170-188. On the date of this poem, see the *Biographia Britannica Literaria* (by the editor of the present work), Anglo-Saxon period, pp. 395, 306.

13 Printed in the *Altdeutsche Blätter* von Moriz Haupt und Heinrich Hoffmann. vol. ii. pp. 99-120, and in the *Reliquiæ Antiquæ*, vol. i. pp. 208-227.

14 Discovered in a MS. at Worcester by Sir Thomas Phillipps, who published a small edition of it, in folio.

15 Edited by Sir Frederick Madden, for the Society of Antiquaries.

> "Cethegrande is a *fis*
> Ꝥe moste Ꝥat in water *is ;*
> Ꝥat tu wuldes seien *get,*
> gef Ꝥu it soꝤe wan it *flet,*" etc.

This kind of poetry appears to have been common until the middle of the thirteenth century ; after which period we only find alliteration in songs, not used in simple alliterative couplets, but mixed up in the same lines with rhyme in an irregular and playful manner.[16] But there appears little room for doubting that during the whole of this time the pure alliterative poetry was in use among the lower classes of society ; and its revival towards the middle of the fourteenth century appears to have been a part of the political movement which then took place. In this point of view, the poem of Piers Ploughman becomes still more worthy of attention as a document of contemporary literary history. The old alliterative verse came so much into fashion at this period that it was adopted for the composition of long romances, of which several still remain.[17] The use of this kind of verse was continued in the fifteenth century, and was imitated in Scotland as late as the time of Dunbar, but the later writers were evidently unacquainted with the strict rules of this species of composition.

The Anglo-Saxons, who used this kind of verse only, wrote their poetry invariably as prose. But the scribe was in the habit of indicating the division of the lines by a dot.

---

[16] Many instances of this will be found in my *Specimens of Lyric Poetry,* composed in England in the reign of Edward the First (Percy Society Publication).

[17] Such as *William and the Werwolf,* edited by Sir Frederick Madden ; the *Romance of Jerusalem ;* that of *Alexander ;* &c.

Among modern scholars a question has arisen as to the propriety of printing the alliterative couplet in two short lines, or in one long one. It appears to me that the mode in which the dot is used in the manuscripts decides the question in favour of the short lines. The manner in which the alliterative couplet is intermixed with the rhyming couplet in the poems of the twelfth and thirteenth centuries (which also are written in the manuscripts in the same form as prose), seems to me a strong confirmation of this opinion ; at least in these last-mentioned cases, the verse must have been considered as written in short lines. As the scribes quitted the custom of writing poetry in their manuscripts as prose, with the divisions of lines indicated by dots, to adopt that of arranging them in lines as we do at present, these short lines were found very inconvenient because they were obliged either to waste a great deal of parchment, or to write in several narrow columns. To remedy this, they fell perhaps gradually into the custom of writing the two parts of the alliterative couplet in one line, always, however, marking the division by a dot. They followed the same method with the shorter rhyming lines, as is the case with the old English Metrical Romance of Horn in a manuscript in the Harleian Collection.[18] All the alliterative poetry of the fourteenth and fifteenth centuries is found written in these long lines, with the dot of

---

[18] MS. Harl. 2253. In this manuscript, and in several others which I have seen the rhyming poems in short lines, whether in English, Latin, or French, are arranged in this manner ; and I have met with instances in which part of a poem has been arranged in this way, and other parts of the same poem have been arranged in short lines, to suit the scribe's convenience. I have a strong impression of having met with an early English manuscript in which a fragment of alliterative verse was written in short couplets.

division in the middle. In the fifteenth century the meaning of this dot appears to have been forgotten, and the system of alliteration so far misunderstood, that the writers thought it only necessary to have *at least* three alliterative words in a long line, without any consideration of their position in the line. I say *at least*, because they not unfrequently inserted four or five alliterative words in the same line, which would certainly have been considered a defect in the earlier writers. It is my opinion, that a modern editor is wrong in printing the verses of Piers Ploughman in long lines, as they stand in the manuscripts, unless he profess to give them as a fac-simile of the manuscripts themselves, or he plead the same excuse of convenience from the shape of his book. In either case, he must carefully preserve the dots of separation in the middle of the lines, which are more inconvenient than the length of the lines, because they interfere with the punctuation of the modern editor. If, as appears to be the case, these dots are merely marks to indicate the division of the couplet, their purpose is much better served by printing the lines in couplets. The construction of the earlier Anglo-Saxon verse, the analogy of the mixed rhyming and alliterative verses of the semi-Saxon poems, and the use of these dots in the middle of the lines in the manuscripts of Piers Ploughman, appear to me convincing proofs that it ought to be printed so. I think moreover that the alliterative verse reads much more harmoniously in the short couplets than in the long lines.

The manuscripts of the Vision of Piers Ploughman are extremely numerous both in public and in private collections. There are at least eight in the British Museum :

there are ten or twelve in the Cambridge Libraries; and they are not less numerous at Oxford. As might be expected in a popular work like this, the manuscripts are in general full of variations; but there are two classes of manuscripts which give two texts that are widely different from each other, those variations commencing even with the first lines of the poem. One of these texts, which was adopted in the early printed editions, is given in the present volumes; the other text was selected for publication by Dr. Whitaker. The following extract, comprising the first lines of the poem,[19] will show how each text begins, and will enable those who possess manuscripts of Piers Ploughman to ascertain at once to which text they belong :—

TEXT I.	TEXT II.
In a somer seson	In a somé seyson,
Whan softe was the sonne,	Whan softe was the sonne,
I shop me into shroudes	Y shop into shrobbis
As I a sheep weere,	As y shepherde were.
In habite as an heremite	In abit az an ermite
Unholy of werkes,	Unholy of werkes,
Wente wide in this world	That wente forthe in the worle
Wonders to here,	Wondres to hure,
Ac on a May morwenynge	And sawe meny cellis
On Malverne hilles	And selcouthe thynges.
Me bifel a ferly,	Ac on a May morwenyng
Of fairye me thoghte.	On Malverne hulles
I was wery for-wandred,	Me by-fel for to slepe,
And wente me to reste	For weyrynesse of wandryng,
Under a broode bank	And in a lande as ich lay
By a bournes syde,	Lenede ich and slepte,
And as I lay and lenede,	And merveylously me mette,
And loked on the watres,	As ich may yow telle.
I slombred into a slepyng,	Al the welthe of this wordle,
It sweyed so murye.	And the woo bothe,

---

[19] *Text I.* is from the edition now offered to the public: *Text II.* from that edited by Dr. Whitaker.

<table>
<tr><td>

Thanne gan I meten
A merveillous swevene,
That I was in a wildernesse
Wiste I nevere where ;
And as I biheld in to the eest
An heigh to the sonne,
I seigh a tour on a toft, etc.

</td><td>

Wynkyng as it were
Wyterly ich saw hyt,
Of truyth and of tricherye,
Of tresonn and of gyle,
Al ich saw slepyng,
As ich shal yow telle.
Esteward ich behulde
After the sonne,
And sawe a tour as ich trowede, etc.

</td></tr>
</table>

Besides such variations as appear in the foregoing specimen, there are in the second text many considerable additions, omissions, and transpositions.   It would not be easy
to account for the existence of two texts differing so much ;
but it is my impression that the first was the one published
by the author, and that the variations were made by some
other person, who was perhaps induced by his own political sentiments to modify passages, and was gradually led
on to publish a revision of the whole.   It is certain that
in some parts of Text II. the strong sentiments or expressions of the first text are softened down.   We may give
as an example of this, the statement of the popular opinion
of the origin and purpose of kingly government :—

<table>
<tr><td>

TEXT I.

Thanne kam ther a kyng,
Knyghthod hym ladde,
Might of the communes
Made hym to regne.
And thanne cam kynde wit,
And clerkes he made,
For to connseillen the kyng,
And the commune save.
The kyng and knyghthod,
And clergie bothe,
Casten that the commune
Sholde hem self fynde.
The commune contreved
Of kynde wit craftes,

</td><td>

TEXT II.

Thanne cam ther a kyng,
Knyghtod hym ladde,
The meche myghte of the men
Made hym to regne.
And thanne cam a kynde witte,
And clerkus he made,
And concience and kynde wit,
And knyghthod to-gederes,
Caste that the comune
Sholde hure comunes fynde.
Kynde wit and the comune
Contrevede alle craftes,
And for most profitable to the puple,
A plouh thei gonne make,

</td></tr>
</table>

And for profit of al the peple
Plowmen ordeyned,
To tilie and to travaille,
As trewe lif asketh.
The kyng and the commune,
And kynde wit the thridde,
Shopen lawe and leautè,
Ech man to knowe his owene.

Wit leil labour to lyve,
Wyl lyve and londe lasteth.

Nobody, I think, can deny that in this instance the doctrine is stated far more distinctly and far more boldly in the first text than in the second. In general the first text is the best, whether we look at the mode in which the sentiments are stated, or at the poetry and language.

As far as I have been able to examine the remaining manuscripts of Piers Ploughman, at London and in the Universities, I think that nearly two-thirds of those which remain are of the *fourteenth* century; and the greater number, particularly of those written in the fourteenth century, present what I have distinguished as the first text, that given in the present volumes. I am by no means inclined to coincide in the reasons which led Dr. Whitaker to prefer the second text; if I were disposed to admit, as barely possible (the supposition is quite a gratuitous one), " that the first edition of this work appeared when its author was a young man, and that he lived and continued in the habit of transcribing to extreme old age" (Pref)., I cannot agree with an editor in adopting a copy which he believes to be " a faithful representation of the work as it came first from the author," and which not only abounds in words and idioms which he afterwards altered, but which contains also " many original passages which the greater maturity of the author's judgment induced him to expunge."

I know only of two manuscripts of the Creed of Piers Ploughman, one in the British Museum (MS. Reg. 18, B. XVII.), the other in the Library of Trinity College, Cambridge, both on paper, and written long after the date of the printed editions, from which they appear to have been copied.

The first printed edition of the Vision was that of Robert Crowley, in 1550; and it was so favourably received, that there is reason for believing that no less than three editions (or rather three impressions[20]) were sold in the course of the year. It is clear that Crowley had obtained an excellent manuscript; the printer has changed the orthography at will, and has evidently altered a word at times, but on the whole this printed text differs very little from the one we now publish.

Three years after the appearance of the Vision, another printer, Reynold Wolfe, published the first edition of the Creed, in the same form as Crowley's edition of the Vision.[21]

After the stormy reign of Mary was past, in the beginning of that of Elizabeth, the call for a new edition, and

---

[20] The title of the second impression is, "The Vision of Pierce Ploughman, nowe the seconde time imprinted by Roberte Crowley, dwellynge in Elye rentes in Holburne. Whereunto are added certayne notes and cotations in the mergyne geryuge light to the Reader, &c. Imprinted at London by Roberte Crowley, dwellyng in Elye rentes in Holburne. The yere of our Lord M.D.L. Cum privilegio ad imprimendum solum." 4to, 125 leaves.

[21] The title consists merely of the words "Pierce the Ploughman's Crede," upon a tablet in the midst of a wood-cut which had evidently been brought from the continent. A fac-simile of the most important part of the cut is given in Mr. Payne Collier's Bibliographical Catalogue of the Library of Lord Francis Egerton p. 235. The colophon, on a separate leaf, is "Imprinted at London. By Reynold Wolfe. Anno Domini M.D.L.IIL" It consists of 16 leaves in 4to.

perhaps the destruction of many copies of the old one, led the well-known printer Owen Rogers to reprint the Vision and the Creed together.[22] The impression was probably large, for it is still by no means a rare book. It was evidently much read during the reign of Elizabeth, and is not unfrequently alluded to by the writers of that age.

No other edition of this popular poem appeared, until it was published by Dr. Whitaker, in 1813,[23] from a manuscript then in the possession of Mr. Heber,[24] which contained the second text, written in a rather broad provincial dialect. This edition was printed in black-letter, in a very large and expensive form. In 1814, a reprint of the old edition of the Creed was published in the same form, as a companion to the Vision. It is not generally known that Dr. Whitaker projected an edition of the same text and paraphrase which are given in his 4to edition, in 8vo, with Roman type instead of black-letter. After a few sheets had been composed, the design was abandoned, as it is

---

[22] The title of this edition is, "The Vision of Pierce Plowman, newlye imprynted after the authours olde copy, with a brefe summary of the principall matters set before every part called Passus. Wherevnto is also annexed the Crede of Pierce Plowman, neuer imprinted with the booke before. ¶ Imprynted at London, by Owen Rogers, dwellyug neare vnto great Saint Bartelmewes gate, at the sygne of the spred Egle. ¶ The yere of our Lord God, a thousand, fyve hundred, thre score and one. The xxi. daye of the Moneth of Februarye. Cum privilegio ad imprimendum solum." 4to. This edition is not foliated, or paged ; and it is remarkable that it is as frequently found without the Creed, as with it. This edition of the Creed is also sometimes found separate.

[23] Whitaker's edition bears the following title,—"Visio Willielmi de Petro Plouhmau, Item Visioues ejusdem de Dowel, Dobet, et Dobest. Or, The Vision of William concerning Piers Plouhman. and The Visions of the same concerning the Origin, Progress, and Perfection of Christian Life, &c. By Thomas Dunham Whitaker, LL.D., &c. 4to. London. Murray, 1813.

[24] This manuscript was bought at Heber's sale for the British Museum, where it is classed as Additional MS. No. 10,574

said, in favour of the larger form. A copy of the proof sheets, formerly belonging to Mr. Haslewood, is now in the possession of Sir Frederick Madden. I am told that a rival edition was also begun, but not persevered in.

An attempt at a modernization, or rather a translation, of Piers Ploughman, was made in the earlier years of the present century, but only a few specimens appear to have been executed. The following lines, which possess some merit (though not very literal or correct), are the modern version the author proposed to give of ll. 2847–2870 of the poem. They were communicated to me by Sir Henry Ellis.

> "Next AVARICE came ; but how he look'd, to say,
> Words do I want that rightly shall portray :
> Like leathern purse his shrivell'd cheeks did shew,
> Thick lipp'd, with two blear eyes and beetle brow :
> In a torn threadbare tabard was he clad,
> Which twelve whole winters now in wear he had ;
> French scarlet 'twas, its colour well it kept,
> So smooth that louse upon its surface crept."

It will be necessary, in conclusion, to say a few words on the edition now offered to the public. Without taking into consideration the inaccuracies and imperfections of Whitaker's edition, its inconvenient size and high price made it altogether inaccessible to the general reader; and there appeared to be a wish for one in a more convenient and less expensive form. At the same time it was desired that a good text of a work so important for the history of our language and literature should be selected. Dr. Whitaker was not well qualified for this undertaking ; he also laboured under many disadvantages ; he had access to only three manuscripts, and those not very good ones ; and he has not chosen the best text even of those. Unless he had some reason to believe that the book was originally written in a particular dialect, he ought to have given a preference to that among the oldest manuscripts which presents the purest language; but we cannot allow that manuscript to be chosen on a ground so capricious as " that the orthography and dialect in which it is written approach very near to that semi-Saxon jargon in the midst of which the editor was brought up, and which he continues to hear daily spoken on the confines of Lancashire, and the West Riding of the county of York." (Pref.) This could not have been the language employed by a monk of Malvern.

The present editor has endeavoured, in the leisure moments which he has been able to snatch from other employments, to supply the deficiency as well, and in as unassuming manner, as he could. He has chosen for his text a manuscript belonging to the valuable library of Trinity College, Cambridge (where its shelf-mark is B. 15, 17), because it appears to him to be the best and oldest manuscript now in existence. It is a fine folio manuscript, on vellum, written in a large hand, undoubtedly contemporary with the author of the poem, and in remarkably pure English, with ornamented initial letters. His object has been to give the poem as popular a form as is consistent with philological correctness. He has added a few notes which occurred to him in the course of editing the text, and which he hopes may render the meaning and allusions sometimes clearer to the general reader, for whom more especially they are intended. They might have been enlarged and rendered more complete, if he had been master of sufficient leisure to enable him to untertake extensive researches.   But there are allusions, as well as words, in both poems to which it would be difficult at present to give any certain explanation.   It has been thought advisable to give in the notes the important variations of the second text, from Dr. Whitaker's edition ; and a few readings are added from a second manuscript in Trinity College Library (R. 3, 14).   The editor has hoped to add to the utility of the book by a copious glossary.   He has been unwillingly obliged to leave a few words without explanation ; all our early alliterative poetry abounds in difficult words.   In this point he has to acknowledge the kind assistance of Sir Frederick Madden, whom no person equals in profound knowledge of English glossography, and than whom no one is more generous to advise and assist those who are in need of his aid.   To Sir Henry Ellis, who kindly lent him his own manuscript notes on Piers Ploughman, the editor also owes his grateful acknowledgments ; and he regrets that at the time he received them the notes were already so far printed as to hinder him from making as much use of them as he could have wished.

London, June 1, 1842.

THE VISION OF PIERS PLOUGHMAN.

THE VISION OF

PIERS PLOUGHMAN.

IN a somer seson
Whan softe was the sonne,
I shoop me into shroudes
As I a sheep weere,
In habite as an heremite
Unholy of werkes,
Wente wide in this world
Wondres to here;
Ac on a May morwenynge
On Malverne hilles   10
Me bifel a ferly,
Of fairye me thoghte.
I was wery for-wandred,
And wente me to reste
Under a brood bank
By a bournes syde;
And as I lay and lenede,
And loked on the watres,
I slombred into a slepyng,
It sweyed so murye.   20

Thanne gan I meten   21
A merveillous swevene,
That I was in a wildernesse,
Wiste I nevere where,
And as I biheeld into the eest
An heigh to the sonne,
I seigh a tour on a toft
Trieliche y-maked,
A deep dale bynethe,
A dongeon therinne,
With depe diches and derke
And dredfulle of sighte.   32
A fair feeld ful of folk
Fond I ther bitwene,
Of alle manere of men,
The meene and the riche,
Werchynge and wandrynge,
As the world asketh.
Some putten hem to the plough,
Pleiden ful selde,
In settynge and sowynge
Swonken ful harde,
And wonnen that wastours   43
With glotonye destruyeth.
And somme putten hem to pride,
Apparailed hem therafter,
In contenaunce of clothynge
Comen degised.
In preires and penaunces
Putten hem manye,
Al for the love of oure Lord
Lyveden ful streyte,
In hope to have after
Hevene riche blisse;   54

As ancres and heremites   55
That holden hem in hire selles,
And coveiten noght in contree
To carien aboute,
For no likerous liflode
Hire likame to plese.
    And somme chosen chaffare;
Thei cheveden the bettre,
As it semeth to our sight
That swiche men thryveth.
    And somme murthes to make,
As mynstralles konne,   66
And geten gold with hire glee,
Giltles, I leeve.
    Ac japeres and jangeleres,
Judas children,
Feynen hem fantasies,
And fooles hem maketh,
And han hire wit at wille
To werken, if thei wolde.
That Poul precheth of hem
I wol nat preve it here;
But *Qui loquitur turpiloquium*   77
Is Luciferes hyne.
    Bidderes and beggeres
Faste aboute yede,
With hire belies and hire bagges
Of breed ful y-crammed;
Faiteden for hire foode,
Foughten at the ale.
In glotonye, God woot,
Go thei to bedde,
And risen with ribaudie,
Tho Roberdes knaves;   88

Sleep and sory sleuthe   89
Seweth hem evere.
   Pilgrymes and palmeres
Plighten hem togidere,
For to seken seint Jame,
And seintes at Rome.
They wenten forth in hire wey,
With many wise tales,
And hadden leve to lyen
Al hire lif after.
   I seigh somme that seiden
Thei hadde y-sought seintes;   100
To ech a tale that thei tolde
Hire tonge was tempred to lye,
Moore than to seye sooth,
It semed bi hire speche.
   Heremytes on an heep
With hoked staves
Wenten to Walsyngham,
And hire wenches after,
Grete lobies and longe
That lothe were to swynke;
Clothed hem in copes,   111
To ben knowen from othere;
And shopen hem heremytes,
Hire ese to have.
   I fond there freres,
Alle the foure ordres,
Prechynge the peple
For profit of hemselve;
Glosed the gospel,
As hem good liked;
For coveitise of copes,
Construwed it as thei wolde.   122

Many of thise maistre freres   123
Now clothen hem at likyng,
For hire moneie and hire marchaun-
Marchen togideres.   [dize
For sith charité hath ben chapman,
And chief to shryve lordes,
Manye ferlies han fallen
In a fewe yeres;
But holy chirche and hii
Holde bettre togidres,
The mooste meschief on molde
Is mountynge wel faste.   134
    Ther preched a pardoner,
As he a preest were;
Broughte forth a bulle
With many bisshopes seles,
And seide that hymself myghte
Assoillen hem alle,
Of falshede, of fastynge,
Of avowes y-broken.
    Lewed men leved it wel,
And liked hise wordes;
Comen up knelynge   145
To kissen hise bulles.
He bouched hem with his brevet,
And blered hire eighen,
And raughte with his rageman
Rynges and broches.
    Thus thei gyven hire gold
Glotons to kepe,
And leveth in swiche losels
As leccherie haunten.
    Were the bisshope y-blessed,
And worth bothe hise eris,   150

His seel sholde noght be sent   157
To deceyve the peple.
Ac it is noght by the bisshope
That the boy precheth ;
For the parisshe preest and the par-
Parten the silver,   [doner
That the poraille of the parisshe
Sholde have, if thei ne were.

Parsons and parisshe preestes
Pleyned hem to the bisshope,
That hire parisshes weren povere
Sith the pestilence tyme,   168
To have a licence and leve
At London to dwelle,
And syngen ther for symonie ;
For silver is swete.

Bisshopes and bachelers,
Bothe maistres and doctours,
That han cure under Crist,
And crownynge in tokene
And signe that thei sholden
Shryven hire parisshens,
Prechen and praye for hem,   179
And the povere fede,
Liggen at Londone
In Lenten and ellis.

Somme serven the kyng,
And his silver tellen
In cheker and in chauncelrie,
Chalangen hise dettes
Of wardes and of wardemotes,
Weyves and streyves.

And somme serven as servauntz
Lordes and ladies,   190

And in stede of stywardes 191
Sitten and demen ;
Hire messe and hire matyns
And many of hire houres
Arn doon un-devoutliche ;
Drede is at the laste,
Lest Crist in consistorie
A-corse ful manye.
   I perceyved of the power
That Peter hadde to kepe,
To bynden and unbynden,
As the book telleth ; 202
How he it lefte with love,
As oure Lord highte,
Amonges foure vertues,
The beste of alle vertues,
That cardinals ben called,
And closynge yates.
There is Crist in his kingdom
To close and to shette,
And to opene it to hem,
And hevene blisse shewe.
   Ac of the cardinals at court 213
That kaughte of that name,
And power presumed in hem
A pope to make,
To han that power that Peter hadde,
Impugnen I nelle ;
For in love and in lettrure
The election bilongeth,
For-thi I kan and kan naught
Of court speke moore.
   Thanne kam ther a kyng,
Knyghthod hym ladde, 224

Might of the communes   225
Made hym to regne.
    And thanne cam kynde wit,
And clerkes he made,
For to counseillen the kyng,
And the commune save.
    The kyng and knyghthod,
And clergie bothe,
Casten that the commune
Sholde hemself fynde.
    The commune contreved
Of kynde wit craftes,   236
And for profit of al the peple
Plowmen ordeyned,
To tilie and to travaille,
As trewe lif asketh.
    The kyng and the commune,
And kynde wit the thridde,
Shopen lawe and leauté,
Ech man to knowe his owene.
    Thanne loked up a lunatik,
A leene thyng with-alle,
And, knelynge to the kyng,   247
Clergially he seide :
    "Crist kepe thee, sire kyng !
And thi kyng-ryche,
And lene thee lede thi lond,
So leauté thee lovye,
And for thi rightful rulyng
Be rewarded in hevene."
    And sithen in the eyr an heigh
An aungel of hevene
Lowed to speke in Latyn,
For lewed men ne koude   258

Jangle ne jugge,   259
That justifie hem sholde,
But suffren and serven ;
For-thi seide the aungel :
Sum rex, sum princeps,
Neutrum fortasse deinceps ;
O qui jura regis
Christi specialia regis,
Hoc quod agas melius,
Justus es, esto pius.
Nudum jus a te
Vestiri vult pietate ;   270
Qualia vis metere,
Talia grana sere.
Si jus nudatur,
Nudo de jure metatur ;
Si seritur pietas,
De pietate metas.
  Thanne greved hym a goliardeis,
A gloton of wordes,
And to the aungel an heigh
Answerde after :
Dum rex a regere   281
Dicatur nomen habere ;
Nomen habet sine re,
Nisi studet jura tenere.
  Thanne gan al the commune
Crye in vers of Latyn,
To the kynges counseil ;
Construe who so wolde :
Præcepta regis
Sunt nobis vincula legis.
  With that ran ther a route
Of ratons at ones,   292

And smale mees myd hem   293
Mo than a thousand,
And comen to a counseil
For the commune profit;
For a cat of a contree
Cam whan hym liked,
And overleep hem lightliche,
And laughte hem at his wille,
And pleide with hem perillousli,
And possed aboute.
" For doute of diverse dredes,
We dar noght wel loke ;   304
And if we grucche of his gamen,
He wol greven us alle,
Cracchen us or clawen us,
And in hise clouches holde,
That us lotheth the lif
Er he late us passe.
Mighte we with any wit
His wille withstonde,
We mighte be lordes o-lofte,
And lyven at oure ese."
    A raton of renoun,   315
Moost renable of tonge,
Seide for a sovereyn
Help to hymselve :
    " I have y-seyen segges," quod
" In the cité of Londone,   [he
Beren beighes ful brighte
Abouten hire nekkes,
And somme colers of crafty werk ;
Uncoupled thei wenten
Bothe in wareyne and in waast
Where hemself liked.   326

And outher while thei arn ellis-
As I here telle;   [where,
Were ther a belle on hire beighe,
By Jhesu, as me thynketh,
Men myghte witen wher thei wente,
And awey renne!"
    "And right so," quod that raton,
"Reson me sheweth,
To bugge a belle of bras,
Or of bright silver,
And knytten it on a coler
For oure commune profit,   338
Wher he ryt or rest,
Or renneth to pleye;
And if hym list for to laike,
Thanne loke we mowen,
And peeren in his presence
The while him pleye liketh:
And, if hym wratheth, be war,
And his way shonye."
    Al this route of ratons
To this reson thei assented.
Ac tho the belle was y-brought, 349
And on the beighe hanged,
Ther ne was raton in al the route,
For al the reaume of Fraunce,
That dorste have bounden the belle
About the cattes nekke,
Ne hangen it aboute the cattes hals,
Al Engelond to wynne.
Alle helden hem un-hardy,
And hir counseil feble;
And leten hire labour lost
And al hire longe studie.   360

   A mous that muche good   361
Kouthe, as me thoughte,
Strook forth sternely,
And stood bifore hem alle,
And to the route of ratons
Reherced thise wordes :
   "Though we killen the cat,
Yet sholde ther come another
To cacchen us and al oure kynde,
Though we cropen under benches.
For-thi I counseille al the commune
To late the cat worthe ;   372
And be we nevere bolde
The belle hym to shewe ;
For I herde my sire seyn,
Is seven yeer y-passed,
Ther the cat is a kitone
The court is ful elenge ;
That witnesseth holy writ,
Who so wole it rede :
Væ terræ ubi puer rex est / etc.
For may no renk ther reste have
For ratons by nyghte ;   383
The while he caccheth conynges,
He coveiteth noght youre caroyne,
But fedeth hym al with venyson :
Defame we hym nevere.
For better is a litel los
Than a long sorwe,
The maze among us alle,
Theigh we mysse a sherewe ;
For many mennes malt
We mees wolde destruye,
And also ye route of ratons   394

Rende mennes clothes,   395
Nere the cat of that court
That can yow over-lepe ;
For hadde ye rattes youre wille,
Ye kouthe noght rule yow selve."
    " I seye for me," quod the mous,
" I se so muchel after,
Shal nevere the cat ne the kiton
By my counseil be greved,
Thorugh carpynge of this coler
That costed me nevere
And though it hadde costned me
Bi-knowen it I nolde,   [catel,
But suffren, as hymself wolde,
To doon as hym liketh,
Coupled and uncoupled
To cacche what thei mowe.
For-thi ech a wis wight I warne,
Wite wel his owene."
    What this metels by-meneth,
Ye men that ben murye
Devyne ye, for I ne dar,
By deere God in hevene.   417
    Yet hoved ther an hundred
In howves of selk,
Sergeantz it bi-semed
That serveden at the barre,
Pleteden for penyes
And poundes the lawe ;
And noght for love of our Lord
Unclose hire lippes ones.
Thow myghtest bettre meete myst
On Malverne hilles,
Than gete a mom of hire mouth,

Til moneie be shewed.   429
   Barons and burgeises,
And bonde-men als,
I seigh in this assemblee,
As ye shul here after :
Baksteres and brewesteres,
And bochiers manye ;
Wollen webbesters,
And weveres of lynnen,
Taillours and tynkers,
And tollers in markettes,
Masons and mynours,   440
And many othere craftes.
Of alle kynne lybbynge laborers
Lopen forth somme,
As dikeres and delveres,
That doon hire dedes ille,
And dryveth forth the longe day
With *Dieu save dame Emme.*
   Cokes and hire knaves
Cryden, "Hote pies, hote !
Goode gees and grys !
Gowe, dyne, gowe !"   451
   Taverners until hem
Trewely tolden the same,
Whit wyn of Oseye,
And reed wyn of Gascoigne,
Of the Ryn and of the Rochel,
The roost to defie.
[Al this I saugh slepynge,
And seve sithes more.]   459

WHAT this mountaigne by-
  meneth   460
  And the merke dale,
  And the feld ful of folk,
  I shal yow faire shewe.
A lovely lady of leere,
In lynnen y-clothed,
Cam doun from a castel
And called me faire,
And seide, "Sone, slepestow?
Sestow this peple,
How bisie thei ben
Alle aboute the maze?   471
The mooste partie of this peple
That passeth on this erthe,
Have thei worship in this world,
Thei wilne no bettre;
Of oother hevene than here
Holde thei no tale."

  I was a-fered of hire face,
Theigh she fair weere,
And seide, "Mercy, madame,
What is this to meene?"

  "The tour on the toft," quod she,
"Truthe is therinne;   483

And wolde that ye wroughte,   484
As his word techeth !
For he is fader of feith,
And formed yow alle
Bothe with fel and with face,
And yaf yow fyve wittes,
For to worshipe hym therwith,
While that ye ben here.
And therfore he highte the erthe
To helpe yow echone,
Of wollene, of lynnen,
Of liflode at nede,   495
In mesurable manere
To make yow at ese ;
And comaunded of his curteisie
In commune three thynges,
Are none nedfulle but tho,
And nempne hem I thynke,
And rekene hem by reson ;
Reherce thow hem after.
  " That oon vesture,
From cold thee to save ;
And mete at meel   506
For mysese of thiselve ;
And drynke whan thow driest ;
Ac do noght out of reson,
That thow worthe the wers
Whan thow werche sholdest.
  " For Lot in hise lif-dayes,
For likynge of drynke,
Dide by hise doughtres
That the devel liked,
Delited hym in drynke
As the devel wolde,   517

And leccherie hym laughte, 518
And lay by hem bothe,
And al he witte it the wyn
That wikked dede.
Inebriamus eum vino, dormiamusque
cum eo, ut servare possimus de
patre nostro semen.
Thorugh wyn and thorugh wom-
Ther was Loth acombred, [men
And there gat in glotonie
Gerles that were cherles.
" For-thi dred delitable drynke,
And thow shalt do the bettre. 530
Mesure is medicine,
Though thow muchel yerne.
It is nought al good to the goost
That the gut asketh,
Ne liflode to thi likame;
For a liere hym techeth,
That is the wrecched world
Wolde thee bitraye.
For the fend and thi flesshe
Folwen togidere. 540
This and that seeth thi soule,
And seith it in thin herte;
And for thow sholdest ben y-war,
I wisse thee the beste."
"Madame, mercy!" quod I,
"Me liketh wel youre wordes;
Ac the moneie of this molde
That men so faste holdeth,
Tel me to whom, madame,
That tresour appendeth." 550
"Go to the gospel," quod she,

"That God seide hymselven ;   552
Tho the poeple hym apposede
With a peny in the temple,
Wheither thei sholde therwith
Worshipe the kyng Cesar.
    "And God asked of hym,
Of whom spak the lettre,
And the ymage was lik
That therinne stondeth.
    "'Cesares,' thei seiden,
'We seen it wel echone.'
    "'*Reddite Cæsari*,' quod God,   563
'That *Cæsari* bifalleth,
Et quæ sunt Dei Deo,
Or ellis ye don ille ;
For rightfully reson
Sholde rule yow alle,
And kynde wit be wardeyn
Youre welthe to kepe,
And tutour of youre tresor,
And take it yow at nede,
For housbondrie and hii
Holden togidres."   574
    Thanne I frayned hire faire,
For hym that me made,
"That dongeon in the dale,
That dredful is of sighte,
What may it be to meene,
Madame, I yow biseche ?"
    "That is the castel of Care ;
Who so comth therinne
May banne that he born was,
To bodi or to soule.
Therinne wonyeth a wight   585

That Wrong is y-hote,   586
Fader of falshede,
And founded it hymselve.
Adam and Eve
He egged to ille;
Counseilled Kaym
To killen his brother;
Judas he japed
With Jewen silver,
And sithen on an eller
Hanged hymselve.
He is lettere of love,   597
And lieth hem alle
That trusten on his tresour;
Bitrayeth he hem sonnest."
    Thanne hadde I wonder in my wit
What womman it weere,
That swiche wise wordes
Of holy writ shewed;
And asked hire on the heighe name,
Er she thennes yede,
What she were witterly
That wissed me so faire.   608
    "Holi chirche I am," quod she,
"Thow oughtest me to knowe;
I underfeng thee first,
And the feith taughte;
And broughtest me borwes
My biddyng to fulfille,
And to loven me leelly
The while thi lif dureth."
    Thanne I courbed on my knees,
And cried hire of grace;
And preide hire pitously   619

Preye for my sinnes,   620
And also kenne me kyndely
On Crist to bi-leve,
That I myghte werchen his wille
That wroghte me to man.
' Teche me to no tresor,
But tel me this ilke,
How I may save my soule,
That seint art y-holden."
    "Whan alle tresors arn tried,"
"Treuthe is the beste ; [quod she,
I do it on *Deus caritas*,   631
To deme the sothe,
It is as dereworthe a drury
As deere God hymselven.
    "Who is trewe of his tonge,
And telleth noon oother,
And dooth the werkes therwith,
And wilneth no man ille,
He is a God by the gospel
A-grounde and o-lofte,
And y-lik to oure Lord,
By seint Lukes wordes.   642
The clerkes that knowen this,
Sholde kennen it aboute,
For cristen and un-cristen
Cleymeth it echone.
    "Kynges and knyghtes
Sholde kepen it by reson,
Riden and rappen doun
In reaumes aboute,
And taken *transgressores*,
And tyen hem faste,
Til treuthe hadde y-termyned   653

Hire trespas to the ende.   654
And that is profession apertli
That apendeth to knyghtes ;
And naught to fasten o friday
In fyve score wynter,
But holden with hym and with here
That wolden alle truthe,
And nevere leve hem for love
Ne for lacchynge of silver.
For David in hise dayes
Dubbed knyghtes,
And dide hem sweren on hirswerdes
To serven truthe evere ;   666
And who so passed that point
Was apostata in the ordre.
"But Crist kyngene kyng
Knyghted ten,
Cherubyn and seraphyn,
Swiche sevene and othere
And yaf hem myght in his majestee,
The murier hem thoughte,
And over his meene meynee
Made hem archangeles ;   676
Taughte hem by the Trinitee
Treuthe to knowe ;
To be buxom at his biddyng,
He bad hem nought ellis.
"Lucifer with legions
Lerned it in hevene ;
But for he brak buxomnesse
His blisse gan he tyne,
And fel fro that felawshipe
In a fendes liknesse,
Into a deep derk helle,   687

To dwelle there for evere ;   688
And mo thousandes myd hym
Than man kouthe nombre
Lopen out with Lucifer
In lothliche forme,
For thei leveden upon hym
That lyed in this manere :
*Ponam pedem in aquilone, et similis
        ero altissimo.*   [be so,
    " And alle that hoped it myghte
Noon hevene myghte hem holde,
But fellen out in fendes liknesse 699
Nyne dayes togideres,
Til God of his goodnesse
Gan stablisse and stynte,
And garte the hevene to stekie
And stonden in quiete.
    "Whan thise wikkede wenten out,
In wonder wise thei fellen ;
Somme in the eyr, somme in erthe,
And somme in helle depe ;
Ac Lucifer lowest lith
Yet of hem alle,   710
For pride that he putte out,
His peyne hath noon ende.
And alle that werchen with wrong,
Wende thei shulle,
After hir deth day
And dwelle with that sherewe.
    " And tho that werche wel,
As holy writ telleth,
And enden as I er seide
In truthe, that is the beste,
Mowe be siker that hire soules 721

Shul wende to hevene,   722
Ther treuthe is in trinitee,
And troneth hem alle.
For-thi I seye, as I seyde er,
By sighte of thise textes,
Whan alle tresors arn tried,
Truthe is the beste ;
Lereth it thise lewed men,
For lettred men it knoweth,
That treuthe is tresor
The trieste on erthe."   [quod I,
  "Yet have I no kynde knowyng."
" Ye mote kenne me bettre,   734
By what craft in my cors
It comseth, and where."
  " Thow doted daffe," quod she,
" Dulle are thi wittes ;
To litel Latyn thow lernedest,
Leode, in thi youthe."
Heu michi ! quia sterilem duxi vitam
    juvenilem.   [she,
  "It is a kynde knowyng," quod
" That kenneth in thyn herte, 744
For to loven thi Lord
Levere than thiselve,
No dedly synne to do,
Deye theigh thow sholdest ;
This I trowe be truthe.
Who kan teche thee bettre,
Loke thow suffre hym to seye,
And sithen lere it after ;
For truthe telleth that love
Is triacle of hevene.
May no synne be on hym seene, 755

That useth that spice, 756
And alle hise werkes be wroughte
With love as hym liste; [thyng,
And lered it Moyses for the leveste
And moost lik to hevene,
And al so the plentee of pees
Moost precious of vertues;
For hevene myghte nat holden it,
It was so hevy of hymself,
Til it hadde of the erthe
Eten his fille.

 "And whan it hadde of this fold 767
Flesshe and blood taken,
Was nevere leef upon lynde
Lighter therafter,
And portatif and persaunt
As the point of a nedle,
That myghte noon armure it lette,
Ne none heighe walles.

 "For-thi is love ledere
Of the Lordes folk of hevene,
And a meene, as the mair is [mune;
Bitwene the kyng and the com-
Right so is love a ledere, 779
And the law shapeth,
Upon man for hise mysdedes
The mercyment he taxeth.
And for to knowen it kyndely
It comseth by myght,
And in the herte there is the heed
And the heighe welle;
For in kynde knowynge in herte,
Ther a myght bigynneth;
And that falleth to the fader 789

That formed us alle,   790
Loked on us with love,
And leet his sone dye
Mekely for oure mysdedes,
To amenden us alle.
And yet wolde he hem no wo
That wroughte hym that peyne,
But mekely with mouthe
Mercy bisoughte,
To have pité of that peple
That peyned hym to dethe.
  "There myghtow sen ensample
In hymself oone,   802
That he was myghtful and meke,
And mercy gan graunte
To hem that hengen hym on heigh
And his herte thirled.
  "For-thi I rede yow, riche,
Haveth ruthe of the povere ;
Though ye be myghtful to mote,
Beeth meke in youre werkes,
For the same mesures that ye mete,
Amys outher ellis,   812
Ye shulle ben weyen therwith
Whan ye wenden hennes.
Eadem mensura qua mensi fueritis,
     remetietur vobis.
  "For though ye be trewe of youre
And treweliche wynne,   [tonge
And as chaste as a child
That in chirche wepeth,
But if ye loven leelly
And lene the povere,
Swich good as God yow sent   823

Goodliche parteth,   824
Ye ne have namoore merite
In masse nor in houres,
Than Malkyn of hire maydenhede
That no man desireth.
    "For James the gentile
Jugged in hise bokes,
That feith withouten the feet
Is right no thyng worthi,
And as deed as a dore-tree,
But if the dedes folwe.   834
Fides sine operibus mortua est, etc.
    "For-thi chastité withouten charité
Worth cheyned in helle ;
It is as lewed as a lampe
That no light is inne.
Manye chapeleyns arn chaste,
Ac charité is aweye ;
Are no men avarouser than hii
Whan thei ben avaunced,
Unkynde to hire kyn,
And to alle cristene
Chewen hire charité,   846
And chiden after moore ;
Swiche chastité withouten charité
Worth cheyned in helle.
    "Manye curatours kepen hem
Clene of hire bodies ;
Thei ben acombred with coveitise,
Thei konne noght doon it from hem,
So harde hath avarice
Y-hasped hem togideres ;
And that is no truthe of the Trinité,
But tricherie of helle,   857

And lernynge to lewed men   858
The latter for to deele.
For-thi thise wordes
Ben writen in the gospel,
Date, et dabitur vobis,
For I deele yow alle,
And that is the lok of love,
And leteth out my grace,
To conforten the carefulle
A-combred with synne.
  " Love is leche of lif,
And next oure Lord selve,   860
And also the graithe gate
That goth into hevene ;
For-thi I seye, as I seide
Er by the textes,
Whan alle tresors ben tried,
Treuthe is the beste.
  "Now have I told thee what truthe
That no tresor is bettre ;   [is,
I may no lenger lenge thee with,
Now loke thee oure Lorde."   870

YET I courbed on my knees,
And cried hire of grace,
And seide, "Mercy, madame,
For Marie love of hevene,
That bar that blisful barn
That boughte us on the rode,
Kenne me by som craft
To knowe the false."
  "Loke up on thi left half,
And lo where he stondeth !
Bothe Fals and Favel,
And hire feeres manye."   891
  I loked on my left half,
As the lady me taughte,
And was war of a womman
Worthiliche y-clothed,
Purfiled with pelure
The fyneste upon erthe,
Y-corouned with a coroune,
The kyng hath noon bettre ;
Fetisliche hire fyngres
Were fretted with gold wyr,
And theron rede rubies
As rede as any gleede,   903

And diamaundes of derrest pris, 904
And double manere saphires,
Orientals and ewages,
Envenymes to destroye.
  Hire robe was ful riche,
Of reed scarlet engreyned,
With ribanes of reed gold
And of riche stones.
Hire array me ravysshed,
Swich richesse saugh I nevere ;
I hadde wonder what she was,
And whos wif she were.   915
  "What is this womman," quod I,
"So worthili atired ?"
  "That is Mede the mayde," quod
"Hath noyed me ful ofte,   [she,
And y-lakked my lemman
That Leautee is hoten,
And bi-lowen hire to lordes
That lawes han to kepe.
  "In the popes paleis
She is pryvee as myselve ;
But soothnesse wolde noght so, 926
For she is a bastarde ;
For fals was hire fader
That hath a fikel tonge,
And nevere sooth seide
Sithen he com to erthe ;
And Mede is manered after hym,
Right as kynde asketh
Qualis pater talis filius.
Bonus arbor bonum fructrum facit.
  "I oughte ben hyere than she,
I kam of a bettre ;   937

My fader the grete God is   938
And ground of alle graces,
So God withouten gynnyng,
And I his goode doughter,
And hath yeven me mercy
To marie with myselve,
And what man be merciful
And leelly me love,
Shal be my lord and I his leef
In the heighe hevene.
    "And what man taketh Mede,
Myn heed dar I legge,   949
That he shal lese for hire love
A lappe of *caritatis*.
    " How construeth David the king
Of men that taketh Mede,
And men of this moolde
That maynteneth truthe,
And how ye shul save yourself,
The sauter bereth witnesse :
*Domine, quis habitabit in taberna-
        culo tuo, etc.*   [maried
    " And now worth this Mede y-
Unto a maused sherewe,   961
To oon fals fikel tonge,
A fendes biyete ;
Favel thorugh his faire speche
Hath this folk enchaunted,
And al is Lieres ledynge,
That she is thus y-wedded.
    " To-morwe worth y-maked
The maydenes bridale,   [wilt,
And there myghtow witen, if thow
Whiche thei ben alle   971

That longen to that lordshipe,   972
The lasse and the moore.
Knowe hem there, if thow kanst,
And kepe thow thi tonge,
And lakke hem noght, but lat hem
Till leauté be justice,   [worthe
And have power to punysshe hem,
Thanne put forth thi reson.
Now I bikenne thee Crist," quod
" And his clene moder,   [she,
And lat no conscience acombre thee
For coveitise of Mede."   983
    Thus lefte me that lady
Liggynge a-slepe ;
And how Mede was y-maried
In metels me thoughte,
That al the riche retenaunce
That regneth with the false,
Were boden to the bridale
On bothe two sides,
Of alle manere of men
The meene and the riche ;
To marien this mayde   994
Were many men assembled,
As of knyghtes and of clerkes,
And oother commune peple,
As sisours and somonours,
Sherreves and hire clerkes,
Bedelles and baillifs,
And brocours of chaffare,
Forgoers and vitaillers,
And advokettes of the arches ;
I kan noght rekene the route
That ran aboute Mede.   1005

Ac Symonie and Cyvylle,   1006
And sisours of courtes,
Were moost pryvee with Mede
Of any men, me thoughte.
Ac Favel was the firste
That fette hire out of boure,
And as a brocour broughte hire
To be with Fals enjoyned.
    Whan Symonye and Cyvylle
Seighe hir bothe wille,
Thei assented, for silver,
To seye as bothe wolde.   1017
    Thanne leep Liere forth, and seide,
" Lo here a chartre ! "
That Gile with hise grete othes
Gaf hem togidere,
And preide Cyvylle to see,
And Symonye to rede it.
    Thanne Symonye and Cyvylle
Stonden forth bothe,
And uufoldeth the feffement
That Fals hath y-maked,
And thus bigynnen thise gomes 1028
To greden ful heighe :
Sciant præsentes et futuri, etc.
    Witeth and witnesseth,
That wonieth upon this erthe,
That Mede is y-maried
Moore for hire goodes
Than for any vertue or fairnesse,
Or any free kynde.
Falsnesse is fayn of hire,
For he woot hire riche ;
And Favel with his fikel speche 1039

Feffeth by this chartre, 1040
To be princes in pride
And poverte to despise,
To bakbite and to bosten,
And bere fals witnesse,
To scorne and to scolde,
And sclaundre to make,
Unbuxome and bolde
To breke the ten hestes.
   And the erldom of Envye
And Wrathe togideres,
With the chastilet of Cheste, 1051
And Chaterynge out of reson.
   The countee of Coveitise,
And alle the costes aboute,
That is Usure and Avarice,
Al I hem graunte,
In bargaynes and in brocages,
With al the burghe of Thefte,
   And al the lordshipe of Leccherie
In lengthe and in brede,
As in werkes and in wordes,
And in waitynges with eighes, 1062
And in wedes and in wisshynges,
And with ydel thoughtes,
There as wil wolde
And werkmanshipe fayleth.
   Glotonye he gaf hem ek,
And grete othes togidere,
And al day to drynken
At diverse tavernes,
And there to jangle and jape,
And jugge hir even cristen ;
And in fastynge dayes to frete 1073

Er ful tyme were,   1074
And thanne to sitten and soupen
Til sleep hem assaille ;
And breden as burghe swyn,
And bedden hem esily,
Til sleuthe and sleep
Sliken hise sydes,   [hem so
And thanne wanhope to awaken
With no wil to amende,
For he leveth be lost,
This is hir laste ende.   1084
    And thei to have and to holde,
And hire heires after,
A dwellynge with the devel,
And dampned be for evere,
With alle the appurtinaunces of
       purgatorie
Into the pyne of helle.
    Yeldynge for this thyng,
At one dayes tyme,
Hire soules to Sathan,
To suffre with hym peynes,   1095
And with hym to wonye with wo
While God is in hevene.
    In witnesse of which thyng,
Wrong was the firste,
And Piers the pardoner
Of Paulynes doctrine,
Bette the bedel
Of Bokyngham shire,
Reynald the reve
Of Rutland sokene,
Maude the millere,
And many mo othere.   1107

In the date of the devel   1108
This dede I ensele,
By sighte of Sire Symonie
And Cyvyles leeve.
Thanne tened hym Theologie,
Whan he this tale herde;
And seide unto Cyvyle,
"Now sorwe mote thow have,
Swiche weddynges to werche,
To wrathe with truthe;
And er this weddynge be wroght,
Wo thee bitide!   1119
"For Mede is muliere
Of Amendes engendred,
And God graunteth to gyve
Mede to Truthe;
And thow hast gyven hire to a gilour;
Now God gyve thee sorwe!
Thi text telleth thee noght so,
Truthe woot the sothe;
For *Dignus est operarius*
His hire to have,
And thow hast fest hire to Fals, 1130
Fy on thi lawe!
For al bi lesynges thow lyvest
And lecherouse werkes.
Symonye and thiself
Shenden holi chirche;
The notaries and ye
Noyen the peple;
Ye shul a-biggen it bothe,
By God that me made!
"Wel ye witen, wernardes,
But if youre wit faille,   1141

That Fals is feithlees   1142
And fikel in hise werkes,
And was a bastarde y-bore
Of Belsabubbes kynne;
And Mede is muliere,
A maiden of goode,
And myghte kisse the kyng
For cosyn, and she wolde.
  " For-thi wercheth by wisdom,
And by wit also;
And ledeth hire to Londone,
There it is y-shewed,   1153
If any lawe wol loke
Thei ligge togideres;
And though justices juggen hire
To be joyned to Fals,
Yet be war of weddynge;
For witty is Truthe,
And Conscience is of his counseil,
And knoweth yow echone,
And if he fynde yow in defaute
And with the false holde,
It shal bi-sitte youre soules   1164
Ful soure at the laste."
  Herto assenteth Cyvyle,
Ac Symonye ne wolde,
Til he hadde silver for his service,
And also the notaries.
  Thanne fette Favel forth
Floryns ynowe,
And bad Gile to gyven
Gold al aboute,
And namely to the notaries
That hem noon ne faille,   1175

And feffe false witnesses 1176
With floryns ynowe,
" For thei may Mede a-maistrye,
And maken at my wille."
  Tho this gold was y-gyve,
Gret was the thonkyng
To Fals and to Favel
For hire faire giftes,
And comen to conforten
From care the false,
And seiden, " Certes, sire,
Cessen shul we nevere, 1187
Til Mede be thi wedded wif
Thorugh wittes of us alle ;
For we have Mede a-maistried
With oure murie speche,
That she graunteth to goon,
With a good wille,
To London, to loken
If the lawe wolde
Juggen yow joyntly
In joie for evere."
  Thanne was Falsnesse fayn, 1198
And Favel as blithe,
And leten somone alle segges
In shires aboute,
And bad hem alle be bown,
Beggers and othere,
To wenden with hem to Westmyn-
To witnesse this dede.   [stre
  Ac thanne cared thei for caples
To carien hem thider,
And Favel fette forth thanne
Foles ynowe, 1209

And sette Mede upon a sherreve
Shoed al newe.
    And Fals sat on a sisour,
That softeli trotted ;
And Favel on a flaterere
Fetisly atired.
    Tho hadde notaries none,
Anoyed thei were,
For Symonye and Cyvylle
Sholde on hire feet gange.
    Ac thanne swoor Symonye,
And Cyvylle bothe,   1221
That somonours sholde be sadeled
And serven hem echone,
And late apparaille thise provisours
In palfreyes wise,
Sire Symonye hymself
Shal sitte upon hir bakkes.
    "Denes and southdenes,
Drawe yow togideres,
Erchdekenes and officials,
And alle youre registrers,
Lat sadle hem with silver   1232
Oure synne to suffre,
As avoutrye and divorses,
And derne usurie,
To bere bisshopes aboute
A-brood in visitynge.
    "Paulynes pryvees
For pleintes in consistorie,
Shul serven myself
That Cyvyle is nempned.
    "And cart-sadle the commissarie,
Oure cart shal he lede,   1243

And fecchen us vitailles. 1244
At *Fornicatores.*

And maketh of Lyere a lang cart
To leden alle thise othere,
As freres and faitours,
That on hire feet rennen."
And thus Fals and Favel
Fareth forth togideres,
And Mede in the middes,
And alle thise men after.
I have no tome to telle
The tail that hire folwed; 1255
Ac Gyle was for-goer,
And gyed hem alle.
Sothnesse seigh hem wel,
And seide but litel,
And priked his palfrey,
And passed hem alle,
And com to the kynges court,
And Conscience it tolde;
And Conscience to the kyng
Carped it after. 1265
"Now, by Crist," quod the kyng,
"And I cacche myghte
Fals or Favel,
Or any of hise feeris,
I wolde be wroken of tho wrecches
That wercheth so ille,
And doon hem hange by the hals,
And alle that hem maynteneth;
Shal nevere man of this molde
Meynprise the leeste,
But right as the lawe wol loke,
Lat falle on hem alle." 1276

And comaunded a constable 1278
That com at the firste,
To attachen tho tyrauntz,
" For any thyng I hote,
And fettreth faste Falsnesse,
For any kynnes giftes,
And girdeth of Gyles heed,
And lat hym go no ferther;
And if ye lacche Lyere,
Lat hym noght ascapen
Er he be put on the pillory,
For any preyere, I hote ;   1289
And bryngeth Mede to me
Maugree hem alle."
Drede at the dore stood,
And the doom herde,
And how the kyng comaunded
Constables and sergeauntz
Falsnesse and his felawshipe
To fettren and to bynden.
Thanne Drede wente wyghtliche,
And warned the False,
And bad hym fle for fere,   1300
And hise felawes alle.
Falsnesse for fere thanne
Fleigh to the ffreres,
And Gyle dooth hym to go,
A-gast for to dye ;
Ac marchauntz metten with hym
And made hym abide,
And bi-shetten hym in hire shoppes
To shewen hire ware,
Apparailed hym as apprentice
The peple to serve.   1311

Lightliche Lyere   1312
Leep awey thanne,
Lurkynge thorugh lanes,
To-lugged of manye.
He was nowher welcome,
For his manye tales,
Over al y-honted,
And y-hote trusse,
Til pardoners hadde pité,
And pulled hym into house.
They wesshen hym and wiped hym,
And wounden hym in cloutes,   1323
And senten hym with seles
On Sondayes to chirches,
And yeven pardoun for pens
Pounde-mele aboute.
   Thanne lourede leches,
And lettres thei sente,
That he sholde wonye with hem
Watres to loke.
   Spycers speken with hym,
To spien hire ware;
For he kouthe of hir craft,   1334
And knewe manye gommes.
   And mynstrales and messagers
Mette with hym ones,
And helden hym an half-yeer
And ellevene dayes.
   Freres with fair speche
Fetten hym pennes,
And for knowynge of comeres
Coped hym as a frere;
Ac he hath leve to lepen out,
As ofte as hym liketh,   1345

And is welcome whan he wile, 1346
And woneth with hem ofte.
　　Alle fledden for fere,
And flowen into hernes;
Save Mede the mayde,
Na-mo dorste abide.
Ac trewely to telle,
She trembled for drede,
And ek wepte and wrong,
Whan she was attached.　　　1355

NOW is Mede the mayde,
And na-mo of hem alle,
With	bedeles	and	with
	baillies
Brought bifore the kyng.
  The kyng called a clerk,
Kan I noght his name,
To take Mede the maide
And maken hire at ese.
" I shal assayen hire myself,
And soothliche appose,
What man of this moolde
That hire were levest.	1367
And if she werche bi wit,
And my wil folwe,
I wol forgyven hire this gilt,
So me God helpe ! "
  Curteisly the clerk thanne,
As the kyng highte,
Took Mede bi the myddel
And broghte hire into chambre ;
And ther was murthe and mynstral-
Mede to plese.	[cie,
  They that wonyeth in Westmyn-
	stre
Worshipeth hire alle,	1380

Gentilliche with joye ; 1381
The justices somme
Busked hem to the bour
Ther the burde dwellede,
To conforten hire kyndely,
By clergies leve ;
And seiden, " Mourne noght, Mede,
Ne make thow no sorwe ;
For we wol wisse the kyng,
And thi wey shape,
To be wedded at thi wille,
And wher thee leef liketh, 1392
For al Consciences cast
Or craft, as I trowe."
   Mildely Mede thanne
Merciede hem alle
Of hire grete goodnesse,
And gaf hem echone
Coupes of clene gold,
And coppes of silver,
Rynges with rubies,
And richesses manye ;
The leeste man of hire meynee 1403
A moton of golde.
Than laughte thei leve
Thise lordes at Mede.
   With that comen clerkes
To conforten hire the same,
And beden hire be blithe ;
" For we beth thyne owene,
For to werche thi wille,
The while thow myght laste."
   Hendiliche heo thanne
Bi-highte hem the same, 1414

To loven hem lelly, 1415
And lordes to make,
And in the consistorie at the court
Do callen hire names;
"Shal no lewednesse lette
The leode that I lovye,
That he ne worth first avaunced;
For I am bi-knowen,
There konnynge clerkes
Shul clokke bi-hynde."
   Thanne cam ther a confessour,
Coped as a frere; 1426
To Mede the mayde
He meved thise wordes,
And seide ful softely,
In shrift as it were,
"Theigh lewed men and lered men
Hadde leyen by thee bothe,
And Falsnesse hadde y-folwed thee
Alle thise fifty wynter,
I shal assoille thee myself
For a seem of whete,
And also be thi bedeman, 1437
And bere wel thi message
Amonges knyghtes and clerkes,
Conscience to torne."
   Thanne Mede for hire mysdedes
To that man kneled,
And shrof hire of hire sherewed-
Shamelees, I trowe; [nesse,
Tolde hym a tale,
And took hym a noble,
For to ben hire bedeman
And hire brocour als. 1448

Thanne he assoiled hire soone,
And sithen he seide,
" We have a wyndow in werchynge
Wole sitten us ful hye,
Woldestow glaze that gable
And grave therinne thy name,
Syker sholde thi soule be
Hevene to have."
" Wiste I that," quod that wom-
" I wolde noght spare   [man,
For to be youre frend, frere,
And faile yow nevere,   1460
While ye love lordes
That lecherie haunten,
And lakketh noght ladies
That loven wel the same.
It is freletee of flesshe,
Ye fynden it in bokes,
And a cours of kynde
Wherof we comen alle.
Who may scape sclaundre,
The scathe is soone amended;
It is synne of the sevene   1471
Sonnest relessed.
Have mercy," quod Mede,
" Of men that it haunteth,
And I shal covere youre kirk,
Youre cloistre do maken,
Wowes do whiten,
And wyndowes glazen,
Do peynten and portraye,
And paie for the makynge,
That every segge shal seye
I am suster of youre house."   1482

Ac God to alle good folk   1483
Swich gravynge defendeth,
To writen in wyndowes
Of hir wel dedes,
An aventure pride be peynted there,
And pomp of the world ;
For Crist knoweth thi conscience,
And thi kynde wille,
And thi cost and thi coveitise,
And who the catel oughte.
   For-thi I lere yow, lordes,
Leveth swiche werkes ;   1494
To writen in wyndowes
Of youre wel dedes,
Or to greden after Goddes men
Whan ye dele doles,
On aventure ye have youre hire here,
And youre hevene als.
Nesciat sinistra quid faciat dextra.
   Lat noght thi left half
Late ne rathe
Wite what thow werchest
With thi right syde ;   1505
For thus by the gospel
Goode men doon hir almesse.
   Maires and maceres,
That menes ben bitwene
The kyng and the comune
To kepe the lawes,
To punysshe on pillories
And pynynge-stooles,
Brewesters and baksters,
Bochiers and cokes,
For thise are men on this molde 1516

That moost harm wercheth   1517
To the povere peple
That percel-mele buggen;
For thei enpoisone the peple
Pryveliche and ofte,
Thei richen thorugh regratrie,
And rentes hem biggen,
With that the povere peple
Sholde putte in hire wombe.
For toke thei on trewely,
Thei tymbred nought so heighe,
Ne boughte none burgages,   1528
Be ye ful certeyne.
   Ac Mede the mayde
The mair hath bi-sought
Of alle swiche selleris
Silver to take,
Or presentz withouten pens,
As pieces of silver,
Rynges or oother richesse,
The regratiers to mayntene;
"For my love," quod that lady,
"Love hem echone,   1539
And suffre hem to selle
Som del ayeins reson."
   Salomon the sage
A sermon he made,
For to amenden maires
And men that kepen lawes;
And tolde hem this teme,
That I telle thynke,
Ignis devorabit tabernacula eorum
      qui libenter accipiunt munera,
      etc.   1550

Among thise lettrede leodes 1551
This Latyn is to mene,
That fir shal falle and brenne
Al to bloo askes
The houses and homes
Of hem that desireth
Yiftes or yeres-yeves
By cause of hire offices.
　The kyng fro the conseil cam,
And called after Mede,
And of sente hire as swithe
With sergeauntz manye, 1562
And broughte hire to boure
With blisse and with joye.
　Curteisly the kyng thanne
Comsed to telle,
To Mede the mayde
He meveth thise wordes,
" Unwittily, womman,
Wroght hastow ofte,
Ac worse wroghtestow nevere
Than tho thow Fals toke.
But I forgyve thee that gilt, 1573
And graunte thee my grace ;
Hennes to thi deeth day
Do so na-moore.
　" I have a knyght Conscience,
Cam late fro biyonde ;
If he wilneth thee to wif,
Wiltow hym have ? "
　" Ye, lord," quod that lady,
" Lord forbede it ellis !
But I be holly at youre heste,
Lat hange me soone." 1584

And thanne was Conscience called
To come and appere
Bifore the kyng and his conseil,
As clerkes and othere.
Knelynge Conscience
To the kyng louted,
To wite what his wille were,
And what he do wolde.
"Woltow wedde this womman,"
"If I wole assente? [quod the kyng,
For she is fayn of thi felaweshipe,
For to be thi make."   1596
Quod Conscience to the kyng,
"Crist it me forbede !
Er I wedde swich a wif,
Wo me bitide !
For she is frele of hire feith,
Fikel of hire speche,
And maketh men mysdo
Many score tymes;
Trust of hire tresor
Bitrayeth ful manye.
"Wyves and widewes   1607
Wantonnes she techeth,
And lereth hem lecherie
That loveth hire giftes.
Youre fader she felled
Thorugh false biheste,
And hath enpoisoned popes,
And peired holy chirche.
Is noght a bettre baude,
By hym that me made !
Bitwene hevene and helle,
In erthe though men soughte.   1618

For she is tikel of hire tail,   1619
And tale-wis of hire tonge ;
As commune as a cartwey
To ech a knave that walketh,
To monkes, to mynstrales,
To meseles in hegges.
  " Sisours and somonours,
Swiche men hire preiseth ;
Sherreves of shires
Were shent if she ne were ;
For she dooth men lese hire lond
And hire lif bothe ;   1630
She leteth passe prisoners,
And paieth for hem ofte,
And gyveth the gailers gold
And grotes togidres,
To unfettre the fals
Fle where hym liketh ;
And taketh the trewe bi the top
And tieth hem faste,
And hangeth hem for hatrede
That harm dide nevere.
  " To be corsed in consistorie 1641
She counteth noght a bene ;
For she copeth the commissarie,
And coteth hise clerkes.
She is assoiled as soone
As hireself liketh ;
And may neigh as muche do
In a monthe one,
As youre secret seel
In sixe score dayes.
For she is pryvee with the pope,
Provisours it knoweth ;   1652

For sire Symonie and hirselve   1653
Seleth hire bulles.
  " She blesseth thise bisshopes,
Theigh thei be lewed ;
Provendreth persones,
And preestes maynteneth,
To have lemmans and lotebies
Alle hire lif daies,
And bryngeth forth barnes
Ayein forbode lawes.
Ther she is wel with the kyng,
Wo is the reaume ;   1664
For she is favourable to fals,
And de-fouleth truthe ofte.
  " By Jhesus ! with hire jeweles
Youre justices she shendeth,
And lith ayein the lawe,
And letteth hym the gate,
That feith may noght have his forth,
Hire floryns go so thikke.
She ledeth the lawe as hire list,
And love-daies maketh,
And doth men lese thorugh hire love,
That lawe myghte wynne
The maze for a mene man,
Though he mote hire evere.
Lawe is so lordlich
And looth to maken ende,
Withouten presentz or pens
She pleseth wel fewe.
  " Barons and burgeises
She bryngeth in sorwe,
And al the comune in care
That coveiten lyve in truthe ;   1686

For clergie and coveitise 1687
She coupleth togidres.
This is the lif of that lady ;
Now Lord gyve hire sorwe !
And alle that maynteneth hire men,
Meschaunce hem bitide !
For povere men may have no power
To pleyne hem, though thei smerte.
Swich a maister is Mede
Among men of goode."
   Thanne mournede Mede,
And mened hire to the kynge 1698
To have space to speke,
Spede if she myghte.
   The kyng graunted hire grace,
With a good wille,
"Excuse thee, if thow kanst ;
I kan na-moore seggen.
For Conscience accuseth thee,
To congeien thee for evere."
   "Nay, lord," quod that lady,
"Leveth hym the werse,
Whan ye witen witterly 1709
Wher the wrong liggeth.
Ther that meschief is gret,
Mede may helpe.
And thow knowest, Conscience,
I kam noght to chide
Ne deprave thi persone,
With a proud herte.
Wel thow woost, wernarde,
But if thow wolt gabbe,
Thow hast hanged on myn half
Ellevene tymes, 1720

G

And also griped my gold,   1721
Gyve it where thee liked;
And whi thow wrathest thee now,
Wonder me thynketh.
Yet I may as I myghte
Menske thee with giftes,
And mayntene thi manhode
Moore than thow knowest.
  " Ac thow hast famed me foule
Bifore the kyng here;
For killed I nevere no kyng
Ne counseiled therafter,   1732
Ne dide as thow demest
I do it on the kynge.
  " In Normandie was he noght
Noyed for my sake;
Ac thow thiself soothly
Shamedest hym ofte,
Crope into a cabane
For cold of thi nayles,
Wendest that wynter
Wolde han y-lasted evere,
And dreddest to be ded   1743
For a dym cloude,
And hyedest homward
For hunger of thi wombe.
  " Withouten pité, pilour,
Povere men thow robbedest;
And bere hire bras at thi bak
To Caleis to selle,
Ther I lafte with my lord,
His lif for to save.
I made his men murye,
And mournynge lette;   1754

I batred hem on the bak,   1755
And boldede hire hertes,
And dide hem hoppe for hope
To have me at wille.
Hadde I ben marchal of his men,
By Marie of hevene !
I dorste have leyd my lif,
And no lasse wedde,
He sholde have be lord of that lond
In lengthe and in brede,
And also kyng of that kith
His kyn for to helpe,   1766
The leeste brol of his blood
A barones piere.
  "Cowardly thow, Conscience,
Conseiledest hym thennes,
To leven his lordshipe
For a litel silver,
That is the richeste reaume
That reyn over-hoveth.
  "It bi-cometh to a kyng
That kepeth a reaume,
To yeve mede to men,   1777
That mekely hym serveth,
To aliens and to alle men,
To honouren hem with giftes ;
Mede maketh hym bi-loved
And for a man holden.
  "Emperours and erles,
And alle manere lordes,
For giftes han yonge men
To renne and to ryde.
  "The pope and alle the prelates
Presentz underfongen,   1788

And medeth men hemselven   1789
To mayntene hir lawes.
  "Sergeauntz for hire servyce,
We seeth wel the sothe,
Taken mede of hir maistres,
As thei mowe acorde.
  "Beggeres for hir biddynge,
Bidden men mede.
  "Mynstrales for hir myrthe,
Mede thei aske.
  "The kyng hath mede of his men,
To make pees in londe.   1800
  "Men that teche children,
Craven after mede.
  "Preestes that prechen the peple
To goode, asken mede,
And massepens and hire mete
At the meel-tymes.
  "Alle kynne craftes men
Craven mede for hir prentices.
  "Marchauntz and Mede
Mote nede go togideres.
No wight, as I wene,   1811
Withouten mede may libbe."
  Quod the kyng to Conscience,
"By Crist! as me thynketh,
Mede is well worthi
The maistrie to have."
  "Nay," quod Conscience to the
And kneled to the erthe,   [kyng,
"Ther are two manere of medes,
My lord, with youre leve.
  "That oon God of his grace
Graunteth in his blisse   1822

To tho that wel werchen,   1823
While thei ben here;
The prophete precheth therof,
And putte it in the Sauter,
Domine, quis habitabit in taberna-
    culo tuo?   [wones,
  "Lord, who shal wonye in thi
And with thyne holy seintes,
Or resten in thyne holy hilles?
This asketh David;
And David assoileth it hymself,
As the Sauter telleth.   1834
Qui ingreditur sine macula et ope-
    ratur justitiam.
  "Tho that entren of o colour,
And of one wille,
And han y-wroght werkes
With right and with reson;
And he that useth noght
The lyf of usurie,
And enformeth povere men,
And pursueth truthe.
Qui pecuniam suam non dedit ad
    usuram, et munera super innoc.
    etc.   [cent,
  "And alle that helpen the inno-
And holden with the rightfulle,
Withouten mede doth hem good,
And the truthe helpeth,
Swiche manere men, my lord,
Shul have this firste mede
Of God at a gret nede,
Whan thei gon hennes.   [lees,
  "Ther is another mede mesure-

That maistres desireth,   1857
To mayntene mysdoers
Mede thei take,
And therof seith the Sauter
In a salmes ende,
In quorum manibus iniquitates
        sunt, dextra eorum repleta est
        muneribus.
  " And he that gripeth hir gold,
So me God helpe !
Shal abien it bittre,
Or the book lieth.   1863
  " Preestes and persons
That plesynge desireth,
That taken mede and moneie
For masses that thei syngeth,
Taken hire mede here,
As Mathew us techeth.
Amen, Amen, recipiebant mercedem
        suam.
  " That laborers and lowe folk
Taken of hire maistres,
It is no manere mede,   1879
But a mesurable hire.
  " In marchaundise is no mede,
I may it wel avowe,
It is a permutacion apertly,
A penyworth for another.
  " Ac reddestow nevere *Regum ?*
Thow recrayed Mede,
Whi the vengeaunce fel
On Saul and on his children ?
God sente to Saul
By Samuel the prophete,   1890

That Agag of Amalec,   1891
And al his peple after,
Sholden deye for a dede
That doon hadde hire eldres.
   "For-thi seide Samuel to Saul,
'God hymself hoteth
Thee be buxom at his biddynge,
His wil to fulfille ;
Weend to Amalec with thyn oost,
And what thow fyndest there sle it,
Burnes and beestes
Bren hem to dethe,   1902
Widwes and wyves,
Wommen and children,
Moebles and un-moebles,
And al thow myght fynde,
Bren it, bere it noght awey,
Be it never so riche,
For mede ne for monee,
Loke thow destruye it,
Spille it and spare it noght,
Thow shalt spede the bettre.'
   "And for he coveited hir catel,
And the kyng spared,
Forbar hym and his beestes bothe,
As the Bible witnesseth,
Oother wise than he was
Warned of the prophete,
God seide to Samuel
That Saul sholde deye,
And al his seed for that synne
Shenfulliche ende.
Swich a meschief Mede made
Saul the kyng to have,   1924

That God hated hym for evere, 1925
And alle hise heires after.
  "The culorum of this cas
Kepe I noght to telle,
On aventure it noyed men,
Noon ende wol I make,
For so is this world went
With hem that han power,
That who so seith hem sothest
Is sonnest y-blamed.
  "Conscience knowe this,
For kynde wit it me taughte,   1934
That Reson shal regne
And reaumes governe,
And right as Agag hadde,
Happe shul somme,
Samuel shal sleen hym,
And Saul shal be blamed,
And David shal be diademed,
And daunten hem alle;
And oon cristene kyng
Kepen hem alle.
Shal na-moore Mede   1947
Be maister, as she is nouthe;
Ac love and lowenesse
And leautee togideres,
Thise shul ben maistres on moolde,
Truthe to save.   [truthe
  "And who so trespaseth ayein
Or taketh ayein his wille,
Leauté shal don hym lawe,
And no lif ellis;
Shall no sergeaunt for his service
Were a silk howve,   1958

Ne no pelure in his cloke   1959
For pledynge at the barre.
Mede of mysdoeres
Maketh manye lordes,
And over lordes lawes
Ruleth the reaumes.
   " Ac kynde love shal come yit,
And conscience togideres,
And make of lawe a laborer ;
Swich love shal arise,
And swich a pees among the peple,
And a perfit truthe,   1970
That Jewes shul wene in hire wit,
And wexen wonder glade,
That Moyses or Messie
Be come into this erthe,
And have wonder in hire hertes
That men beth so trewe.
   " Alle that beren baselarde,
Brood swerd or launce,
Ax outher hachet,
Or any wepene ellis,
Shal be demed to the deeth,   1981
But if he do it smythye
Into sikel or to sithe,
To shaar or to kultour ;
Conflabunt gladios suos in vomeres,
    etc.
   " Ech man to pleye with a plow,
Pykoise or spade,
Spynne or sprede donge,
Or spille hymself with sleuthe.
   " Preestes and persons
With *Placebo* to hunte,   1992

And dyngen upon David   1993
Eche day til eve.
Huntynge or haukynge
If any of hem use,
His boost of his benefice
Worth by-nomen hym after.
Shal neither kyng ne knyght,
Constable ne meire,
Overlede the commune,
Ne to the court sompne,
Ne putte hem in panel
To doon hem plighte hir truthe;
But after the dede that is doon
Oon doom shal rewarde,
Mercy or no mercy,
As truthe wole acorde.   [court,
    "Kynges court and commune
Consistorie and chapitle,
Al shal be but oon court,
And oon baron be justice.
Thanne worth Trewe-tonge a tidy
That tened me nevere;   [man,
Batailles shul none be,   2015
Ne no man bere wepene;
And what smyth that any smytheth,
Be smyte therwith to dethe.
*Non levabit gens contra gentem
      gladium, etc.*
    "And er this fortune falle,
Fynde men shul the worste,
By sixe sonnes and a shipe,
And half a shef of arwes,
And the myddel of a moone,
Shal make the Jewes to torne,   2020

And Sarzynes for that sighte   2027
Shul synge *Gloria in excelsis, etc.*
For Makometh and Mede
Mys-happe shul that tyme,
For *melius est bonum nomen quam*
    divitiæ multæ."
   Al so wroth as the wynd
Weex Mede in a while,
" I kan no Latyn," quod she,
" Clerkes wite the sothe ;
Se what Salomon seith
In Sapience bokes,   2038
That thei that gyven giftes
The victorie wynneth,
And moost worshipe hadde ther
As holy writ telleth :   [with
Honorem adquiret qui dat munera,
    etc."   [science,
  " Leve wel, lady," quod Con-
" That thi Latyn be trewe ;
Ac thow art lik a lady
That radde a lesson ones,
Was *omnia probate,*   2049
And that plesed hire herte ;
For that lyne was no lenger
At the leves ende.
Hadde she loked that oother half,
And the leef torned,
She sholde have founden fele wordes
Folwynge therafter,
Quod bonum est tenete ;
Truthe that text made.
And so ferde ye, madame,
Ye kouthe na-moore fynde,   2060

Tho ye loked on Sapience   2061
Sittynge in youre studie.
This text that ye han told
Were good for lordes ;
Ac yow fayled a konnynge clerk
That kouthe the leef han torned.
And if ye seche Sapience eft,
Fynde shul ye that folweth,
A ful teneful text
To hem that taketh mede ;
And that is *animam autem aufert
      accipientium, etc.,*   2072
And that is the tail of the text ;
Of that that she shewed,
That theigh we wynne worshipe,
And with mede have victorie,
The soule that the sonde taketh
By so muche is bounde."   2073

Passus Quartus de Visione, ut
supra.

"CESSETII," seith the kyng,
    " I suffre yow no lenger ;
    Ye shul saughtne for sothe,
    And serve me bothe.
Kis hire," quod the kyng,
" Conscience, I hote."   [science,
    " Nay, by Crist !" quod Con-
" Congeye me er for evere,
But Reson rede me therto,
Rather wol I deye."   [the kyng,
    " And I comaunde thee," quod
To Conscience thanne,
" Rape thee to ryde,   2091
And Reson thow fecche ;
Comaunde hym that he come
My counseil to here,
For he shal rule my reaume
And rede me the beste,
And acounte with thee, Conscience,
So me Crist helpe !
How thow lernest the peple,
The lered and the lewed."
    " I am fayn of that foreward,"
Seide the freke thanne,   2102

And ryt right to Reson,   2103
And rouneth in his ere,
And seide as the kyng bad,
And sithen took his leve.
  " I shal arraye me to ryde," quod
" Reste thee a while."   [Reson,
And called Caton his knave,
Curteis of speche,
And also Tomme Trewe-tonge,—
" Tel me no tales,
Ne lesynge to laughen of,
For I loved hem nevere ;   2114
And set my sadel upon Suffre,
Til I se my tyme,
And lat warroke hym wel
With witty-wordes gerthes,
And hange on hym the hevy brydel
To holde his heed lowe,
For he wol make ' wehee ! '
Twies er he be there."
  Thanne Conscience upon his
Carieth forth faste,   [capul
And Reson with hym ryt,   2125
Rownynge togideres,
Whiche maistries Mede
Maketh on this erthe.
  Oon Waryn Wisdom,
And Witty his feere,
Folwed hym faste,
For thei hadde to doone   [rye,
In th'escheker and in the chaunce-
To ben descharged of thynges ;
And riden faste, for Reson sholde
Rede hem the beste,   2136

For to save hem for silver   2137
From shame and from harmes.
And Conscience knew hem wel,
Thei loved coveitise ;
And bad Reson ryde faste,
And recche of hir neither.
"Ther are wiles in hire wordes,
And with Mede thei dwelleth ;
Ther as wrathe and wranglynge is,
Ther wynne thei silver ;
Ac where is love and leautee,
Thei wol noght come there.   2148
Contritio et infelicitas in viis eorum,
        etc.
    "Thei ne yeveth noght of God
One goose wynge.
Non est timor Dei ante oculos
        eorum, etc.
    "For woot God thei wolde do
For a dozeyne chicknes,   [moore
Or as manye capons,
Or for a seem of otes,
Than for the love of oure Lord, 2159
Or alle hise leeve seintes.
For-thi Reson lat hem ride,
Tho riche by hemselve,
For Conscience knoweth hem noght,
Ne Crist, as I trowe."
And thanne Reson rood faste
The righte heighe gate,
As Conscience hym kenned,
Til thei come to the kynge.
    Curteisly the kyng thanne
Com ayeins Reson,   2170

And bitwene hymself and his sone
Sette hym on benche;
And wordeden wel wisely
A gret while togideres.
  And thanne com Pees into par-
And putte forth a bille,   [lement.
How Wrong ayeins his wille
Hadde his wif taken,
And how he ravysshede Rose
Reginaldes loove,
And Margrete of hir maydenhede
Maugree hire chekes.   2182
"Bothe my gees and my grys
Hise gadelynges feccheth,
I dar noght for fere of hem
Fighte ne chide.
He borwed of me Bayard,
He broughte hym hom nevere,
Ne no ferthyng therfore,
For ought I koude plede.
He maynteneth hise men
To murthere myne hewen,
Forstalleth my feires,   2193
And fighteth in my chepyng,
And breketh up my bernes dore,
And bereth awey my whete,
And taketh me but a taillé
For ten quarters of otes;
And yet he beteth me therto,
And lyth by my mayde.
I am noght hardy for hym
Unnethe to loke."
  The kyng knew he seide sooth,
For Conscience hym tolde   2204

That Wrong was a wikked luft, 2205
And wroghte muche sorwe.
Wrong was afered thanne,
And Wisdom he soughte,
To maken pees with hise pens;
And profred hym manye,
And seide, "Hadde I love of my lord
Litel wolde I recche,   [the kyng,
Theigh Pees and his power
Pleyned hym evere."
Tho wente Wisdom
And sire Waryn the Witty,   2216
For that Wrong hadde y-wroght
So wikked a dede,
And warnede Wrong tho
With swich a wis tale,
"Who so wercheth by wille,
Wrathe maketh ofte;
I sey it by myself,
Thow shalt it wel fynde;
But if Mede it make,
Thi meschief is uppe,
For bothe thi lif and thi lond 2227
Lyth in his grace."
Thanne wowede Wrong
Wisdom ful yerne,
To maken pees with his pens,
Handy dandy payed.
Wisdom and Wit thanne
Wenten togidres,
And token Mede myd hem
Mercy to wynne.
Pees putte forth his heed,
And his panne blody,   2233

" Withouten gilt, God it woot,   2239
Gat I this scathe ;
Conscience and the commune
Knowen the sothe."
    Ac Wisdom and Wit
Were aboute faste,
To overcomen the kyng
With catel, if thei myghte.
    The kyng swor by Crist,
And by his crowne bothe,
That Wrong for hise werkes
Sholde wo tholie ;   2250
And comaundede a constable
To casten hym in irens,
And lete hym noght thise seven yer
Seen his feet ones.
    " God woot," quod Wisdom,
" That were noght the beste ;
And he amendes nowe make,
Lat maynprise hym have,
And be borgh for his bale,
And buggen hym boote,
And so amenden that is mys-do   2261
And evere moore the bettre."
    Wit acorded therwith,
And seide the same,
" Bettre is that boote
Bale a-doun brynge,
Than bale be y-bet,
And boote never the bettre."
    And thanne gan Mede to mengen
And mercy she bi-soughte,   [hire,
And profrede Pees a present
Al of pure golde :   2272

" Have this, man, of me," quod she,
" To amenden thi scathe,
For I wol wage for Wrong
He wol do so na-moore."
   Pitously Pees thanne
Preyde to the kynge,
To have mercy on that man
That mys-dide hym so ofte;
" For he hath waged me wel,
As Wisdom hym taughte,
And I forgyve hym that gilt
With a good wille,   2284
So that the kyng assente,
I kan seye no bettre;
For Mede hath me amendes maad,
I may na-moore axe."
   " Nay," quod the kyng tho,
" So me Crist helpe!
Wrong wendeth noght so a-wey,
Erst wole I wite moore.
For lope he so lightly,
Laughen he wolde;
And eft the boldere be   2295
To bete myne hewen;
But Reson have ruthe on hym,
He shal reste in my stokkes;
And that as longe as he lyveth,
But lownesse hym borwe."
   Som men radde Reson tho
To have ruthe on that shrewe,
And for to counseille the kyng,
And Conscience after;
That Mede moste be maynpernour
Reson thei bi-soughte.   2306

" Reed me noght," quod Reson,
" No ruthe to have,
Til lordes and ladies
Loven alle truthe,
And haten alle harlotrie,
To heren or to mouthen it.
  "Til Parnelles purfille
Be put in hire hucche,
And childrene cherissynge
Be chastynge with yerdes,
And harlottes holynesse
Be holden for an hyne.   2318
  "Til clerkene coveitise be
To clothe the povere and fede,
And religiouse romeris
Recordare in hir cloistres,
As seynt Beneyt hem bad,
Bernard and Fraunceis,
And til prechours prechynge
Be preved on hemselve.
  "Til the kynges counseil
Be the commune profit,
Til bisshopes bayardes   2329
Ben beggeris chaumbres,
Hire haukes and hire houndes
Help to povere religious.
  "And til seint James be sought
There I shal assigne,
That no man go to Galis
But if he go for evere ;—
And alle Rome renneres,
For robberes biyonde,
Bere no silver over see
That signe of kyng sheweth,   2340

Neither grave ne ungrave,   2341
Gold neither silver,
Upon forfeture of that fee,
Who so fynt it at Dovere,
But if he be marchaunt or his man,
Or messager with lettres,
Provysour or preest,
Or penaunt for hise synnes.
  "And yet," quod Reson, "by the
I shal no ruthe have,   [Rode!
While Mede hath the maistrie
In this moot-halle.   2352
Ac I may shewe ensamples,
As I se outher while,
I seye it by myself," quod he,
"And it so were
That I were kyng with coroune
To kepen a reaume,
Sholde nevere Wrong in this world,
That I wite myghte,
Ben unpunysshed in my power,
For peril of my soule,
Ne gete my grace for giftes,   2363
So me God save!
Ne for no mede have mercy,
But mekenesse it make;
For *nullum malum* the man
Mette with *inpunitum*,
And bad *nullum bonum*
Be *irremuneratum*.
  "Lat youre confessour, sire kyng,
Construe this unglosed;
And if ye werchen it in werk,
I wedde myne eris,   2374

That lawe shal ben a laborer   2375
And lede a-feld donge,
And love shal lede thi lond,
As the leef liketh."
    Clerkes that were confessours
Coupled hem togideres,
Al to construe this clause,
And for the kynges profit,
Ac noght for confort of the com-
Ne for the kynges soule ;   [mune,
For I seigh Mede in the moot-halle
On men of lawe wynke,   2386
And thei laughynge lope to hire,
And left Reson manye.
Waryn Wisdom
Wynked upon Mede,
And seide, " Madame, I am youre
What so my mouth jangle ;   [man,
I falle in floryns," quod that freke,
" And faile speche ofte."
    Alle rightfulle recordede
That Reson truthe tolde ;
And Wit acorded therwith,   2397
And comendede hise wordes,
And the mooste peple in the halle,
And manye of the grete,
And leten Mekenesse a maister,
And Mede a mansed sherewe.
    Love leet of hire light,
And leauté yet lasse,
And seiden it so heighe
That al the halle it herde,
" Who so wilneth hire to wif,
For welthe of hire goodes,   2408

But he be knowe for a cokewold, 2409
Kut of my nose."
  Mede mornede tho,
And made hevy chere,
For the mooste commune of that
Called hire an hore.   [court
Ac a sisour and a somonour
Sued hire faste,
And a sherreves clerk
Bisherewed at the route ;
" For ofte have I," quod he,
" Holpen yow at the barre,   2420
And yet yeve ye me nevere
The worth of a risshe."
  The kyng callede Conscience,
And afterward Reson,
And recordede that Reson
Hadde rightfully shewed ;
And modiliche upon Mede
With myght the kyng loked ;
And gan wexe wroth with lawe,
For Mede almoost hadde shent it ;
And seide, " thorugh lawe, as I
I lese manye eschetes ;   [leve !
Mede overmaistreth lawe,
And muche Truthe letteth.
Ac Reson shal rekene with yow,
If I regne any while,
And deme yow bi this day,
As ye han deserved.
Mede shal noght maynprise yow,
By the Marie of hevene !
I wole have leauté in lawe,
And lete be al youre janglyng ; 2442

And as moost folk witnesseth wel, 2443
Wrong shal be demed."
  Quod Conscience to the kyng,
"But the commune wole assente,
It is ful hard, by myn heed!
Hertoo to brynge it,
Alle youre lige leodes
To lede thus evene."   [rode!"
  "By hym that raughte on the
Quod Reson to the kynge,
"But if I rule thus youre reaume,
Rende out my guttes,   2454
If ye bidden buxomnesse
Be of myn assent."
  "And I assente," seith the kyng,
"By seinte Marie my lady!
By my counseil commune,
Of clerkes and of erles ;
Ac redily, Reson,
Thow shalt noght ride fro me,
For, as longe as I lyve,
Lete thee I nelle."
  "I am al redy," quod Reson,
"To reste with yow evere ;
So Conscience be of oure counseil,
I kepe no bettre."
  "And I graunte," quod the kyng,
"Goddes forbode ellis !
Als longe as oure lyf lasteth,
Lyve we togideres."   2472

THE kyng and hise knyghtes
　　To the kirke wente,
　　To here matyns of the day
　　And the masse after.
Thanne waked I of my wynkyng,
And wo was withalle,
That I ne hadde slept sadder,
And y-seighen moore.
Ac er I hadde faren a furlong,
Feyntise me hente,
That I ne myghte ferther a foot
For defaute of slepynge,
And sat softely a-doun,　　　　2485
And seide my bileve,
And so I bablede on my bedes,
Thei broughte me a-slepe.
And thanne saugh I muche moore
Than I bifore of tolde,
For I seigh the feld ful of folk,
That I bifore of seide,
And how Reson gan arayen hym
Al the reaume to preche,
And with a cros afore the kyng
Comsede thus to techen.　　　　2496

He preved that thise pestilences
Were for pure synne,
And the south-westrene wynd
On Saterday at even
Was pertliche for pure pride,
And for no point ellis;
Pyries and plum-trees
Were puffed to the erthe,
In ensaumple that the segges
Sholden do the bettre;
Beches and brode okes
Were blowen to the grounde,   2508
Turned upward hire tailes,
In tokenynge of drede
That dedly synne er domes-day
Shal for-doon hem alle.

Of this matere I myghte
Mamelen ful longe;
Ac I shal seye as I saugh,
So me God helpe!
How pertly afore the peple
Reson bigan to preche.

He bad Wastour go werche,   2519
'What he best kouthe,
And wynnen his wastyng
With som maner crafte.

He preide Pernele
Hir purfil to lete,
And kepe it in hire cofre
For catel at hire nede.

Tomme Stowne he taughte
To take two staves,
And fecche Felice hom
Fro the wynen pyne.   2530

He warnede Watte   2531
His wif was to blame,
For hire heed was worth half marc,
And his hood noght worth a grote;
And bad Bette kutte
A bough outher tweye,
And bete Beton therwith,
But if she wolde werche.
    And thanne he chargede chapmen
To chastizen hir children,
Late no wynnyng hem for-wanye
While thei be yonge,   2542
Ne for no poustee of pestilence
Plese hem noght out of reson.
"My sire seide so to me,
And so dide my dame,
That the levere child
The moore loore bihoveth;
And Salomon seide the same,
That *Sapience* made,
Qui parcit virgæ, odit filium.
The Englissh of this Latyn is,
Who so wole it knowe   2553
Who so spareth the spring,
Spilleth hise children."
    And sithen he prechede prelates
And preestes togideres,
"That ye prechen to the peple,
Preve it on yowselve,
And dooth it in dede,
It shal drawe yow to goode;
If ye leven as ye leren us,
We shul leve yow the bettre."
    And sithen he radde Religion 2564

Hir rule to holde ;   2565
" Lest the kyng and his conseil
Youre comunes apeire,
And be stywardes of youre stedes,
Til ye be ruled bettre."

  And sithen he counseiled the kyng
His commune to lovye :
" It is thi trewe tresor.
And tryacle at thy nede."

  And sithen he preide the pope
Have pite on holy chirche,
And er he gyve any grace,   2576
Governe first hymselve.

  " And ye that han lawes to kepe,
Lat truthe be youre coveitise.
Moore than gold outher giftes.
If ye wol God plese :
For who so contrarieth Truthe,
He telleth in the gospel.
That God knoweth hym noght,
Ne no seynt of hevene.
Amen dico vobis, nescio vos.

  " And ye that seke seynt James.
And seyntes of Rome.
Seketh seynt Truthe,
For he may save yow alle ;
Qui cum patre et filio,
That faire hem bi-falle
That seweth my sermon."
And thus seyde Reson.

  Thanne ran Repentaunce,
And reherced his teme :
And garte Wille to wepe
Water with hise eighen.   2588

Pernele Proud-herte   2599
Platte hire to the erthe,
And lay longe er she loked,
And "Lord, mercy!" cryde,
And bi-highte to hym
That us alle made,
She sholde unsowen hir serk,
And sette there an heyre,
To affaiten hire flesshe
That fiers was to synne.
"Shal nevere heigh herte me hente,
But holde I wole me lowe   2610
And suffre to be mys-seyd,
And so dide I nevere;
And now I wole meke me,
And mercy biseche,
For al this I have
Hated in myn herte."
    Thanne Lechour seide, "Allas!"
And on oure Lady he cryde,
To maken mercy for hise mys-dedes
Bitwene God and his soule;
With that he sholde the Saterday,
Seven yer therafter,
Drynke but myd the doke,
And dyne but ones.
    Envye with hevy herte
Asked after shrifte,
And carefully *mea culpa*
He comsed to shewe.
He was as pale as a pelet,
In the palsy he semed;
And clothed in a kaurymaury,
I kouthe it nought discryve,   2632

In kirtel and courtepy,   2633
And a knyf by his syde;
Of a freres frokke
Were the fore-sleves;
And as a leek that hadde y-leye
Longe in the sonne,
So loked he with lene chekes
Lourynge foule.

    His body was to-bollen for wrathe,
That he boot hise lippes;   [fust,
And wryngynge he yede with the
To wreke hymself he thoughte   2644
With werkes or with wordes,
Whan he seyghe his tyme.
Ech a word that he warpe
Was of a neddres tonge;
Of chidynge and of chalangynge
Was his chief liflode,
With bakbitynge and bismere,
And berynge of fals witnesse.

    "I wolde ben y-shryve," quod this
"And I for shame dorste; [sherewe,
I wolde be gladder, by God!   2655
That Gybbe hadde meschaunce,
Than though I hadde this wouke y-
A weye of Essex chese.   [wonne
    "I have a neghebore by me,
I have anoyed hym ofte,
And lowen on hym to lordes
To doon hym lese his silver,
And maad his frendes be his foon
Thorugh my false tonge;
His grace and his goode happes
Greven me ful soore.   2666

" Bitwene manye and manye 2667
I make debate ofte,
That bothe lif and lyme
Is lost thorugh my speche.
And whan I mete hym in market
That I moost hate,
I hailse hym hendely,
As I his frend were ;
For he is doughtier than I,
I dar do noon oother ;
Ac hadde I maistrie and myght,
God woot my wille !   2678
   " And whan I come to the kirk,
And sholde knele to the roode,
And preye for the peple
As the preest techeth,
For pilgrymes and for palmeres,
For al the peple after,
Thanne I crye on my knees
That Crist gyve hem sorwe,
That beren awey my bolle
And my broke shete.
   " Awey fro the auter thanne 2689
Turne I myne eighen,
And bi-holde Eleyne
Hath a newe cote ;
I wisshe thanne it were myn,
And al the web after.
   " And of mennes lesynge I laughe,
That liketh myn herte ;
And for hir wynnynge I wepe,
And waille the tyme ;
And deme that thei doon ille,
There I do wel werse.   2700

Who so under-nymeth me here 2701
I hate hym dedly after;
I wolde that ech a wight
Were my knave,
For who so hath moore than I,
Than angreth me soore.
And thus I lyve love-lees,
Lik a luther dogge;
That al my body bolneth,
For bitter of my galle.
    "I myghte noght ete many yeres
As a man oughte,   2712
For envye and yvel wil
Is yvel to defie.
May no sugre ne swete thyng
Aswage my swellyng?
Ne no *diapenidion*
Dryve it fro myn herte?
Ne neither shrifte ne shame,
But who so shrape my mawe?"
    "Yis redily," quod Repentaunce,
And radde hym to the beste,
"Sorwe of synnes   2723
Is savacion of soules."
    "I am sory," quod that segge,
"I am but selde oother,
And that maketh me thus megre,
For I ne may me venge.
    "Amonges burgeises have I be
Dwellyng at Londone,
And gart bakbityng be a brocour
To blame mennes ware;
Whan he solde and I nought,
Thanne was I redy   2734

To lye and to loure on my neghebore,
And to lakke his chaffare ;
I wole amende this, if I may,
Thorugh myght of God almyghty."
  Now awaketh Wrathe,
With two white eighen ;
And nevelynge with the nose,
And his nekke hangyng.
  " I am Wrathe," quod he,
" I was som tyme a frere,
And the coventes gardyner
For to graffen impes ;   2746
On lymitours and listres
Lesynges I ymped,
Til thei beere leves of lowe speche,
Lordes to plese,
And sithen thei blosmede a-brood
In boure to here shriftes ;
And now is fallen therof a fruyt,
That folk han wel levere
Shewen hire shriftes to hem,
Than shryve hem to hir persons.
  "And now persons han perceyved
That freres parte with hem,
Thise possessioners preche
And deprave freres.
  "And freres fyndeth hem in de-
As folk bereth witnesse,   [faute,
That whan thei preche the peple
In many places aboute,
I Wrathe walke with hem,
And wisse hem of my bokes.
Thus thei speken of my spiritualté,
That either despiseth oother,   2768

Til thei be bothe beggers   2769
And by my spiritualté libben,
Or ellis al riche
And ryden aboute.
I Wrathe reste nevere,
That I ne moste folwe
This wikked folk,
For swich is my grace.
  "I have an aunte to nonne,
And an abbesse bothe;
Hir hadde levere swowe or swelte,
Than suffre any peyne,   2780
  "I have be cook in hir kichene,
And the covent served
Manye monthes with hem,
And with monkes bothe.
I was the prioresse potager,
And othere povere ladies,
And maad hem joutes of janglyng,
That dame Johane was a bastard,
And dame Clarice a knyghtes dough-
Ac a cokewold was hir sire;   [ter,
And dame Pernele a preestes fyle,
Prioresse worth she nevere,
For she hadde child in chirie-tyme,
Al our chapitre it wiste.
  "Of wikkede wordes
I Wrathe hire wortes made,
Til 'thow lixt' and 'thow lixt'
Lopen out at ones,
And either hite oother
Under the cheke;
Hadde thei had knyves, by Crist
Hir either hadde kild oother.

" Seint Gregory was a good pope,
And hadde a good forwit,
That no prioresse were preost,
For that he ordeyned ;   [firste day,
They hadde thanne ben *infames* the
Thei kan so yvele hele conseil.
" Among monkes I myghte be,
Ac many tyme I shonye it ;
For there ben manye felle frekes
My feeris to aspie,
Bothe priour and suppriour
And oure *pater abbas ;*   2814
And if I telle any tales,
Thei taken hem togideres,
And doon me faste frydayes
To breed and to watre,   [hous
And am chalanged in the chapitre
As I a child were,
And baleised on the bare ers,
And no brech bitwene.
For-thi have I no likyng
With tho leodes to wonye.
I ete there unthende fisshe,   2825
And feble ale drynke ;
Ac outher while whan wyn cometh,
Thanne I drynke wyn at eve,
And have a flux of a foul mouth
Wel fyve dayes after.
Al the wikkednesse that I woot
By any of oure bretheren,
I couthe it in oure cloistre,
That al oure covent woot it."
" Now repente thee," quod Repent-
" And reherce thow nevere [aunce,

Counseil that thow knowest   2837
By contenaunce ne by right ;
And drynk nat over delicatly,
Ne to depe neither,
That thi wille by cause therof
To wrathe myghte turne.
Esto sobrius," he seide,
And assoiled me after,
And bad me wilne to wepe
My wikkednesse to amende.

    And thanne cam Coveitise,
Kan I hym naght discryve,   2848
So hungrily and holwe
Sire Hervy hym loked.
He was bitel-browed,
And baber-lipped also,
With two blered eighen
As a blynd hagge ;
And as a letheren purs
Lolled hise chekes,
Wel sidder than his chyn
Thei chyveled for elde ;
And as a bonde-man of his bacon
His berd was bi-draveled,
With an hood on his heed,
A lousy hat above,
And in a tawny tabard
Of twelf wynter age,
Al so torn and baudy,
And ful of lys crepyng,
But if that a lous couthe
Han lopen the bettre,   [welthe,
She sholde noght han walked on that
So was it thred-bare.   2870

"I have ben coveitous," quod this
"I bi-knowe it here,   [caytif,
For som tyme I served
Symme-atte-Style,
And was his prentice y-plight
His profit to wayte.
    "First I lerned to lye,
A leef outher tweyne ;
Wikkedly to weye
Was my firste lesson ;
To Wy and to Wynchestre
I wente to the feyre,   2882
With many manere marchaundise,
As my maister me highte.
Ne hadde the grace of gyle y-go
Amonges my chaffare,
It hadde ben unsold this seven yer,
So me God helpe !
    "Thanne drough I me among dra-
My donet to lerne,   [piers,
To drawe the liser along,
The lenger it semed ;
Among the riche rayes   2893
I rendred a lesson,
To broche hem with a pak-nedle,
And playte hem togideres,
And putte hem in a presse,
And pyne hem therinne,
Til ten yerdes or twelve
Hadde tolled out thrittene.
    "My wif was a webbe,
And wollen cloth made ;
She spak to spynnesteres
To spynnen it oute,   2904

Ac the pound that she paied by 2905
Peised a quatron moore
Than myn owene auncer,
Who so weyed truthe.
　"I boughte hire barly-malt,
She brew it to selle,
Peny ale and puddyng ale
She poured togideres,
For laborers and for lowe folk
That lay by hymselve.
　"The beste ale lay in my bour,
Or in my bed-chambre ;　　　2916
And who so bummed therof,
Boughte it therafter,
A galon for a grote,
God woot, no lesse !
And yet it cam in cuppe-mele,
This craft my wif used.
Rose the Regrater
Was hire righte name ;
She hath holden hukkerye
Al hire lif tyme.
Ac I swere now, so thee ik !　2927
That synne wol I lete,
And nevere wikkedly weye,
Ne wikke chaffare use ;
But wenden to Walsyngham,
And my wif als,
And bidde the Roode of Bromholm
Brynge me out of dette."
　"Repentedestow evere ?" quod
　　Repentaunce,
"Or restitucion madest." [quod he,
　"Yis, ones I was y-herberwed,"

" With an heep of chapmen,   2938
I roos whan thei were a-reste
And riflede hire males."
    " That was no restitucion," quod
        Repentaunce,
" But a robberis thefte ;
Thow haddest be the bettre worthi
Ben hanged therfore,
Than for al that
That thow hast here shewed."
    " I wende riflynge were restitu-
        cion," quod he,   2947
" For I lerned nevere rede on boke ;
And I kan no Frensshe, in feith,
But of the fertheste ende of North-
        folk."   [Repentaunce,
    " Usedestow evere usurie ?" quod
" In al thi lif tyme."
    " Nay sothly," he seide,
" Save in my youthe
I lerned among Lumbardes
And Jewes a lesson,
To weye pens with a peis,   2957
And pare the hevyeste.
And lene it for love of the cros,
To legge a wed and lese it.
Swiche dedes I dide write,
If he his day breke,
I have mo manoirs thorugh rerages,
Than thorugh *miseretur et commo-*
    " I have lent lordes   [*dat.*
And ladies my chaffare,
And ben hire brocour after,
And bought it myselve ;   2968

Eschaunges and chevysaunces   2969
With swich chaffare I dele,
And lene folk that lese wole
A lippe at every noble,
And with Lumbardes lettres
I ladde gold to Rome,
And took it by tale here,
And tolde hem there lasse."
   " Lentestow evere lordes,
For love of hire mayntenaunce ? "
   " Ye, I have lent to lordes,
Loved me nevere after,   2980
And have y-maad many a knyght
Bothe mercer and draper,
That payed nevere for his prentis-
Noght a peire gloves."   [hode
   " Hastow pité on povere men,
That mote nedes borwe ? "
   " I have as muche pité of povere
As pedlere hath of cattes,   [men,
That wolde kille hem, if he cacche
       hem myghte,
For coveitise of hir skynnes."   2990
   " Artow   manlich   among   thi
       neghebores
Of thi mete and drynke ? "
   " I am holden," quod he, " as
As hound is in kichene,   [hende
Amonges my neghebores, namely,
Swiche a name ich have."
   " Now God lene thee nevere,"
       quod Repentaunce,
" But thow repente the rather,
The grace on this grounde   2999

Thi good wel to bi-sette,   3000
Ne thyne heires after thee
Have joie of that thow wynnest,
Ne thyne executours wel bi-sette
The silver that thow hem lěvest ;
And that was wonne with wrong
With wikked men be despended.
For were I frere of that hous
Ther good feith and charité is,
I nolde cope us with thi catel,
Ne oure kirk amende,
Ne have a peny to my pitaunce,   3011
So God my soule save !
For the beste book in oure hous,
Theigh brent gold were the leves,
And I wiste witterly
Thow were swich as thow tellest.
Servus es alterius,
Dum fercula pinguia quæris ;
Pane tuo potius
Vescere, liber eris.
   " Thow art an unkynde creature,
I kan thee noght assoille,   3022
Til thow make restitucion
And rekene with hem alle ;
And sithen that Reson rolle it
In the registre of hevene,
That thow hast maad ech man good,
I may thee noght assoile.
Non dimittitur peccatum, donec re-
    stituatur oblatum.
   " For alle that han of thi good,
Have God my trouthe !
Ben holden at the heighe doom   3033

To helpe thee to restitue ;   [sooth,
And who so leveth noght this be
Loke in the Sauter glose,
In *Miserere mei, Deus,*
Wher I mene truthe ;
Ecce enim veritatem dilexisti, etc.
Shal nevere werkman in this world
Thryve with that thow wynnest.
Cum sancto sanctus eris ;
Construwe me this on Englisshe."

Thanne weex that shere we in wan-
And wolde han hanged hym ; [hope,
Ne hadde Repentaunce the rather
Reconforted hym in this manere.
" Have mercy in thi mynde,
And with thi mouth biseche it ;
For Goddes mercy is moore
Than alle hise othere werkes.
And al the wikkednesse in this world
That man myghte werche or thynke,
Nis na-moore to the mercy of God,
Than in the see a gleede.
Omnis iniquitas quantum ad miseri-
cordiam Dei, est quasi scintilla
in medio maris.
"For-thi have mercy in thy mynde,
And marchaundise leve it ;
For thow hast no good ground
To gete thee with a wastel,
But if it were with thi tonge,
Or ellis with thi two hondes.
For the good that thow hast geten
Bigan al with falshede,   [with,
And as longe as thow lyvest ther-

Thow yeldest noght, but borwest.
  "And if thow wite nevere to
Ne whom to restitue,   [whiche,
Ber it to the bisshope,
And bid hym of his grace
Bi-sette it hymself,
As best is for thi soule;
For he shal answere for thee
At the heighe dome,
For thee and for many mo
That man shal yeve a rekenyng,
What he lerned yow in Lente, 3079
Leve thow noon oother,
And what he lente yow of oure Lordes
To lette yow fro synne."   [good
  Now bi-gynneth Gloton
For to go to shrifte,
And karieth hym to kirke-warde
His coupe to shewe;
And Beton the brewestere
Bad hym good morwe,
And asked at hym with that,
Whider-ward he wolde.   3090
  "To holy chirche," quod he,
"For to here masse,
And sithen I wole be shryven,
And synne na-moore."   [she,
  "I have good ale, gossib," quod
"Gloton, woltow assaye?"   [he,
  "Hastow oughtin thipurs?" quod
"Any hote spices?"   [she,
  "I have pepir and piones," quod
"And a pound of garleek,
And a ferthyng-worth of fenel-seed

For fastynge dayes."   3102
  Thanne goth Glotin in,
And grete othes after.
Cesse the souteresse
Sat on the benche ;
Watte the warner,
And his wif bothe ;
Tymme the tynkere,
And tweyne of his prentices ;
Hikke the hakeney-man,
And Hughe the nedlere ;
Clarice of Cokkeslane,   3113
And the clerk of the chirche ;
Dawe the dykere,
And a dozeyne othere.
  Sire Piers of Pridie,
And Pernele of Flaundres ;
A ribibour, a ratoner,
A rakiere of Chepe,
A ropere, a redyng-kyng,
And Rose the dyssheres ;
Godefray of Garlekhithe,
And Griffyn the Walshe ;   3124
And upholderes an heep,
Erly by the morwe,
Geve Gloton with glad chere
Good ale to hanselle.
  Clement the Cobelere
Caste of his cloke,
And at the newe feire
He nempned it to selle,
  Hikke the hakeney-man
Hitte his hood after,
And bad Bette the bocher   3135

Ben on his syde.   3136
    Ther were chapmen y-chose
This chaffare to preise,
That who so hadde the hood
Sholde han amendes of the cloke.
    Two risen up in rape,
And rouned togideres,
And preised thise peny-worthes
A-part by hemselve;
Thei kouthe noght by hir con-
Acorden in truthe,   [science
Til Robyn the ropere   3147
Aroos by the southe,
And nempned hym for a nounpere,
That no debat nere.
    Hikke the hostiler
Hadde the cloke,
In covenaunt that Clement
Sholde the cuppe fille,
And have Hikkes hood hostiler,
And holden hym y-served.
And who so repented rathest
Sholde aryse after,   3158
And greten sire Gloton
With a galon ale.
    There was laughynge and lour-
And "lat go the cuppe;"   [ynge,
And seten so till even-song,
And songen umwhile,
Til Gloton hadde y-glubbed
A galon and a gille.
Hise guttes bigonne to gothelen
As two gredy sowes;
He pissed a potel   3169

In a pater-noster while,   3170
And blew his rounde ruwet
At his rugge-bones ende,
That alle that herde that horn
Held hir noses after,
And wisshed it hadde been wexed
With a wispe of firses.

He myghte neither steppe ne
Er he his staf hadde ;   [stonde,
And thanne gan he to go
Like a gle-mannes bicche,
Som tyme aside,   3181
And som tyme arere,
As who so leith lynes
For to lacche foweles.

And whan he drough to the dore,
Thanne dymmed his eighen ;
He. stumbled on the thresshfold,
And threw to the erthe.
Clement the cobelere
Kaughte hym by the myddel,
For to liften hym o-lofte ;
And leyde hym on his knowes. 3192
Ac Gloton was a gret cherl,
And a grym in the liftyng,
And koughed up a cawdel
In Clementes lappe ;
Is noon so hungry hound
In Hertford shire
Dorste lape of that levynges,
So un-lovely thei smaughte.

With al the wo of this world,
His wif and his wenche
Baren hym hom to his bed,   3203

And broughte hym therinne ;   3204
And after al this excesse
He hadde an accidie,
That he sleep Saterday and Sonday,
Til sonne yede to reste.
    Thanne waked he of his wynk-
And wiped hise eighen ;   [yng,
The firste word that he warpe
Was " where is the bolle ? "
His wif gan edwyte hym tho,
How wikkedly he lyvede ;
And Repentaunce right so   3215
Rebuked hym that tyme,
" As thow with wordes and werkes
Has wroght yvele in thi lyve,
Shryve thee, and be shamed therof,
And shewe it with thi mouthe."
    " I Gloton," quod the grom,
" Gilty me yelde,   [tonge,
That I have trespased with my
I kan noght telle how ofte ;
Sworen Goddes soule,
And so me God helpe !   3226
There no nede was,
Nyne hundred tymes.
    " And over-seyen me at my soper,
And som tyme at nones,
That I Gloton girte it up
Er I hadde gon a myle,
An y-spilt that myghte be spared
And spended on som hungry ;
Over delicatly on fastyng-dayes
Dronken and eten bothe,
And sat som tyme so longe there,

That I sleep and eet at ones.   3233
For love of tales in tavernes
And for drynke, the moore I dyned;
And hyed to the mete er noon,
Whan fastyng-days were."
   " This shewynge shrift," quod
      Repentaunce,
"Shal be meryt to the."
   And thanne gan Gloton greete,
And gret doel to make,
For his luther lif
That he lyved hadde;   3248
And avowed to faste,
" For hunger or for thurste,
Shal nevere fyssh on Fryday
Defyen in my wombe,
Til abstinence myn aunte
Have gyve me leeve ;
And yet have I hated hire
Al my lif tyme."   [bered,
   Thanne cam Sleuthe al bi-sla-
With two slymy eighen ;
" I moste sitte," seide the segge,
" Or ellis sholde I nappe.
I may noght stonde ne stoupe,
Ne withoute a stool knele ;
Were I brought a-bedde,
But if my tail-ende it made,
Sholde no ryngynge do me ryse
Er I were ripe to dyne."
He bigan Benedicite with a bolk,
And his brest knokked,
And raxed and rored,
And rutte at the laste.   3270

" What, awake, renk !" quod Re-
    pentaunce,
" And rape thee to shryfte."
  " If I sholde deye bi this day,
Me list nought to loke ;
I kan noght parfitly my pater-noster,
As the preest it syngeth ;
But I kan rymes of Robyn Hood,
And Randolf erl of Chestre ; [Lady
Ac neither of oure Lord ne of oure
The leeste that evere was maked.

  " I have maad avowes fourty,
And foryete hem on the morwe ;
I perfournede nevere penaunce
As the preest me highte ;
Ne right sory for my synnes
Yet was I nevere.
And if I bidde any bedes,
But if it be in wrathe,
That I telle with my tonge
Is two myle fro myn herte.
I am ocupied eche day,
Haly-day and oother,   3292
With ydel tales at the ale,
And outher while at chirche ;
Goddes peyne and his passion
Ful selde thenke I on it.

  " I visited nevere feble men,
Ne fettred folk in puttes ;
I have levere here an harlotrye,
Or a somer game of souters,
Or lesynge to laughen at
And bi-lye my neghebores,
Than al that evere Marc made, 3303

Mathew, Johan, and Lucas.   3304
And vigilies and fastyng-dayes,
Alle thise late I passe ;
And ligge a-beddle in Lenten,
And my lemman in myne armes,
Til matyns and masse be do,
And thanne go to the freres.
Come I to *Ite, missa est*,
I holde me y-served ;
I nam noght shryven som tyme,
But if siknesse it make,
Nought twyes in two yer,   3315
And thanne up gesse I shryve me.
  " I have be preest and parson
Passynge thritty wynter,
And yet can I neyther solne ne
Ne seintes lyves rede ;   [synge,
But I kan fynden in a feld,
Or in a furlang, an hare,
Bettre than in *Beatus vir*,
Or in *Beati omnes*,
Construe oon clause wel
And kenne it to my parisshens.
I kan holde love-dayes,
And here a reves rekenyng ;
Ac in canon nor in decretals
I kan noght rede a lyne.
  " If I bigge and borwe aught,
But if it be y-tailed,
I foryete it as yerne ;
And if men me it axe
Sixe sithes or sevene,
I forsake it with othes ;
And thus tene I trewe men   3337

Ten hundred tymes.   3338
  "And my servauntz som tyme
Hir salarie is bi-hynde ;
Ruthe it is to here the rekenyng,
Whan we shul rede acountes.
So with wikked wil and wrathe,
My werkmen I paye.
  "If any man dooth me a bienfait,
Or helpeth me at nede,
I am unkynde ayeins curteisie,
And kan nought understounden it ;
For I have and have had   3349
Som del haukes maneres,
I am noght lured with love, [thombe.
But ther ligge aught under the
  "The kyndenesse that myn even
Kidde me fernyere,   [cristene
Sixty sithes I Sleuthe
Have foryete it siththe.
In speche and in sparynge of speche
Y-spilt many a tyme
Bothe flessh and fissh,
And manye othere vitailles,   3360
Both bred and ale,
Buttre, melk, and chese,
For-sleuthed in my service
Til it myghte serve no man.
  "I ran aboute in youthe,
And yaf me naught to lerne,
And evere siththe have I be beggere
For my foule sleuthe.
*Heu michi! quia sterilem vitam duxi
      juvenilem."* [Repentaunce ;
  "Repentedestow noght ?" quod

And right with that he swowned,
Til *Vigilate* the veille
Fette water at hise eighen,
And flatte it on his face,
And faste on hym cryde,
And seide, "Ware thee, for Wan-
Wolde thee bi-traye,   [hope
'I am sory for my synnes'
Seye to thiselve,
And beet thiself on the brest,
And bidde hym of grace ;
For is no gilt here so gret   3383
That his goodnesse nys moore."
    Thanne sat Sleuthe up,
And seyned hym swithe,
And made a vow to-fore God
For his foule sleuthe.
"Shal no Sonday be this seven yer,
But siknesse it lette,
That I ne shal do me er day
To the deere chirche ;
And here matyns and masse,
As I a monk were,   3394
Shal noon ale after mete
Holde me thennes,
Til I have even-song herd,
I bi-hote to the roode !
And yet wole I yelde ayein,
If I so much have,
Al that I wikkedly wan
Sithen I wit hadde.
    "And though my liflode lakke,
Leten I nelle,
That ech man ne shal have his,

Er I hennes wende;   [menaunt,
And with the residue and the re-
Bi the Rode of Chestre !
I shal seken Truthe erst
Er I se Rome."
     Roberd the robbere
On *Reddite* loked,
And for ther was noght wherof,
He wepte swithe soore ;
Ac yet the synfulle sherewe
Seide to hymselve,
" Crist, that on Calvarie   3417
Upon the cros deidest,
Tho Dysmas my brother
Bi-soughte yow of grace,
And haddest mercy on that man
For *memento* sake,
So rewe on this robbere
That *reddere* ne have,
Ne nevere wene to wynne
With craft that I owe ;
But for thi muchel mercy
Mitigacion I bi-seche,   3428
Ne dampne me noght at domes-day
For that I dide so ille."
     What bi-fel of this feloun
I kan noght faire shewe ;
Wel I woot he wepte faste
Water with bothe hise eighen,
And knoweliched his gilt
To Crist yet eft soones,
That *Pœnetentia* his pik
He sholde polshe newe,
And lepe with hym over lond   3439

Al his lif tyme,   3440
For he hadde leyen by *Latro*
Luciferis aunte.   [ruthe,
    And thanne hadde Repentaunce
And redde hem alle to knele ;
" For I shal bi-seche for alle synfulle
Our Saveour of grace,
To amenden us of oure mysdedes,
And do mercy to us alle."
    " Now God," quod he, " that of
        thi goodnesse
Bi-gonne the world to make,   3450
And of naught madest aught, and
Moost lik to thiselve,   [man
And sithen suffredest for to synne,
A siknesse to us alle,
And al for the beste, as I bi-leve,
What evere the book telleth.
O felix culpa ! O necessarium pec-
        catum Adæ ! etc.
    " For thorugh that synne thi sone
Sent was to this erthe,
And bicam man of a maide,   3461
Mankynde to save :
And madest thiself with thi sone
And us synfulle y-liche
Faciamus hominem ad imaginem
        nostram. Et alibi. Qui manet
        in caritate, in Deo manet, et
        Deus in eo.
    " And siththe with thi selve sone
In oure secte deidest,
On Good-Fryday, for mannes sake,
At ful tyme of the daye,   3472

Ther thiself ne thi sone   3473
No sorwe in deeth feledest,
But in oure secte was the sorwe,
And thi sone it ladde.
Captivam duxit captivitatem.
  " The sonne for sorwe therof
Lees light of a tyme,
Aboute mydday whan moostlightis,
And meel-tyme of seintes,
Feddest with thi fresshe blood
Oure fore-fadres in derknesse.
Populus qui ambulabat in tenebris,
    vidit lucem magnam.
  " And thorugh the light that lepe
Lucifer was blent.   [out of thee
And blewe alle thi blessed
Into the blisse of paradys.
  " The thridde day after
Thow yedest in oure sute,
A synful Marie the seigh,
Er seynte Marie thi dame ;
And al to solace synfulle
Thow suffredest it so were.   3495
Non veni vocare justos sed pecca-
    tores ad pœnitentiam.
  " And al that Marc hath y-maad,
Mathew, Johan, and Lucas,
Of thyne doughty dedes
Was doon in oure armes.
Verbum caro factum est, et habita-
    vit in nobis.
  " And by so muche me semeth
The sikerer we mowe
Bidde and bi-seche,   3506

If it be thi wille,   3507
That art oure fader and oure brother,
Be merciable to us,
And have ruthe on thise ribaudes
That repenten hem here soore,
That evere thei wrathed thee in this
In word, thought, or dedes." [world,
    Thanne hent Hope an horn
Of *Deus, tu conversus vivificabis,*
And blew it with *Beati quorum
Remissæ sunt iniquitates,*
That alle seintes in hevene'   3518
Songen at ones.
*Homines et jumenta salvabis, quem-
    admodum multiplicasti miseri-
    cordiam tuam.*
    A thousand of men tho
Thrungen togideres,
Cride upward to Crist,
And to his clene moder,
To have grace to go with hem
Truthe to seke.
    Ac there was wight noon so wys
The wey thider kouthe,
But blustreden forth as beestes
Over bankes and hilles;
Til late was and longe
That thei a leode mette,
Apparailled as a paynym
In pilgrymes wise.
He bar a burdoun y-bounde
With a brood liste,
In a withwynde wise
Y-wounden aboute;   3540

A bolle and a bagge   3541
He bar by his syde,
And hundred of ampulles
On his hat seten,
Signes of Synay,
And shelles of Galice,
And many a crouche on his cloke,
And keyes of Rome,
And the vernycle bi-fore,
For men sholde knowe
And se bi hise signes
Whom he sought hadde.   3552
   This folk frayned hym first,
Fro whennes he come.
   "Fram Syny," he seide,
"And fram oure Lordes sepulcre ;
In Bethlem and in Babiloyne,
I have ben in bothe ;
In Armonye and Alisaundre,
In manye othere places.
Ye may se by my signes,
That sitten on myn hatte,
That I have walked ful wide   3563
In weet and in drye,
And sought goode seintes
For my soules helthe."
   "Knowestow aught a corsaint,
That men calle Truthe ?
Kondestow aught wissen us the wey,
Wher that wye dwelleth ? "
   " Nay, so me God helpe ! "
Seide the gome thanne,
" I seigh nevere palmere,
With pyk ne with scrippe,   3574

Asken after hym er   3575
Til now in this place."
  "Peter!" quod a plowman,
And putte forth his hed,
"I knowe hym as kyndely
As clerk doth hise bokes;
Conscience and kynde wit
Kenned me to his place,
And diden me suren hym sikerly
To serven hym for evere,
Bothe to sowe and to sette,
The while I swynke myghte.   3586
I have ben his folwere
Al this fifty wynter,
Bothe y-sowen his seed,
And suwed hise beestes,
Withinne and withouten
Waited his profit.
I dyke and I delve,
I do that Truthe hoteth;
Som tyme I sowe,
And som tyme I thresshe;
In taillours craft and tynkeris craft,
What Truthe kan devyse,
I weve and I wynde,
And do what Truthe hoteth,
For though I seye it myselfe,
I serve hym to paye;
I have myn hire wel,
And outher whiles moore.
He is the presteste paiere
That povere men knoweth;
He ne withhalt noon hewe his hire,
That he ne hath it at even;   3608

He is as lowe as a lomb,   3609
And lovelich of speche ;
And if ye wilneth to wite
Where that he dwelleth,
I shal wisse you witterly
The wey to his place."

    " Ye, leve Piers," quod thise pil-
And profred hym huyre,   [grimes,
For to wende with hem
To Truthes dwellyng-place.

    "Nay, by my soules helpe !"quod
And gan for to swere,   [Piers,
" I nolde fange a ferthyng.
For seint Thomas shryne ;
Truthe wolde love me the lasse
A long tyme therafter ;
Ac if yow wilneth to wende wel,
This is the wey thider.

    " Ye moten go thorugh Meke-
Both men and wyves,   [nesse,
Til ye come into Conscience,
That Crist wite the sothe
That ye loven oure Lord God   3631
Levest of alle thynges,
And thanne youre neghebores next
In none wise apeire,
Other wise than thow woldest
He wroughte to thiselve.

    "And so boweth forth by a brook,
Beth-buxom-of-speche,
Til he fynden a ford,
Youre-fadres-honoureth,
Honora patrem et matrem, etc.
Wadeth in that water,   3642

And wasshe yow wel therinne, 3643
And ye shul lepe the lightloker
Al youre lif tyme;
And so shaltow se Swere-noght,-
But-if-it-be-for-nede,-
And-nameliche-on-ydel-
The-name-of-God-almyghty.
"Thanne shaltow come by a croft,
But come thow noght therinne;
That croft hatte Coveite-noght-
Mennes-catel-ne-hire-wyves,-
Ne-noon-of-hire-servauntz-   3654
That-noyen-hem-myghte;
Loke ye breke no bowes there,
But if it be youre owene.
" Two stokkes ther stondeth,
Ac stynte ye noght there,
Thei highte Stele-noght and Sle-
Strik forth by bothe,   [noght,
And leve hem on thi lift half,
And loke noght therafter,
And hold wel thyn hali-day
Heighe til even.   3605
" Thanne shaltow blenche at a
Bere-no-fals-witnesse,   [bergh,
He is frythed in with floryns
And othere fees manye;
Loke thow plukke no plaunte there,
For peril of thi soule;
Thanne shul ye see Seye-sooth,-
So-it-be-to-doone,-
In-good-manere,-ellis-noght-
For-no-mannes-biddyng.
"Thanne shaltow come to a court

As cler as the sonne ;   3677
The moot is of Mercy
The manoir aboute,
And alle the walles ben of Wit,
To holden Wil oute,
And kerneled wit Cristendom,
Mankynde to save,
Botrased with Bileef-so,-
Or-thow-beest-noght-saved.

   "And alle the houses ben hiled,
Halles and chambres,
With no leed but with love,   3688
And lowe speche as bretheren ;
The brugg is of Bidde-wel,-
The-bet-may-thow-spede ;
Ech piler is of penaunce,
Of preieres to seyntes ;
Of almes-dedes are the hokes
That the gates hangen on.

   "Grace hatte the gatewarde,
A good man for sothe ;
His man hatte Amende-yow,
For many men hym knoweth ; 3699
Telleth hym this tokene,
That Truthe wite the sothe ;
' I perfourned the penaunce
That the preest me enjoyned,
And am ful sory for my synnes,
And so I shal evere,
Whan I thynke theron,
Theigh I were a pope.'

   "Biddeth Amende-yow meke hym
Til his maister ones,
To wayven up the wiket   3710

That the womman shette,   3711
Tho Adam and Eve
Eten apples un-rosted.
Per Evam cunctis clausa est, et per
     Mariam virginem patefacta est.
  " For he hath the keye and the
Though the kyng slepe.   [cliket,
And if grace graunte thee
To go in this wise,
Thow shalt see in thiselve
Truthe in thyn herte,
In a cheyne of charité   3722
As thow a child were,
To suffren hym and segge noght
Ayein thi sires wille.
  " And be war thanne of Wrathe-
That is a wikked sherewe ;   [thee,
He hath envye to hym
That in thyn herte sitteth,
And poketh forth pride
To preise thiselven.
The boldnesse of thi bienfetes
Maketh thee blynd thanne ;   3733
And thanne worstow dryven out as
And the dore closed,   [dew,
Keyed and cliketted,
To kepe thee withouten ;
Happily an hundred wynter
Er thow eft entre.
Thus mgyhtestow lesen his love,
To lete wel by thiselve,
And nevere happily eft entre,
But grace thow have.
  "And ther are seven sustren 3744

That serven Truthe evere,   3745
And arn porters of the posternes
That to the place longeth.
  "That oon hatte Abstinence,
And Humilité another;
Charité and Chastité
Ben hise chief maydenes;
Pacience and Pees
Muche peple thei helpeth;
Largenesse the lady,
She let in ful manye,
Heo hath holpe a thousand out
Of the develes punfolde;
And who is sib to thise sevene,
So me God helpe!
He is wonderly welcome,
And faire underfongen.
And but if ye be sibbe
To some of thise sevene,   [Piers,
It is ful hard, by myn heed!" quod
" For any of yow alle
To geten in-going at any gate there,
But grace be the moore."   3767

  " Now by Crist!" quod a kutte-
" I have no kyn there."   [purs,
" Nor I," quod an ape-ward,
" By aught that I kan knowe."
" Wite God!" quod a wafrestere,
" Wiste I this for sothe,
Sholde I nevere ferther a foot,
For no freres prechyng."

  " Yis," quod Piers the Plowman,
And poked hem alle to goode,
" Mercy is a maiden there   3778

Hath myght over alle ;   3779
And she is sib to alle synfulle,
And hire sone also,
And thorugh the help of hem two
Hope thow noon oother,
Thow myght gete grace there,
So thow go bi-tyme."

   "Bi seint Poul!" quod a pardoner,
"Peraventure I be noght knowe
        there ;   [vettes,
I wol go fecche my box with my bre-
And a bulle with bisshopes lettres."

   " By Crist!" quod a commune
        womman,
"Thi compaignie wol I folwe ;
Thow shalt seye I am thi suster,
I ne woot where thei bicome."   3793

" THIS were a wikkede wey,
    But who so hadde a gyde,
    That wolde folwen us ech
      a foot ; "
Thus this folke hem mened.
   Quod Perkyn the Plowman,
" By seint Peter of Rome !
I have an half acre to erie
By the heighe weye ;
Hadde I eryed this half acre,
And sowen it after,
I wolde wende with yow,
And the wey teche."   3805
   "This were a long lettyng,"
Quod a lady in scleyre,
" What sholde we wommen
Werche the while ? "   [Piers,
   "Somme shul sowe the sak," quod
" For shedyng of the whete ;
And ye, lovely ladies,
With youre longe fyngres,
That ye have silk and sandel
To sowe, whan tyme is ;
Chesibles for chapeleyns,
Chirches to honoure.   3817

" Wyves and widewes,   3818
Wolle and flex spynneth ;
Maketh cloth, I counseille yow,
And kenneth so youre doughtres ;
The nedy and the naked,
Nymeth hede how thei liggeth,
And casteth hem clothes,
For so comaundeth Truthe.
For I shal leven hem liflode,
But if the lond faille,
Flesshe and breed bothe
To riche and to poore,   3829
As long as I lyve,
For the Lordes love of hevene ;
And alle manere of men   [beth,
That thorugh mete and drynke lib-
Helpeth hym to werche wightliche,
That wynneth youre foode."

   " By Crist !" quod a knyght thoo,
" He kenneth us the beste ;
Ac on the teme, trewely,
Taught was I nevere ;   3840
But kenne me," quod the knyght,
" And by Crist I wole assaye !"

   " By seint Poul !" quod Perkyn,
" Ye profre yow so faire,
That I shal swynke and swete,
And sowe for us bothe,
And othere labours do for thi love
Al my lif tyme,
In covenaunt that thow kepe
Holy kirke and myselve
Fro wastours and fro wikked men
That this world destruyeth.   3851

And go hunte hardiliche 3852
To hares and to foxes,
To bores and to brokkes
That breken doun myne hegges ;
And so affaite thi faucons
Wilde foweles to kille ;
For swiche cometh to my croft,
And croppeth my whete.”
   Curteisly the knyght thanne
Comsed thise wordes ;
“ By my power, Piers ! ” quod he,
“ I plighte thee my trouthe, 3863
To fulfille this forwarde,
Though I fighte sholde ;
Als longe as I lyve
I shal thee mayntene.”
   “ Ye, and yet a point,” quod
“ I preye yow of moore, [Piers,
Loke ye tene no tenaunt,
But Truthe wole assente ;
And though ye mowe amercy hem,
Lat mercy be taxour,
And mekenesse thi maister, 3874
Maugree Medes chekes.
And though povere men profre yow
Presentes and giftes,
Nyme it noght, an aventure
Ye mowe it noght deserve ;
For thow shalt yelde it ayein
At one yeres tyme,
In a ful perilous place,
Purgatorie it hatte. [men,
   “ And mys-bede noght thi bonde-
The bettre may thow spede ; 3885

Though he be thyn underlyng here,
Wel may happe in hevene
That he worth worthier set,
And with moore blisse.
Amice, ascende superius.
For in charnel at chirche
Cherles ben yvel to knowe,
Or a knyght from a knave there,
Knowe this in thyn herte.
And that thow be trewe of thi tonge,
And tales that thow hatie,
But if thei ben of wisdom or of wit
Thi werkmen to chaste.
Hold with none harlotes,
Ne here noght hir tales,
And namely at the mete
Swiche men eschuwe ;
For it ben the develes disours,
I do the to understonde."

"I assente, by seint Jame !"
Seide the knyght thanne,
" For to werche by thi wordes
The while my lif dureth."   3908

" And I shal apparaille me," quod
" In pilgrymes wise,   [Perkyn,
And wende with yow I wile,
Til we fynde Truthe ;
And caste on my clothes
Y-clouted and hole,
My cokeres and my coffes,
For cold of my nailes ;
And hange myn hoper at myn hals
In stede of a scryppe.
A busshel of bred corn   3919

Brynge me therinne;   3920
For I wol sowe it myself,
And sithenes wol I wende
To pilgrymage, as palmeres doon,
Pardon for to have.
And who so helpeth me to erie
And sowen here er I wende,
Shal have leve, by oure Lorde!
To lese here in hervest,
And make hem murie thermyd,
Maugree who so bi-gruccheth it.
And alle kynne crafty-men,   3931
That konne lyven in truthe,
I shal fynden hem fode,
That feithfulliche libbeth.
  "Save Jagge the jogelour,
And Jonette of the stuwes,
And Danyel the dees-pleyere,
And Denote the baude,
And frere the faitour,
And folk of hire ordre,
And Robyn the ribaudour
For hise rusty wordes.   3942
Truthe tolde me ones,
And bad me telle it after,
Deleantur de libro viventium,
I sholde noght dele with hem,
For holy chirche is hote of hem
No tithe to take;
Qui cum justis non scribantur;
They ben ascaped good aventure,
God hem amende!"
  Dame Werch-whan-tyme-is
Piers wif highte;   3953

His doughter highte Do-right-so,-
Or-thi-dame-shal-thee-bete ;
His sone highte Suffre-thi-sove-
To-haven-hir-wille,-   [reyns-
Deme-hem-noght,-for-if-thow-doost,-
Thow-shalt-it-deere-abugge.
Lat God y-worthe with al,
For so his word techeth ;
For now I am old and hoor,
And have of myn owene,
To penaunce and to pilgrimage
I wol passe with thise othere.   3965
    "For-thi I wole er I wende
Do write my biqueste,
In Dei nomine, Amen,
I make it myselve ;
He shal have my soule,
That best hath deserved it ;
And fro the fend it defende,
For so I bileve,
Til I come to hise acountes,
As my Credo me telleth,
To have a relees and a remission,
On that rental I leve.
    "The kirke shal have my caroyne,
And kepe my bones ;
For of my corn and catel
She craved the tithe ;
I paide it ful prestly,
For peril of my soule.
For-thi is he holden I hope
To have me in his masse,
And mengen in his memorie
Amonges alle cristene.   3987

" My wif shal have of that I wan
With truthe, and na-moore,
And dele among my doughtres,
And my deere children ;
For though I deye to day,
My dettes are quyte ;
I bar hom that I borwed,
Er I to bedde yede.   [remenaunt,
 " And with the residue and the
By the Rode of Lukes !
I wol worshipe therwith
Truthe by my lyve,   3999
And ben his pilgrym atte plow,
For povere mennes sake.
My plow-foot shall be my pikstaf,
And picche a-two the rotes,
And helpe my cultour to kerve
And clense the furwes."
    Now is Perkyn and hise pilgrimes
To the plow faren ;
To erie his half acre
Holpen hym manye ;
Dikeres and delveres   4010
Digged up the balkes.
Therwith was Perkyn a-payed,
And preised hem faste.
    Othere werkmen ther were
That wroghten ful yerne ;
Ech man in his manere
Made hymself to doone,
And somme to plese Perkyn
Piked up the wedes.
    At heigh prime Piers
Leet the plowgh stonde,   4021

To over-sen hem hymself,   4022
And who so best wroghte
He sholde be hired therafter,
Whan hervest tyme come.
    And thanne seten somme,
And songen atte nale,
And holpen ere this half acre
With " How, trolly lolly."
    " Now, by the peril of my soule!"
All in pure tene,   [quod Piers,
" But ye arise the rather
And rape yow to werche,   4033
Shal no greyn that groweth
Glade yow at nede,
And though ye deye for doel,
The devel have that reccheth."
    Tho were faitours a-fered,
And feyned hem blynde ;
Somme leide hir legges a-liry,
As swiche losels konneth,
And made hir mone to Piers,
And preide hym of grace ;
" For we have no lymes to laboure
Lord, y-graced be the ;   [with,
Ac we preie for yow, Piers,
And for youre plowgh bothe,
That God of his grace
Youre greyn multiplie,
And yelde yow for youre almesse
That ye gyve us here ;
For we may noght swynke ne swete,
Swich siknesse us eyleth."
    "If it be sooth," quod Piers, "that
I shal it soone aspie.   [ye seyn,

Ye ben wastours, I woot wel,   4056
And Truthe woot the sothe;
And I am his olde hyne,
And highte hym to warne,
Whiche thei were in this world
Hise werkmen apeired.
Ye wasten that men wynnen
With travaille and with tene;
Ac Truthe shal teche yow
His teme to dryve,
Or ye shul eten barley breed,
And of the broke drynke.   4067
  "But if he be blynd or broke-
Or bolted with irens,   [legged,
He shall ete whete breed,
And drynke with myselve,
Til God of his goodnesse
Amendement hym sende.
Ac ye myghte travaille, as Truthe
And take mete and hyre,   [wolde,
To kepe kyen in the feld,
The corn fro the beestes,
Diken or delven,   4078
Or dyngen upon sheves,
Or helpe make morter,
Or bere muk a-feld.
  "In lecherie and in losengerie
Ye lyven, and in sleuthe;
And al is thorugh suffraunce,
That vengeaunce yow ne taketh.
  "Ac ancres and heremites
That eten noght but at nones,
And na-moore er the morwe,
Myn almesse shul thei have,   4089

And of catel to kepe hem with, 4090
That han cloistres and chirches.
  " Ac Robert Renaboute
Shal noght have of myne,
Ne postles, but thei preche konne
And have power of the bisshope ;
Thei shul have payn and potage,
And make hemself at ese,
For it is an unreasonable religion
That hath right noght of certein."
    And thanne gan Wastour to
        wrathen hym,   4100
And wolde have y-foughte ;
And to Piers the Plowman
He profrede his glove ;
A bretoner, a braggere,
A-bosted Piers als,
And bad hym go pissen with his
" For-pynede sherewe !   [plowgh,
Wiltow or neltow,
We wol have oure wille
Of thi flour and of thi flesshe,
Fecche whanne us liketh ;   4111
And maken us murye thermyde,
Maugree thi chekes."
    Thanne Piers the Plowman
Pleyned hym to the knyghte,
To kepen hym as covenaunt was
Fro cursede sherewes,   [kynnes
And fro thise wastours wolves-
That maketh the world deere ;
" For tho wasten and wynnen noght,
And that ilke while   [peple,
Worth nevere plentee among the

The while my plowgh liggeth." 4123
  Curteisly the knyght thanne,
As his kynde wolde,
Warnede Wastour,
And wissed hym bettre,
" Or thow shalt abigge by the lawe,
By the ordre that I bere ! "
  " I was noght wont to werche,"
    quod Wastour,
" And now wol I noght bigynne : "
And leet light of the lawe,
And lasse of the knyghte ;   4133
And sette Piers at a pese,
And his plowgh bothe ;
And manaced Piers and his men,
If thei mette eft soone. [quod Piers,
  " Now, by the peril of my soule ! "
" I shal apeire yow alle ; "
And houped after Hunger,
That herde hym at the firste,
" A-wreke me of thise wastours,"
    quod he,
" That this world shendeth."   4143
  Hunger in haste thoo
Hente Wastour by the wombe,
And wrong him so by the wombe,
That bothe hise eighen watrede.
  He buffeted the bretoner
Aboute the chekes,
That he loked lik a lanterne
Al his lif after.
He bette hem so bothe,
He brast ner hire guttes ;
Ne hadde Piers with a pese loof 4154

Preyed Hunger to cesse,   4155
They hadde be dolven,
Ne deme thow noon oother.
  "Suffre hem lyve," he seide,
"And lat hem ete with hogges,
Or ellis benes or bren
Y-baken togideres,
Or ellis melk and mene ale;"
Thus preied Piers for hem.
  Faitours for fere herof
Flowen into bernes,
And flapten on with flailes   4166
Fro morwe til even;
That Hunger was noght so hardy
On hem for to loke,
For a potful of peses
That Piers hadde y-maked.
  An heep of heremytes
Henten hem spades,
And kitten hir copes,
And courtepies hem maked,
And wente as werkmen
With spades and with shoveles 4177
And dolven and dikeden,
To dryve awey hunger.
  Blynde and bed-reden
Were bootned a thousande,
That seten to begge silver,
Soone were thei heeled;
For that was bake for bayarde,
Was boote for many hungry;
And many a beggere for benes
Buxum was to swynke;
And eche a povere man wel a-paied

Er hunger thee take,   4324
And sende thee of his sauce
To savore with thi lippes ;
And keep som til soper-tyme,
And sitte noght to longe,
And rys up er appetit
Have eten his fille.
Lat noght sire Surfet
Sitten at thi borde.
Leve hym noght, for he is lecherous,
And likerous of tunge,
And after many maner metes   4335
His mawe is a-fyngred.

   " And if thow diete thee thus,
I dar legge myne eris,
That Phisik shal hise furred hodes
For his fode selle,
And his cloke of Calabre,
With alle the knappes of golde,
And be fayn, by my feith !
His phisik to lete,
And lerne to laboure with lond,
For liflode is swete.   4346
For murthereris are manye leches,
Lord hem amende !   [drynkes,
They do men deye thorugh hir
Er destynee it wolde."
" By seint Poul ! " quod Piers,
" Thise arn profitable wordes !
Wend now, Hunger, whan thow
That wel be thow evere !   [wolt,
For this is a lovely lesson,
Lord it thee for-yelde ! "

   " Bi-hote God ! " quod Hunger,

" Hennes ne wole I wende,   4358
Til I have dyned bi this day,
And y-dronke bothe."
   " I have no peny," quod Piers,
" Pulettes to bugge,
Ne neither gees ne grys,
But two grene cheses,
A fewe cruddes and creme,
And an haver cake,
And two loves of benes and bran
Y-bake for my fauntes ;
And yet I seye, by my soule !   4369
I have no salt bacon,
Ne no cokeney, by Crist !
Coloppes for to maken.
   " Ac I have percile and porettes,
And manye cole plauntes,
And ek a cow and a calf,
And a cart mare
To drawe a-feld my donge,
The while the droghte lasteth ;
And by this liflode we mote lyve
Til Lammesse tyme.   4380
And by that, I hope to have
Hervest in my crofte,
And thanne may I dighte thi dyner,
As me deere liketh."
   Al the povere peple tho
Pescoddes fetten,
Benes and baken apples
Thei broghte in hir lappes,
Chibolles and chervelles,
And ripe chiries manye,
And profrede Piers this present 4391

To plese with Hunger.   4392
  Al Hunger eet in haste,
And axed after moore.
Thanne povere folk, for fere,
Fedden Hunger yerne,
With grene poret and pesen,
To poisone hym thei thoghte.
By that it neghed neer hervest,
And newe corn cam to chepyng;
Thanne was folk fayn,
And fedde Hunger with the beste,
With goode ale, as Gloton taghte,
And garte Hunger go slepe.
  And tho wolde Wastour noght
But wandren aboute,   [werche,
Ne no beggere ete breed
That benes inne were,
But of coket and cler-matyn,
Or ellis of clene whete;
Ne noon halfpeny ale
In none wise drynke,   [neste
But of the beste and of the brun-
That in burghe is to selle.   4414
  Laborers that have no land
To lyve on but hire handes,
Deyned noght to dyne a day
Nyght-olde wortes;
May no peny ale hem paye,
Ne no pece of bacone,
But if it be fresshe flessh outher
Fryed outher y-bake,   [fisshe,
And that *chaud* and *plus chaud*,
For chillynge of hir mawe;
And but if he be heighliche hyred;

Ellis wole he chide,   4426
And that he was werkman wroght
Waille the tyme,
Ayeins Catons counseil
Comseth he to jangle.
*Paupertatis onus patienter ferre me-
        mento.*
  He greveth hym ageyn God,
And gruccheth ageyn Reson,
And thanne corseth he the kyng,
And al his counseil after,
Swiche lawes to loke   4437
Laborers to greve.
Ac whiles Hunger was hir maister,
Ther wolde noon of hem chide,
Ne stryven ayeins his statut,
So sterneliche he loked.

  Ac I warne yow, werkmen,
Wynneth whil ye mowe,
For Hunger hiderward
Hasteth hym faste.
He shal a-wake with water
Wastours to chaste ;
Er fyve be fulfilled,
Swich famyn shal a-ryse,
Thorugh flodes and thorugh foule
Fruytes shul faille,   [wedres
And so seide Saturne,
And sente yow to warne.

  Whan ye se the sonne a-mys,
And two monkes heddes,
And a mayde have the maistrie,
And multiplie by eighte,
Thanne shal deeth with-drawe, 4459

And derthe be justice,   4460
And Dawe the dykere
Deye for hunger;
But God of his goodnesse
Graunte us a trewe.   4464

Passus Septimus de Visione, ut
supra.

REUTHE herde telle her
    And to Piers he sente,
    To maken his teme
    And tilien the erthe,
And purchaced hym a pardone
A pœna et a culpa,
For hym and for hise heires,
For evere moore after,
And bad hym holde hym at home,
And erien hise leyes.
And alle that holpen hym to erye,
To sette or to sowe,
Or any oother mestier   4477
That myghte Piers availle,
Pardon with Piers Plowman
Truthe hath y-graunted.
   Kynges and knyghtes,
That kepen holy chirche,
And rightfully in remes
Rulen the peple,
Han pardon thorugh purgatorie
To passen ful lightly,
With patriarkes and prophetes
In paradis to be felawe.   4483

Bysshopes y-blessed,   4489
If thei ben as thei sholde,
Legistres of bothe lawes,
The lewed therwith to preche,
And in as muche as thei mowe
Amenden alle synfulle,
Arn peres with the Apostles,
This pardon Piers sheweth,
And at the day of dome
At the heighe deys sitte.
  Marchauntz in the margyne
Hadde manye yeres,   4500
Ac noon *a pœna et a culpa*
The pope nolde hem graunte,
For thei holde noght hir hali-dayes
As holy chirche techeth,
And for thei swere by hir soule,
And so God moste hem helpe,
Ayein clene Conscience,
Hir catel to selle.
  Ac under his secret seel
Truthe sente hem a lettre,
That thei sholde buggen boldely
That hem best liked,
And sithenes selle it ayein,
And save the wynnyng,
And amende meson-dieux thermyd,
And mys-eise folk helpe,
And wikkede weyes
Wightly amende,
And do boote to brugges
That to-broke were,
Marien maydenes,
Or maken hem nonnes,   4522

Povere peple and prisons   4523
Fynden hem hir foode,
And sette scolers to scole,
Or to som othere craftes,
Releve religion,
And renten hem bettre ;
" And I shal sende yow myselve
Seint Michel myn archangel,
That no devel shal yow dere,
Ne fere yow in youre deying,
And witen yow fro wanhope,
If ye wol thus werche,   4534
And sende youre soules in saufté
To my seintes in joye."
    Thanne were marchauntz murie,
Manye wepten for joye,
And preiseden Piers the Plowman,
That purchaced this bulle.
    Men of lawe leest pardon hadde,
That pleteden for Mede ;
For the Sauter saveth hem noght,
Swiche as take giftes,
And nameliche of innocentz   4545
That noon yvel ne konneth.
Super innocentem munera non ac-
        cipies.
    Pledours sholde peynen hem
To plede for swiche and helpe ;
Princes and prelates
Sholde paie for hire travaille.
A regibus et principibus erit merces
        corum.
    Ac many a justice and jurour
Wolde for Johan do moore   4556

Than *pro Dei pietate*,   4557
Leve thow noon oother.
  Ac he that spendeth his speche,
And speketh for the povere
That is innocent and nedy,
And no man apeireth,
Conforteth hym in that caas
Withouten coveitise of giftes,
And sheweth lawe for oure Lordes
As he it hath y-lerned,   [love,
Shal no devel at his deeth day
Deren hym a myte,   4568
That he ne worth saaf and his soule,
The Sauter bereth witnesse :
Domine, quis habitabit in taberna-
    culo tuo ?
  Ac to bugge water, ne wynd,
Ne wit, ne fir the ferthe,
Thise foure the fader of hevene
Made to this foold in commune.
Thise ben Truthes tresores
Trewe folk to helpe,
That nevere shul wexe ne wanye,
Withouten God hymselve.
  Whan thei drawen on to deye,
And indulgences wolde have,
Hir pardon is ful petit
At hir partyng hennes,
That any mede of mene men
For hir motyng taketh.
Ye legistres and lawieres,
Holdeth this for truthe,
That if that I lye,
Mathew is to blame,   4590

For he bad me make yow this,   4591
And this proverbe me tolde,
Quodcunque vultis ut faciant vobis
    homines, facite eis.
  Alle libbynge laborers
That lyven with hir hondes,
That treweliche taken,
And treweliche wynnen,
And lyven in love and in lawe,
For hir lowe hertes
Haveth the same absolucion
That sent was to Piers.   4602
    Beggeres ne bidderes
Ne beth noght in the bulle,
But if the suggestion be sooth
That shapeth hem to begge.
For he that beggeth or bit,
But if he have nede,
He is fals with the feend,
And defraudeth the nedy;
And also he bi-gileth the gyvere,
Ageynes his wille;
For if he wiste he were noght nedy,
He wolde gyve that another
That were moore nedy than he,
So the nedieste sholde be holpe.
Caton kenneth me thus,
And the clerc of stories;
Cui des videto,
Is Catons techyng.
  And in the stories he techeth
To bistowe thyn almesse.
Sit elemosina tua in manu tua,
    donec studes cui des.   4624

Ac Gregory was a good man, 4625
And bad us gyven alle
That asketh for his love
That us al leneth.
Non eligas cui miserearis, ne forte
prætereas illum qui meretur
accipere. Quia incertum est
pro quo Deo magis placeas.
For wite ye nevere who is worthi,
Ac God woot who hath nede ;
In hym that taketh is the trecherie,
If any treson walke. 4636
For he that yeveth, yeldeth,
And yarketh hym to reste ;
And he that biddeth, borweth,
And bryngeth hymself in dette.
For beggeres borwen evere mo,
And hir borgh is God almyghty,
To yelden hem that yeveth hem,
And yet usure moore.
Quare non dedisti pecuniam meam
ad mensam, ut ego veniam cum
usuris exigere ? 4647
For-thi biddeth noght, ye beg-
But if ye have gret nede ; [geres,
For who so hath to buggen hym
The book bereth witnesse, [breed,
He hath y-nough that hath breed
y-nough,
Though he have noght ellis.
Satis dives est, qui non indiget pane.
Lat usage be youre solas,
Of seintes lyves redyng,
The book banneth beggerie, 4657

And blameth hem in this manere : 4658
*Junior fui, et jam senui, et non vidi
    justum derelictum, nec semen
    ejus, etc.*
    For ye lyve in no love,
Ne no lawe holde ;
Manye of yow ne wedde noght
The womman that ye with deele,
But as wilde bestes with ' wehee ! '
Worthen uppe and werchen,
And bryngen forth barnes,
That bastardes men calleth ;   4669
Or the bak or som boon
He breketh in his youthe,
And siththe goon faiten with youre
For evere moore after.   [fauntes
Ther is moore mys-shapen peple
Amonges thise beggeres,
Than of alle manere men
That on this moolde walketh.
And thei that lyve thus hir lif,
Mowe lothe the tyme
That evere thei were men wroght,
Whan thei shal hennes fare.
Ac olde men and hore,
Than help-lees ben of strengthe,
And wommen with childe
That werche ne mowe,
Blynde and bed-reden,
And broken hire membres,
That taken thise myschiefs meke-
As mesels and othere,   [liche,
Han as pleyn pardon
As the plowman hymselve.   4691

For love of hir lowe hertes,　　4692
Oure Lord hath hem graunted
Hir penaunce and hir purgatorie
Here on this erthe.
　"Piers," quod a preest thoo,
"Thi pardon moste I rede ;
For I wol construe ech clause,
And kenne it thee on Englisshe."
　And Piers at his preiere
The pardon unfoldeth ;
And I by-hynde hem bothe
Biheld al the bulle,　　4703
And in two lynes it lay,
And noght a leef more,
And was writen right thus,
In witnesse of Truthe :
*Et qui bona egerunt, ibunt in vitam
　　eternam.*
Qui vero mala, in ignem eternum.
　"Peter," quod the preest thoo,
"I kan no pardon fynde,
But do wel and have wel,
And God shal have thi soule,　　4714
And do yvel and have yvel,
Hope thow noon oother,
But after thi deeth-day
The devel shal have thi soule."
And Piers for pure tene
Pulled it a-tweyne,
And seide *Si ambulavero in medio
　　umbræ mortis, non timebo mala,
　　quoniam tu mecum es.*
　"I shal cessen of my sowyng,"
　　quod Piers,　　4725

"And swynke noght so harde, 4726
Ne aboute my bely joye
So bisy be na-moore;
Of preieres and of penaunce
My plough shal ben herafter,
And wepen whan I sholde slepe,
Though whete-breed me faille.

"The prophete his payn eet
In penaunce and in sorwe,
By that the Sauter seith,
So dide othere manye;
That loveth God lelly, 4737
His liflode is ful esy.
Fuerunt mihi lacrimæ meæ panes
die ac nocte.

"And but if Luc lye,
He lereth us by foweles,
We sholde noght be to bisy
Aboute the worldes blisse;
Ne soliciti sitis,
He seith in the Gospel,
And sheweth us by ensamples
Us selve to wisse. 4748
The foweles in the feld,
Who fynt hem mete at wynter?
Have thei no gerner to go to,
But God fynt hem alle."

"What!" quod the preest to
"Peter! as me thynketh, [Perkyn,
Thow art lettred a litel :—
Who lerned thee on boke?"

"Abstynence the abbesse," quod
"Myn a.b.c. me taughte; [Piers,
And Conscience cam afterward,
And kenned me muche moore." 4760

" Were thow a preest," quod he,
" Thou myghtest preche where thou
As divinour in divinité,   [sholdest,
With *Dixit insipiens* to thi teme."
" Lewed lorel ! " quod Piers,
" Litel lokestow on the Bible ;
On Salomons sawes
Selden thow biholdest :
*Ejice derisores et jurgia cum eis, ne
    crescant, etc.*"
The preest and Perkyn
Opposeden either oother.   4772
And I thorugh hir wordes a-wook,
And waited aboute,
And seigh the sonne in the south
Sitte that tyme,
Mete-lees and monei-lees
On Malverne hulles,
Musynge on this metels,
And my wey ich yede.

MANY tyme this metels
    Hath maked me to studie
Of that I seigh slepynge,
If it so be myghte,
And also for Piers the Plowman
Ful pencif in herte,
And which a pardon Piers hadde
Al the peple to conforte,
And how the preest impugned it
With two propre wordes.
Ac I have no savour in songewarie,
For I se it ofte faille ;
Caton and canonistres
Counseillen us to leve   4794

To sette sadnesse in songewarie, 4795
For *sompnia ne cures.*
    Ac for the book Bible
Bereth witnesse
How Daniel divined
The dreem of a kyng,
That was Nabugodonosor
Nempned of clerkes.
    Daniel seide, " Sire kyng,
Thi dremels bitokneth
That unkouthe knyghtes shul come
Thi kyngdom to cleyme ;   4806
Amonges lower lordes
Thi lond shal be departed."
And as Daniel divined,
In dede it fel after ;
The kyng lees his lordshipe,
And lower men it hadde.
    And Joseph mette merveillously
How the moone and the sonne
And the ellevene sterres
Hailsed hym alle.
    Thanne Jacob jugged   4817
Josephes swevene.
" Beau fitz," quod his fader,
" For defaute we shullen,
I myself and my sones,
Seche thee for nede."
    It bifel as his fader seide,
In Pharaoes tyme,
That Joseph was justice
Egipte to loke ;
It bifel as his fader tolde,
Hise frendes there hym soughte,
And al this maketh me   4829

On this metels to thynke.   4830
And how the preest preved
No pardon to Do-wel,
And demed that Do-wel
Indulgences passed,
Biennals and triennals,
And bisshopes lettres;
And how Do-wel at the day of dome
Is digneliche underfongen,
And passeth al the pardon
Of seint Petres cherche.

   Now hath the pope power   4841
Pardon to graunte the peple,
Withouten any penaunce
To passen into hevene;
This is oure bileve,
As lettred men us techeth:
Quodcumque ligaveris super ter-
    ram, erit ligatum et in cœlis,
    etc.

   And so I leve leelly,
Lordes forbode ellis!
That pardon and penaunce   4852
And preieres doon save
Soules that have synned
Seven sithes dedly;
Ac to truste to thise triennals,
Trewely me thynketh,
Is noght so siker for the soule,
Certes, as is Do-wel.

   For-thi I rede yow, renkes,
That riche ben on this erthe,
Upon trust of youre tresor
Triennals to have,
Be ye never the bolder   4864

To breake the .x. hestes ;   4365
And namely ye maistres,
Meires and jugges,
That have the welthe of this world
And for wise men ben holden,
To purchace yow pardon
And the popes bulles.
At the dredful dome,
Whan dede shulle rise,
And comen alle to-fore Crist
Acountes to yelde,
How thow laddest thi lif here,   4370
And hise lawes keptest,
And how thow didest day by day,
The doom wole reherce.
A poke ful of pardon there,
Ne provincials lettres,
Theigh ye be founde in the fraternité
Of alle the foure ordres,
And have indulgences double-fold,
But if Do-wel yow helpe,
I sette youre patentes and youre
At one pies hele.   [pardon
    For-thi I counseille alle Cristene
To crie God mercy,
And Marie his moder
Be oure meene bitwene,
That God gyve us grace here,
Er we go hennes,
Swiche werkes to werche
While we ben here,
That after oure deeth-day
Do-wel reherce
At the day of dome,
We dide as he highte.   4390

THUS y-robed in russet   4000
I romed aboute
Al a somer seson
For to seke Do-wel;
And frayned ful ofte
Of folk that I mette,
If any wight wiste
Wher Do-wel was at inne;
And what man he myghte be
Of many man I asked.
    Was nevere wight, as I wente,
That me wisse kouthe   4011
Where this leode lenged,
Lasse ne moore;
Til it bi-fel on a Friday
Two freres I mette,
Maistres of the menours,
Men of grete witte.
I hailsed hem hendely,
As I hadde y-lerned,
And preide hem *par charité*,
Er thei passed ferther,
If thei knewe any contree
Or costes, as thei wente,   4023

"Where that Do-wel dwelleth   4924
Dooth me to witene."
For thei be men of this moolde
That moost wide walken,
And knowen contrees and courtes,
And many kynnes places,
Bothe princes paleises
And povere mennes cotes,
And Do-wel and Do-yvele
Wher thei dwelle bothe.

    "Amonges us," quod the Me-
"That man is dwellynge,   [nours,
And evere hath, as I hope,
And evere shal herafter."

    "*Contra*," quod I as a clerc,
And comsed to disputen,
And seide hem soothly,
"*Septies in die cadit justus.*"

    Sevene sithes, seith the book,
Synneth the rightfulle;
And who so synneth," I seide,
"Dooth yvele, as me thynketh;
And Do-wel and Do-yvele   4946
Mowe noght dwelle togideres.
Ergo he nys noght alwey
Amonges yow freres;
He is outher while ellis where
To wisse the peple."

    "I shal seye thee, my sone,"
Seide the frere thanne,
"How seven sithes the sadde man
On a day synneth;
By a forbisne," quod the frere,
"I shal thee faire shewe.   4957

Lat brynge a man in a boot   4958
Amydde the brode watre,
The wynd and the water
And the boot waggyng
Maketh the man many a tyme
To falle and to stonde ;
For stonde he never so stif,
He stumbleth if he meve,
Ac yet is he saaf and sound,
And so hym bihoveth.
For if he ne arise the rather,
And raughte to the steere,   4969
'The wynd wolde with the water
The boot over throwe ;
And thanne were his lif lost,
Through lachesse of hymselve.
"And thus it falleth," quod the frere,
" By folk here on erthe ;
The water is likned to the world
That wanyeth and wexeth ;
The goodes of this grounde arn lik
To the grete wawes,
That as wyndes and wedres   4980
Walketh aboute ;
The boot is likned to oure body
That brotel is of kynde,
That thorugh the fend and the flesshe
And the frele worlde
Synneth the sadde man
A day seven sithes.

    " Ac dedly synne doth he noght,
For Do-wel hym kepeth ;
And that is charité the champion,
Chief help ayein synne ;   4991

For he strengheth men to stonde, 4992
And steereth mannes soule,
And though the body bowe
As boot dooth in the watre,
Ay is thi soule saaf,
But if thow wole thiselve
Do a deedly synne,
And drenche so thi soule,
God wole suffre wel thi sleuthe,
If thiself liketh.
For he yaf thee a yeres-gyve,
To yeme wel thiselve,   5003
And that is wit and free-wil,
To every wight a porcion,
To fleynge foweles,
To fisshes and to beestes ;
Ac man hath moost therof,
And moost is to blame,
But if he werche wel therwith,
As Do-wel hym teacheth." [quod I,
  "I have no kynde knowyng,"
" To conceyven alle youre wordes ;
Ac if I may lyve and loke,   5014
I shal go lerne bettre."

  "I bikenne thee Crist," quod he,
" That on cros deyde ! "
And I seide, " The same
Save yow fro myschaunce,
And gyve yow grace on this grounde
Goode men to worthe ! "

AND thus I wente wide wher
  Walkyng myn one,
    wilde wildernesse,   5024

And by a wodes side ;   5025
Blisse of the briddes
Broughte me a-slepe,
And under a lynde upon a launde
Lened I a stounde,
To lythe the layes
Tho lovely foweles made.
Murthe of hire mouthes
Made me ther to sleple ;
The marveillouseste metels
Mette me thanne
That ever dremed wight   5036
In world, as I wene.
    A muche man, as me thoughte,
And lik to myselve,
Cam and called me
By my kynde name.
    "What artow ?" quod I tho,
"That thow my name knowest."
    "That thou woost wel," quod he,
"And no wight bettre."
    "Woot I what thow art ?"
"Thought," seide he thanne ;   5047
"I have sued thee this seven yeer,
Seye thow me no rather."
    "Artow Thought," quod I thoo,
"Thow koudest me wisse,
Where that Do-wel dwelleth,
And do me that to knowe."
    "Do-wel and Do-bet,
And Do-best the thridde," quod he,
"Arn thre fair vertues,
And ben noght fer to fynde.
Whe so is trewe of his tunge,   5058

And of his two handes,   5059
And thorugh his labour, or thorugh
His liflode wynneth,   [his land,
And is trusty of his tailende,
Taketh but his owene,
And his noght dronklewe ne dedey-
Do-wel hym folweth.   [nous,
     "Do-bet dooth right thus :
Ac he dooth muche moore ;
He is as lowe as a lomb,
And lovelich of speche,
And helpeth alle men   5070
After that hem nedeth.
The bagges and the bigirdles,
He hath to-broke hem alle,
That the erl Avarous
Heeld and hise heires.
And thus with Mammonaes moneie
He hath maad hym frendes,
And is ronne to religion,
And hath rendred the Bible,
And precheth to the peple
Seint Poules wordes :   5081
Libenter suffertis insipientes, cum
     sitis ipsi sapientes.
     "And suffreth the unwise
With yow for to libbe ;
And with glad wille dooth hem good,
For so God yow hoteth.
     "Do-best is above bothe,
And bereth a bisshopes crosse,
Is hoked on that oon ende
To halie men fro helle ;
A pik is on that potente,   5092

To putte a-down the wikked   5093
That waiten any wikkednesse
Do-wel to tene.
And Do-wel and Do-bet
Amonges hem han ordeyned,
To crowne oon to be kyng
To rulen hem bothe;
That if Do-wel or Do-bet
Dide ayein Do-best,
Thanne shal the kyng come
And casten hem in irens,
And but if Do-best bede for hem,
Thei to be ther for evere.
  "Thus Do-wel and Do-bet,
And Do-best the thridde,
Crouned oon to the kyng
To kepen hem alle,
And to rule the reme
By hire thre wittes,
And noon oother wise
But as thei thre assented."
  I thonked Thoght tho,
That he me thus taughte.   5115
" Ac yet savoreth me noght thi sey-
I coveite to lerne   [ing;
How Do-wel, Do-bet, and Do-best
Doon among the peple."
  "But Witkonne wisse thee," quod
" Wher tho thre dwelle, [Thoght,
Ellis woot I noon that kan
That now is alyve."
  Thoght and I thus
Thre daies we yeden,
Disputyng upon Do-wel   5126

Day after oother;   5127
And ere we were war,
With Wit gonne we mete.
He was long and lene,
Lik to noon other;
Was no pride on his apparaille,
Ne poverte neither;
Sad of his semblaunt,
And of softe chere.
I dorste meve no matere
To maken hym to jangle,
But as I bad Thoght thoo   5138
Be mene bitwene,
And pute forth som purpos
To preven hise wittes,
What was Do-wel fro Do-bet,
And Do-best from hem bothe.
    Thanne Thoght in that tyme
Seide thise wordes:
" Where Do-wel, Do-bet,
And Do-best ben in londe,
Here is Wil wolde wite,
If Wit koude teche hym;
And wheither he be man or womman
This man fayn wolde aspie,
And werchen as thei thre wolde,
Thus is his entente."   5153

"SIRE   Do-wel   dwelleth,"
                [quod Wit,   5154
   " Noght a day hennes,
   In a castel that Kynde made
   Of four kynnes thynges ;
Of erthe and of eyr it is maad,
Medled togideres,
With wynd and with water
Witterly enjoyned.
Kynde hath closed therinne
Craftily withalle
A lemman that he loveth
Lik to hymselve ;   5165
Anima she hatte.
Ac envye hir hateth,
A proud prikere of Fraunce,
Princeps hujus mundi,
And wolde wynne hire awey
With wiles, and he myghte.
   " Ac Kynde knoweth this wel,
And kepeth hire the bettre,
And dooth hire with sire Do-wel,
Is duc of thise marches.
   " Do-bet is hire damyselle,
Sire Do-weles doughter,   5177

To serven this lady leelly   5178
Bothe late and rathe.
   "Do-best is above bothe,
A bisshopes peere ;
That he bit moot be do,
He ruleth hem alle.
Anima, that lady,
Is lad by his leryng.
Ac the constable of that castel,
That kepeth al the wacche,
Is a wis knyght withalle,
Sire Inwit he hatte,   5189
And hathe fyve faire sones
Bi his firste wyve ;
Sire Se-wel, and Sey-wel,
And Here-wel the hende,
Sire Werch-wel-with-thyn-hand,
A wight man of strengthe,
And sire Godefray Go-wel ;
Grete lordes, for sothe.
Thise fyve ben set
To kepe this lady *Anima*,
Til Kynde come or sende   5200
To saven hire for evere."   [quod I,
   "What kynnes thyng is Kynde?"
"Kanstow me telle ?"   [tour
   "Kynde," quod Wit, "is a crea-
Of alle kynnes thynges,
Fader and formour
Of al that evere was maked ;
And that is the grete God
That gynnyng hadde nevere,
Lord of lif and of light,
Of lisse and of peyne.   5211

Aungeles and alle thyng   5212
Arn at his wille;
Ac man is hym moost lik
Of marc and of shafte;
For thorugh the word that he spak
Woxen forth beestes.
Dixit et facta sunt.
  "And made man likkest
To hymself one,
And Eve of his ryb-bon,
Withouten any mene,
For he was synguler hymself; 5223
And seide *faciamus*,
As who seith moore moot herto
Than my word oone,
My myght moot helpe
Forth with my speche.
Right as a lord sholde make lettres,
And hym lakked parchemyn,
Though he koude write never so wel,
If he hadde no penne,
The lettre, for al the lordshipe,
I leve were nevere y-maked.   5234
  "And so it semeth by hym,
As the Bible telleth,
There he seide *Dixit et facta sunt*,
He moste werche with his word,
And his wit shewe.
And in this manere was man maad,
Thorugh myght of God almighty,
With his word and werkmanshipe,
And with lif to laste.
And thus God gaf hym a goost,
Thorugh the godhede of hevene, 5245

And of his grete grace   5246
Graunted hym blisse,
And that is lif that ay shal laste
To al his lynage after.
And that is the castel that Kynde
Caro it hatte,   [made,
And is as muche to mene
As man with a soule ;
And that he wroghte with werk,
And with word bothe,
Thorgh myght of the magesté
Man was y-maked.   5257
  " Inwit and alle wittes
Closed ben therinne,
For love of the lady *Anima*,
That lif is y-nempned ;
Over al in mannes body
He walketh and wandreth.
And in the herte is hir hoom
And hir mooste reste.
  " Ac Inwit is in the heed,
And to the herte he loketh ;
What *Anima* is leef or looth,   5268
He lat hire at his wille ;
For after the grace of God,
The gretteste is Inwit.
  " Muche wo worth that man
That mys-ruleth his Inwit ;
And that ben glotons glubberes,
Hir God is hire wombe.
Quorum deus venter est.
  " For thei serven Sathan,
Hir soules shal he have.
That lyven synful lif here,   5279

Hir soule is lich the devil ; 5280
And alle that lyven good lif
Are lik to God almyghty,
Qui manet in caritate, in Deo manet,
    etc.
"Alas ! that drynke shal for-do
That God deere boughte,
And dooth God forsaken hem
That he shoop to his liknesse.
Amen dico vobis, nescio vos. Et alibi :
    Et dimisi eos secundum desideria
    eorum. 5291
"Fools that fauten Inwit,
I fynde that holy chirche
Sholde fynden hem that hem fauted,
And fader-lese children,
And widewes that han noght wher-
To wynnen hem hir foode,   [with
Madde men, and maydenes
That help-lese were,
Alle thise lakken Inwit,
And loore bihoveth.
"Of this matere I myghte 5302
Make a long tale,
And fynde fele witnesses
Among the foure doctours ;
And that I lye noght of that I lere
Luc bereth witnesse.   [thee,
"God-fadres and god-modres,
That seen hire god-children
At mys-eise and at myschief,
And mowe hem amende,
Shul have penaunce in purgatorie
But thei hem helpe. 5713

For moore bilongeth to the litel barn,
Er he the lawe knowe,
Than nempnynge of a name,
And he never the wiser.
Sholde no cristene creature
Cryen at the yate,
Ne faille payn ne potage,
And prelates dide as thei sholden.
A Jew wolde noght se a Jew
Go janglyng for defaute,
For alle the mebles on this moolde,
And he amende it myghte.   5325
   " Alas ! that a cristene creature
Shal be unkynde til another ;
Syn Jewes, that we jugge
Judas felawes,
Eyther of hem helpeth oother
Of that that hem nedeth.
Whi nel we cristene
Of Cristes good be as kynde
As Jewes, that ben oure lores-men ?
Shame to us alle !
The commune for hir unkyndenesse,
I drede me, shul abye.
   " Bisshopes shul be blamed
For beggeres sake.
He is wors than Judas,
That gyveth a japer silver,
And biddeth the beggere go,
For his broke clothes.
Proditor est prælatus cum Juda,
   qui patrimonium Christi mimis
   distribuit.   Et alibi : Perni-
   ciosus dispensator est, qui res

*pauperum Christi inutiliter
consumit.*

" He dooth noght wel that dooth
thus,
Ne drat noght God almyghty ;
He loveth noght Salomons sawes,
That sapience taughte.
Initium sapientiæ, timor Domini.
"That dredeth God, he dooth wel ;
That dredeth him for love,
And noght for drede of vengeaunce,
Dooth therfore the bettre.
"He dooth best that with-draweth
By daye and by nyghte,   [hym
To spille any speche
Or any space of tyme.
*Qui offendit in uno, in omnibus est
reus.*
" Lesynge of tyme,
Truthe woot the sothe,
Is moost y-hated upon erthe
Of hem that ben in hevene ;
And siththe to spille speche,   5369
That spicerie is of grace,
And Goddes gle-man,
And a game of hevene.
Wolde nevere the feithful fader
This fithele were un-tempred,
Ne his gle-man a gedelyng,
A goere to tavernes.
" To alle trewe tidy men
That travaille desiren,
Oure Lord loveth hem and lent
Loude outher stille   5380

Grace to go to hem,   5381
And of-gon hir liflode.
Inquirentes autem Dominum non
minuenter omni bono.
    " Trewe wedded libbynge folk
In this world is Do-wel,
For thei mote werche and wynne,
And the world sustene.
For of hir kynde thei come
That confessours ben nempned,
Kynges and knyghtes,
Kaysers and cherles,   5392
Maidenes and martires,
Out of o man come.
The wif was maad the weye
For to helpe werche ;
And thus was wedlok y-wroght
With a mene persone,
First, by the fadres wille,
And the frendes conseille ;
And sithenes by assent of hemself,
As thei two myghte acorde.
And thus was wedlok y-wroght,
And God hymself it made
In erthe and in hevene,
Hymself bereth witnesse.
    " Ac fals folk feyth-lees,
Theves and lyeres,
Wastours and wrecches,
Out of wedlok, I trowe,
Conceyved ben in yvel tyme,
As Caym was on Eve ;
Of swiche synfulle sherewes
The Sauter maketh mynde :   5414

Concepit in dolore, et peperit ini-
quitatem, etc.
 "And alle that come of that Caym,
Come to yvel ende.
And God sente to Seem,
And seide by an aungel,
'Thyn issue in thyn issue
I wol that thei be wedded,
And noght thi kynde with Caymes
Y-coupled nor y-spoused.'
 "Yet some, ayein the sonde
Of oure Saveour of hevene,   5426
Caymes kynde and his kynde
Coupled togideres,
Til God wrathed for hir werkes,
And swich a word seide,
'That I makede man
It me for-thynketh.'
Pœnitet me fecisse hominem.
 "And com to Noe anon,
And bad hym noght lette:
'Swith go shape a ship
Of shides and of bordes ;   5437
Thyself and thi sones,
And sithen youre wyves,
Busketh yow to that boot,
And bideth ye therinne,
Til fourty daies be fulfild,
That the flood have y-wasshen
Clene awey the corsed blood
That Caym hath y-maked.
 "'Beestes that now ben
Shul banne the tyme
That evere that cursed Caym   5448

Coom on this erthe ;   5449
Alle shul deye for hise dedes,
By dales and by hulles,
And the foweles that fleen
Forth with othere beestes,
Excepte oonliche
Of ech kynde a couple,
That in thi shyngled ship
Shul ben y-saved.'
Here a-boughte the barn
The bel-sires giltes,
And alle for hir fadres   5460
Thei ferden the werse ;
The Gospel is her ayein,
In o degré, I fynde :
Filius non portabit iniquitatem pa-
*   tris, et pater non portabit ini-*
*   quitatem filii, etc.*
  " Ac I fynde if the fader
Be fals and a sherewe,
That som del the sone
Shal have the sires tacches.
  " Impe on an ellere,   5471
And if thyn appul be swete,
Muchel merveille me thynketh ;
And moore of a sherewe
That bryngeth forth any barn,
But if he be the same,
And have a savour after the sire ;
Selde sestow oother.
Nunquam colligitur de spinis uva,
*   nec de tribulis ficus.*
  " And thus thorugh cursed Caym
Cam care upon erthe ;   5482

And al for thei wroghte wedlokes 5483
Ayein Goddes wille.
For-thi have thei maugré of hir ma-
That marie so hir children. [riages
For some, as I se now,
Sooth for to telle,
For coveitise of catel
Un-kyndely ben wedded;
As careful concepcion
Cometh of swiche mariages,
As bi-fel of the folk
That I bifore of tolde,   5494
Therfore goode sholde wedde goode,
Though thei no good hadde;
'I am *via et veritas*,' seith Crist,
'I may avaunce yow alle.'
   "It is an uncomly couple,
By Crist! as me thynketh,
To yeven a yong wenche
To an old feble,
Or wedden any wodewe
For welthe of hir goodes,
That nevere shal barn bere   5505
But if it be in hir armes.
Many a peire, sithen the pestilence,
Han plight hem tegideres,
The fruyt that brynge forth
Arn foule wordes,
In jelousie joye-lees,
And janglynge on bedde,
Have thei no children but cheeste,
And clappyng hem bitwene.
And though thei do hem to Dun-
But if the devel helpe,   [mowe,

To folwen after the flicche,   5517
Fecche thei it nevere ;
And but thi bothe be for-swore,
That bacon thei tyne.
  " For-thei I counseille alle cristene
Coveite noght be wedded
For coveitise of catel,
Ne of kyn-rede riche ;
Ac maidenes and maydenes
Macche yow togideres,
Wodewes and wideweres
Wercheth the same ;   5528
For no londes, but for love,
Loke ye be wedded,
And thanne gete ye the grace of God,
And good y-nough to lyve with.
  " And every maner seculer
That may noght continue,
Wisely goo wedde,
And ware hym fro synne ;
For lecherie in likynge
Is lyme-yerd of helle.
Whiles thow art yong,   5539
And thi wepene kene,
Wreke thee with wyvyng,
If thow wolt ben excused.
Dum sis vir fortis,
Ne des tua robora scortis ;
Scribitur in portis,
Meretrix est janua mortis.
  " Whan ye han wyved, beth war
And wercheth in tyme ;
Noght as Adam and Eve,
Whan Caym was engendred.   5550

For in un-tyme, trewely, 5551
Bitwene man and womman,
Ne sholde no bourde or bedde be;
But if thei bothe were clene
Bothe of lif and of soule,
And in perfit charité,
That ilke derne dede do
No man ne sholde.
And if thei leden thus hir lif,
It liketh God almyghty;
For he made wedlok first,
And hymself it seide : 5562
Bonum est ut unusquisque uxorem
  suam habeat, propter fornica-
  tionem. [geten
 "And thei that other gates ben
For gedelynges arn holden,
As fals folk fondlynges,
Faitours and lieres,
Ungracious to gete good
Or love of the peple,
Wandren and wasten
What thei cacche mowe, 5573
Ayeins Do-wel thei doon yvel,
And the devel serve;
And after hir deeth day
Shul dwelle with the same,
But God gyve hem grace here
Hemself to amende.
 "Do-wel my frend is,
To doon as lawe techeth;
To love thi frend and thi foo,
Leve me, that is Do-bet;
To gyven and to yemen 5584

Bothe yonge and olde,   5585
To helen and to helpen,
Is Do-best of alle.
    " And Do-wel is to drede God,
And Do-bet to suffre,
And so cometh Do-best of bothe,
And bryngeth adoun the mody,
And that is wikked wille
That many a werk shendeth,
And dryveth awey Do-wel
Thorugh dedliche synnes."   5595

THANNE hadde Wit a wif,
Was hote dame Studie,
That lene was of lere,
And of liche bothe;
She was wonderly wroth
That Wit me thus taughte;
And, al starynge dame Studie
Sterneliche loked.

"Wel artow wis," quod she to Wit,
"Any wisdomes to telle
To flatereres or to fooles,
That frenetike ben of wittes." 5607
And blamed hym and banned hym,
And bad hym be stille,
With swiche wise wordes
To wissen any sottes.
And seide, "*Noli mittere*, man,
Margery perles
Among hogges, that han
Hawes at wille;
Thei doon but dryvele theron,
Draf were hem levere
Than al the precious perree
That in paradis wexeth. 5619

I seye it by swiche," quod she, 5620
"That sheweth by hir werkes,
That hem were levere lond
And lordshipe on erthe,
Or richesse, or rentes,
And reste at hir wille,
Than alle the sooth sawes
That Salomon seide evere.
  " Wisdom and wit now
Is noght worth a kerse,
But if it be carded with coveitise,
As clotheres kemben hir wolle. 5631
Who so can contreve deceites
And conspire wronges,
And lede forth a love-day
To lette with truthe,
He that swiche craftes can
To counseil is cleped.
Thei lede lordes with lesynges,
And bi-lieth Truthe.
  " Job the gentile
In his gestes witnesseth,
That wikked men thei welden 5642
The welthe of this worlde ;
And that thei ben lordes of ech a lond
That out of lawe libbeth.
Quare impii vivunt, bene est omni-
  bus qui prævaricantur et inique
  agunt.
  "The Sauter seith the same
By swiche that doon ille :
Ecce ipsi peccatores abundantes in
  sæculo obtinuerunt divitias.
  "Lo ! seith holy lettrure,   5653

Whiche beth thise sherewes? 5654
Thilke that God gyveth moost,
Leest good thei deleth ;
And moost un-kynde to the com-
That moost catel weldeth.   [mune
Quæ perfecisti destruxerunt, justus
        autem, etc.
  " Harlotes for hir harlotrie
May have of hir goodes,
And japeris and jogelours,
And jangleris of gestes.
  " Ac he that hath holy writ 5665
Ay in his mouthe,
And kan telle of Tobye,
And of twelve apostles,
Or prechen of the penaunce
That Pilat wikkedly wroghte
To Jhesu the gentile,
That Jewes to-drowe ;
Litel is he loved
That swich a lesson sheweth,
Or daunted or drawe forth,
I do it on God hymselve.   5676
  "But thoo that feynen hem foolis,
And with faityng libbeth,
Ayein the lawe of oure Lord,
And lyen on hemselve,
Spitten and spuen,
And speke foule wordes,
Drynken and drevelen,
And do men fer to gape,
Likne men, and lye on hem,
That leneth hem no giftes ;
Thei konne na-moore mynstralcie

Ne musik men to glade,   5688
Than Munde the millere
Of *Multa fecit Deus.*
Ne were hir vile harlotrye,
Have God my trouthe!
Sholde nevere kyng ne knyght,
Ne chanon of seint Poules,
Gyve hem to hir yeres-gyve
The gifte of a grote.
    "Ac murthe and mynstralcie
Amonges men is nouthe
Lecherie, losengerye,   5699
And losels tales,
Glotonye and grete othes,
This murthe thei lovyeth.
    "Ac if thei carpen of Crist,
Thise clerkes and thise lewed
At mete in hir murthe,
Whan mynstrals beth stille,
Thanne telleth thei of the Trinité
A tale outher tweye,
And bryngen forth a balled reson,
And taken Bernard to witnesse,
And putten forth a presumpcion
To preve the sothe.
Thus thei dryvele at hir deys
The Deitee to knowe,
And gnawen God with the gorge,
Whanne hir guttes fullen.
    "Ac the carefulle may crie
And carpen at the yate,
Bothe a-fyngred and a-furst,
And for chele quake;
Is ther noon to nyme hym neer,

His anoy to amende,   5722
But hunten hym as an hound,
And hoten hym go thennes.
Litel loveth he that Lord
That lent hym al that blisse,
That thus parteth with the povere
A percell whan hym nedeth.
Ne were mercy in meene men
Moore than in riche,
Mendinauntz mete-lees
Myghte go to bedde.
God is muche in the gorge   5733
Of thise grete maistres,
Ac amonges meene men
His mercy and hise werkes.
And so seith the Sauter,
I have seighen it ofte :
Ecce audivimus eam in Effrata, in-
    venimus eam in campis silvæ.
  " Cleikes and othere kynnes men
Carpen of God faste,
And have hym muche in the mouth ;
Ac meene men in herte.   5744
  " Freres and faitours
Han founde swiche questions,
To plese with proude men,
Syn the pestilence tyme ;
And prechen at seint Poules
For pure envye of clerkes ;
That folk is noght fermed in the feith,
Ne free of hire goodes,
Ne sory for hire synnes ;
So is pride woxen,
In religion and in al the reme, 5755

Amonges riche and povere,   5756
That preieres have no power
The pestilence to lette.
And yet the wrecches of this world
Is noon y-war by oother;
Ne for drede of the deeth
With-drawe noght hir pride;
Ne beth plentevouse to the povere,
As pure charité wolde;
But in gaynesse and in glotonye
For-glutten hir good hemselve,
And breketh noght to the beggere
As the Book techeth:
Frange esurienti panem tuum, etc.
And the moore he wynneth and welt
Welthes and richesse,
And lordeth in londes,
The lasse good he deleth.
    "Tobye telleth yow noght so,
Taketh hede, ye riche,
How the book Bible
Of hym bereth witnesse.
Si tibi sit copia, abundanter tribue.
Si autem exiguum, illud impertiri
        stude libenter.
    "Who so hath muche, spende
So seith Tobye;   [manliche,
And who so litel weldeth,
Rule hym therafter.
For we have no lettre of oure lif,
How longe it shal dure,
Swiche lessons lordes sholde
Lovye to here,
And how he myghte moost meynee

Manliche fynde.   5790
  " Nought to fare as a fithelere or
For to seke festes   [a frere,
Homliche at othere mennes houses,
And hatien hir owene.
Elenge is the halle
Ech day in the wike,
Ther the lord ne the lady
Liketh noght to sitte.
Now hath ech riche a rule
To eten by hymselve
In a pryvee parlour,   5801
For povere mennes sake,
Or in a chambre with a chymenee,
And leve the chief halle
That was maad for meles,
Men to eten inne,
And al to spare to spende
That spille shal another.
  " I have y-herd heighe men,
Etynge at the table,
Carpen, as thei clerkes were,
Of Crist, and of hise myghtes ; 5812
And leyden fautes upon the fader
That formede us alle,
And carpen ayein clerkes
Crabbede wordes,
Why wolde oure Saveour suffre
Swich a worm in his blisse,
That bigiled the womman,
And the man after,
Thorugh whiche wiles and wordes
Thei wente to helle,
And al hir seed for hir synne   5823

The same deeth suffrede.   5824
   " Here lyeth youre lore,
Thise lordes gynneth dispute,
Of that the clerkes us kenneth
Of Crist by the Gospel :
Filius non portabit iniquitatem pa-
        tris, etc.
   " Why sholde we that now ben,
For the werkes of Adam,
Roten and to-rende ?
Reson wolde it nevere.
Unusquisque portabit onus suum, etc.
   " Swiche motyves thei mene,
Thise maistres in hir glorie,
And maken men in mys-bileve
That muse muche on hire wordes,
Ymaginatif herafterwarde
Shal answere to hir purpos.
   " Austyn to swiche argueres
Telleth this teme :
Non plus sapere quam oportet.
   " Wilneth nevere to wite
Why that God wolde   5846
Suffre Sathan
His seed to bigile ;
Ac bileveth lelly
In the loore of holy chirche,
And preie hym of pardon
And penaunce in thi lyve,
And for his muche mercy
To amende yow here.
For alle that wilneth to wite
The weyes of God almyghty,
I wolde his eighe were in his ers,

And his fynger after,   5858
That evere wilneth to wite
Why that God wolde
Suffre Sathan
His seed to bigile,
Or Judas to the Jewes
Jhesu bitraye.
Al was as thow woldest,
Lord, y-worshiped be the !
And al worth as thow wolt,
What so we dispute.
    " And tho that useth thise hany-
To blende mennes wittes,   [lons
What is Do-wel fro Do-bet,
That deef mote he worthe,
Siththe he wilneth to wite
Whiche thei ben bothe,
But if he lyve in the lif
That longeth to Do-wel.
For I dar ben his bolde borgh,
That do-bet wole he nevere,
Theigh Do-best drawe on hym
Day after oother."   5880
    And whan that Wit was y-war
What dame Studie tolde,
He bicom so confus,
He kouthe noght loke,
And as doumb as deeth,
And drough hym arere ;
And for no carpyng I kouthe after,
Ne knelyng to the grounde,
I myghte gete no greyn
Of his grete wittes.
But al laughynge he louted,   5891

And loked upon Studie   5892
In signe that I sholde
Bi-secchen hire of grace.
   And whan I was war of his wille,
To his wif gan I loute,
And seide, "Mercy, madame,
Youre man shal I worthe
As longe as I lyve,
Bothe late and rathe,
For to werche youre wille
The while my lif dureth,
With that ye kenne me kyndely
To knowe what is Do-wel."
   "For thi mekenesse, man," quod
"And for thi mylde speche, [she,
I shal kenne thee to my cosyn
That Clergie is hoten.
He hath wedded a wif
Withinne thise sixe monthes,
Is sib to seven artz,
Scripture is hir name.
They two, as I hope,
After my techyng,   5914
Shullen wissen thee to Do-wel,
I dar it undertake."
   Thanne was I al so fayn,
As fowel of fair morwe,
And gladder than the gle-man
That gold hath to gifte;
And asked hire the heighe wey
Where that Clergie dwelte,
"And tel me som tokene," quod I,
"For tyme is that I wende."
   "Aske the heighe wey," quod she,

" Hennes to Suffre-   5926
Both-wele-and-wo,
If that thow wolt lerne,
And ryd forth by Richesse,
Ac rest thow noght therinne ;
For if thow couplest thee therwith,
To Clergie comestow nevere.
   " And also the likerouse launde
That Lecherie hatte,   .
Leve it on thi left half
A large myle or moore,
Til thow come to a court,   5937
Kepe-wel-thi-tunge-
Fro-lesynges-and-lither-speche-
And-likerouse-drynkes.
   " Thanne shaltow se Sobretee,
And Sympletee-of-speche,
That ech wight be in wille
His wit thee to shewe ;
And thus shaltow come to Clergie,
That kan manye thynges.
   " Seye hym this signe,
I sette hym to scole,   5948
And that I grete wel his wif,
For I wroot hire manye bokes,
And sette hire to Sapience,
And to the Sauter glose ;
Logyk I lerned hire,
And manye othere lawes,
And alle musons in musik
I made hire to knowe.
   " Plato the poete
I putte first to boke,
Aristotle and othere mo   5959

To argue I taughte.   5960
  " Grammer for girles
I garte first to write,
And bette hem with a baleys,
But if thei wolde lerne,
  " Of alle kynne craftes
I contreved tooles,
Of carpentrie, of kerveres,
And compased masons,
And lerned hem level and lyne,
Though I loke dymme.
  " Ac Theologie hath tened me
Ten score tymes ;
The moore I muse therinne
The mystier it seemeth,
And the depper I devyne
The derker me it thynketh.
It is no science, for sothe,
For to sotile inne ;
A ful lethi thyng it were,
If that love nere ;
Ac for it leteth best bi-love,
I love it the bettre.   5982
For there that love is ledere,
Ther lakked nevere grace.
Loke thow love lelly,
If thee liketh Do-wel ;
For Do-bet and Do-best
Ben of Loves kynne.
  " In oother science it scith,
I seigh it in Caton :   [*amicus,*
*Qui simulat verbis, nec corde est fidus
Tu quoque fac simile, sic ars delu-
    ditur arte.*   5993

" Who so gloseth as gyloursdoon,
Go me to the same ;
And so shaltow fals folk
And feith-lees bigile.
This is Catons kennyng
To clerkes that he lereth.
" Ac Theologie techeth noght so,
Who so taketh yeme ;
He kenneth us the contrarie,
Ayein Catons wordes.
For he biddeth us be as bretheren,
And bidde for our enemys.   6010
And loven hem that lyen on us,
And lene hem whan hem nedeth,
And do good ayein yvel,
God hymself it hoteth.
*Dum tempus habemus, operemur
     bonum ad omnes, maxime autem
     ad domesticos fidei.*
Poul preched the peple
That perfitnesse lovede,
To do good for Goddes love,
And gyven men that asked,   6015
And namely to swiche
As suwen oure bileve,
And alle that lakketh us, or lyeth,
Oure Lord techeth us to lovye.
And noght to greven hem that grev-
God hymself forbad it,   [eth us,
Mihi vindictam, et ego retribuam.
" For-thi loke thow lovye,
As longe as thow durest ;
For is no science under sonne
So sovereyn for the soule.   6026

" Ac astronomye is an hard thyng,
And yvel for to knowe ;
Geometrie and geomesie,
So gynful of speche,
Whoso thynketh werchewith thotwo
Thryveth ful late,
For sorcerie is the sovereyn book
That to tho sciences bilongeth.
" Yet ar ther fibicches in forceres
Of fele mennes makyng,
Experimentz of alkenamye
The peple to deceyve ;   6028
If thow thynke to do-wel,
Deel therwith nevere.
" Alle thise sciences I myself
Sotilede and ordeynede,
And founded hem formest
Folk to deceyve.
Tel Clergie this tokene,
And Scripture after,
To counseille thee kyndely
To knowe what is Do-wel."
I seide, "Graunt mercy, madame,"
And mekely hir grette ;
And wente wightly awey
Withoute moore lettyng,
And til I com to Clergie
I koude nevere stynte ;
And grette the goode man,
As Studie me taughte,
And afterwardes the wif,
And worshiped hem bothe,
And tolde hem the tokenes
That me taught were.   6060

Was nevere gome upon this ground,
Sith God made the worlde,
Fairer under-fongen,
Ne frendlier at ese,
Than myself, soothly,
Soone so he wiste
Than I was of Wittes hous,
And with his wif, dame Studie.
   I seide to hem soothly
That sent was I thider,
Do-wel and Do-bet
And Do-best to lerne.   [Clergie,
   "It is a commune lyf," quod
"On holy chirche to bileve,
With alle the articles of the feith
That falleth to be knowe;
And that is to bileve lelly,
Bothe lered and lewed,
On the grete God
That gynnyng hadde nevere,
And on the soothfast Sone
That saved mankynde
Fro the dedly deeth   6083
And devel's power,
Thorugh the help of the Holy Goost,
The which goost is of bothe,
Thre persones, ac noght
In plurel nombre;
For al is but oon God,
And ech is God hymselve.
Deus pater, Deus filius, Deus spiritus
    sanctus.
God the fader, God the sone,
God holy goost of bothe,   6094

Makere of mankynde,   6095
And of beestes bothe.
  " Austyn the olde
Herof made bokes,
And hymself ordeyned
To sadde us in bileve.
Who was his auctour?
Alle the foure euvangelistes,
And Crist cleped hymself so,
The euvangelistes bereth witnesse.
  " Alle the clerkes under Crist
Ne koude this assoille ;   6106
But thus it bi-longeth to bileve
To lewed that willen do-wel.
For hadde nevere freke fyn wit
The feith to dispute,
Ne man hadde no merite,
Myghte it ben y-preved.
Fides non habet meritum, ubi hu-
    mana ratio præbet experimen-
    tum.
  "Thanne is Do-bet to suffre
For the soules helthe,   6117
Al that the book bit
Bi holi cherches techyng ;
And that is, man, bi thy myght,
For mercies sake.
Loke thow werche it in werk,
That thi word sheweth,
Swich as thow semest in sighte
Be in assay y-founde.
Appare quod es, vel esto quod ap-
    pares.
  " And lat no body be   6128

By thi beryng bigiled,　　　　6129
But be swich in thi soule
As thow semest withoute.
　"Thanne is Do-best to be boold
To blame the gilty,
Sythenes thow seest thiself
As in soule clene ;
Ac blame thow nevere body,
And thow be blame worthy.
Si culpare velis,
Culpabilis esse cavebis ;
Dogma tuum sordet,　　　　6140
Cum te tua culpa remordet.
　"God in the Gospel
Grevously repreveth
Alle that lakketh any lif,
And lakkes han hemselve.
Qui consideras festucam in oculo
　　fratris tui, trabem in oculo tuo,
　　etc.
　"Why menestow thi mood for a
In thi brotheres eighe,　　　[mote
Sithen a beem in thyn owene　6151
A-blyndeth thiselve.
Ejice primo trabem in oculo tuo,
　　etc.
Which letteth thee to loke
Lasse outher more.
　"I rede ech a blynd bosarde
Do boote to hymselve,
For abbotes and for priours,
And for alle manere prelates,
As persons and parisshes preestes
That preche sholde and teche　6162

Alle maner men to amenden   6163
Bi hire myghtes.
  "This text was told yow,
To ben y-war, er ye taughte,
That ye were swiche as ye seye,
So salve with othere ;
For Goddesword wolde noght be lost,
For that wercheth evere ;
If it availled noght the commune,
It myghte availle yowselve.
  "Ac it semeth now soothly
To the worldes sighte,   6174
That Goddes word wercheth noght
On lered ne on lewed,
But in swich a manere
As Marc meneth in the gospel :
*Dum cæcus ducit cæcum, ambo in
    foveam cadunt.*
  "Lewed men may likne yow thus,
That the beem lith in youre eighen ;
And the festu is fallen
For youre defaute,
In alle maner men,   6185
Thorugh mausede preestes.
The Bible bereth witnesse
That the folk of Israel
Bittre a-boughte the giltes
Of two badde preestes,
Offyn and Fynes,
For hir coveitise,
Archa Dei mys-happed,
And Ely brak his nekke.   [heron.
  "For-thi ye corectours claweth
And corecteth first yowselve   6196

And thanne mowe ye safly seye, 6197
As David made in the Sauter,
Existimasti inique quod ero tui
    similis, arguam te, et statuam
    contra faciem tuam.
    "And thanne shul burel clerkes
        ben abasshed
To blame yow or to greve,
And carpen noght as thei carpe now,
Ne calle yow doumbe houndes.
Canes non valentes latrare. [word,
And drede to wrathe yow in any
Youre werkmanshipe to lette,
And be prester at youre preiere,
Than for a pound of nobles.
And al for youre holynesse,
Have ye this in herte.
    "In scole there is scorn,
But if a clerk wol lerne,
And gret love and likyng,
For ech of hem loveth oother.
    "Ac now is Religion a rydere,
A romere aboute,   6218
A ledere of love-dayes,
And a lond-buggere,
A prikere on a palfrey
Fro manere to manere,
An heepe of houndes at his ers
As he a lord were.
And but if his knave knele
That shal his coppe brynge,
He loureth on hym, and asketh hym
Who taughte hym curteisie.
    "Litel hadde lordes to doon, 6229

To gyve lond from hire heires   6230
To religiouse, that han no routhe,
Though it reyne on hir auters.
　"In many places ther thei ben
By hemself at ese   [persons,
Of the povere have thei no pité;
And that is hir charité.
Ac thei leten hem as lordes
Hire londes lyen so brode.
　" Ac ther shal come a kyng,
And confesse yow religiouses,
And bete yow as the Bible telleth 6241
For brekynge of youre rule;
And amende monyals,
Monkes and chanons,
And puten to hir penaunce
Ad pristinum statum ire;
And barons with erles beten hem,
Thorugh *Beatus-virres* techyng,
That hir barnes claymen
And blame yow foule.
Hi in curribus et hi in equis ipsi
　　　obligati sunt, etc.   6252
　"And thanne freres in hir fray-
Shul fynden a keye   [tour
Of Costantyns cofres,
In which is the catel
That Gregories god-children
Han yvele despended.
　" And thanne shal the abbot of
　　　Abyngdone,
And al his issue for evere,
Have a knok of a kyng,
And incurable the wounde.   6263

" That this worth sooth, seke ye
That ofte over-se the Bible :
*Quomodo cessavit exactor, quievit
     tributum, contrivit Dominus
     baculum impiorum et virgam
     dominantium cædentium plaga
     insanabili.*
" Ac er that kyng come,
Caym shal awake.
But Do-wel shal dyngen hym adoun,
And destruye his myghte." [quod I,
    " Thanne is Do-wel and Do-bet,"
" *Dominus* and knyghthode."
    " I nel noght scorne," quod
" But if scryveynes lye ; [Scripture,
Kynghod ne knyghthod,
By noght I kan a-wayte,
Helpeth noght to hevene-ward
Oone heris ende ;
Ne richesse right noght,
Ne reautee of lordes.
Poul preveth it impossible
Riche men to have hevene.   6286
Salomon seith also
That silver is worst to lovye :
*Nihil iniquius quam amare pecu-
     niam.*
And Caton kenneth us to coveiten it
Naught but as nede techeth,
*Dilige denarium, sed parce dilige
     formam.*
And patriarkes and prophetes,
And poetes bothe,
Writen to wissen us   6297

To wilne no richesse,   6298
And preiseden poverte with pacience;
The apostles bereth witnesse
That thei han eritage in hevene,
And by trewe righte;
Ther riche men no right may cleyme,
But of ruthe and grace."
  " *Contra*," quod I, " by Crist !
That kan I repreve,
And preven it by Peter,
And by Poul bothe,
That is baptized beth saaf,   6309
Be he riche or povere." [Scripture,
  " That is *in extremis*," quod
" Amonges Sarzens and Jewes,
They mowen be saved so,
And that is oure bileve,
That an un-cristene in that caas
May cristen an hethen ;
And for his lele bileve,
Whan he the lif tyneth,
Have the heritage of hevene
As any man cristene.   6320
  " Ac cristene men withoute moore
Maye noght come to hevene ;
For that Crist for cristene men
Deide and confermed the lawe,
That who so wolde and wilneth
With Crist to arise,
Si cum Christo surexistis, etc.
He sholde lovye and leve,
And the lawe fulfille.
That is, love thi lord God
Levest aboven alle ;   6331

And after, alle cristene creatures
In commune, ech man oother ;
And thus bi-longeth to lovye,
That leveth be saved.
And but we do thus in dede,
At the day of dome
It shal bi-sitten us ful soure
The silver that we kepen ;
And oure bakkes that mothe-eten be,
And seen beggeris go naked ;
Or delit in wyn and wilde fowel,
And wite any in defaute.   6343
For every cristene creature
Sholde be kynde til oother,
And sithen hethen to helpe,
In hope of amendement.
    " God hoteth heighe and lowe
That no man hurte oother ;
And seith, ' Slee noght that sem-
To myn owene liknesse, [blable is
But if I sende thee som tokene ; '
And seith ' *Non mœchaberis.*
Is slee noght, but suffre,   6354
And al for the beste ;   [torie
For I shal punysshe hem in purga-
Or in the put of helle,
Ech man for hise mysdedes,
But mercy it lette.' "

    " THIS is a long lesson," quod I,
        " And litel am I the wiser ;
Where Do-wel is or Do-bet,
Derkliche ye shewen.
Manye tales ye tellen   6364

That Theologie lerneth ;   6365
And that I man maad was,
And my name y-entred
In the legende of lif
Longe er I were,   [nesse,
Or ellis un-writen for som wikked-
As Holy Writ witnesseth :
Nemo ascendit ad cœlum, nisi qui
        de cœlo descendit.
  "I leve it wel," quod I, "by oure
And on no lettrure bettre. [Lord !
For Salomon the sage,   6376
That Sapience taughte,
God gat hym grace of wit,
And alle hise goodes after ;
He demed wel and wisely,
As Holy Writ telleth.
Aristotle and he,
Who wissed men bettre ?
Maistres that of Goddes mercy
Techen men and prechen,
Of hir wordes thei wissen us
For wisest as in hir tyme,   6387
And al holy chirche
Holdeth hem bothe y-dampned.
  " And if I sholde werche by hir
To wynne me hevene,   [werkes
That for hir werkes and wit
Now wonyeth in pyne,
Thanne wroughe I un-wisly,
What so evere ye preche.
  " Ac of fele witty, in feith,
Litel ferly I have,
Though hir goost be un-gracious 6393

God for to plese.   6399
For many men on this moolde
Moore setten hir hertes
In good than in God ;
For-thi hem grace failleth
At hir mooste meschief,
Whan thei shal lif lete.
As Salomon dide, and swiche othere
That shewed grete wittes ;
Ac hir werkes, as holy writ seith,
Were evere the contrarie.
For-thi wise witted men,   6410
And wel y-lettrede clerkes,
As thei seyen hemself,
Selde doon therafter.
Super cathedra Moysi, etc.
    " Ac I wene it worth of manye,
As was in Noes tyme,
Tho he shoop that shipe
Of shides and of bordes ;
Was nevere wrighte saved that
        wroghte theron,
Ne oothir werkman ellis,   6421
But briddes, and beestes,
And the blissed Noe,
And his wif with hise sones,
And also hire wyves ;
Of wightes that it wroghte
Was noon of hem y-saved.
    " God leve it fare noght so bi folk
That the feith techeth
Of holi chirche, that herberwe is,
And Goddes hous to save,
And shilden us from shame therinne,

As Noes ship dide beestes ;   6433
And men that maden it
A-mydde the flood a-dreynten.
The culorum of this clause
Curatours is to mene,   [make
That ben carpenters holy kirk to
For Cristes owene beestes :
Homines et jumenta salvabis, Do-
      mine, etc.
  "On Good Friday I fynde
A felon was y-saved,
That hadde lyved al his lif   6444
With lesynges and with thefte ;
And for he beknede to the cros,
And to Crist shrof him,
He was sonner y-saved
Than seint Johan the Baptist ;
And or Adam or Ysaye,
Or any of the prophetes,
That hadde y-leyen with Lucifer
Many longe yeres,
A robbere was y-raunsoned
Rather than thei alle,   [torie,
Withouten any penaunce of purga-
To perpetuel blisse.
  "Than Marie Maudeleyne
What womman dide werse ?
Or who worse than David,
That Uries deeth conspired ?
Or Poul the apostle,
That no pité hadde
Muche cristene kynde
To kille to dethe ?
And now ben thise as sovereyns
With seintes in hevene,   6467

Tho that wroughte wikkedlokest 6468
In world tho thei were.
And tho that wisely wordeden,
And writen manye bokes
Of wit and of wisedom,
With dampned soules wonye.
That Salomon seith, I trowe be sooth
And certein of us alle :
*Sunt justi atque sapientes et opera
    eorum in manu Dei sunt, etc.*
  "Ther are witty and wel libbynge,
Ac hire werkes ben y-hudde   6479
In the hondes of almyghty God,
And he woot the sothe,
Wherfore a man worth allowed there,
And hise lele werkes,
Or ellis for his yvel wille,
And for envye of herte,
And be allowed as he lyved so ;
For by the luthere men knoweth
    the goode.
  "And wherby wiste men which
If alle thyng blak were ? [were whit,
And who were a good man,
But if ther were som sherewe ?
For-thi lyve we forth with othere
I leve fewe ben goode ;   [men,
For *quant* oportet *vient en place,*
Il n'y ad que pati.
And he that may al amende,
Have mercy on us alle !
For sothest word that ever God seide
Was tho he seide *Nemo bonus.*
  " Clergie tho of Cristes mouth
Comended was it litel ;   6501

For he seide to seint Peter,   6502
And to swiche as he lovede,
Cum steteritis ante reges et præ-
       sides, etc.
Though ye come bifore kynges
And clerkes of the lawe,
Beth noght abasshed,
For I shal be in youre mouthes,
And gyve yow wit and wille,
And konnyng to conclude
Hem alle that ayeins yow
Of Cristendom disputen.   6513
    " David maketh mencion,
He spak amonges kynges,   [hym
And myghte no kyng over-comen
As by konnynge of speche,
But wit and wisedom
Wan nevere the maistrie,
Whan man was at meschief,
Withoute the moore grace.
    " The doughtieste doctour
And devinour of the Trinitee
Was Austyn the olde,   6524
And heighest of the foure,
Seide thus in a sermon,
I seigh it writen ones :
Ecce ipsi idiotæ irapiunt cœlum, ubi
       nos sapientes in inferno mer-
       gimur.
    " And is to mene to men,
Moore ne lesse,
Arn none rather y-ravysshed
Fro the righte bileve,
Than are thise konnynge clerkes
That konne manye bokes.   6536

" Ne none sonner saved,   6537
Ne sadder of bileve,
Than plowmen and pastours,
And othere commune laborers ;
Souteres and shepherdes,
And othere lewed juttes,
Percen with a pater-noster
The paleys of hevene,
And passen purgatorie penaunce-lees
At her hennes partyng
Into the blisse of paradis,
For hir pure bileve,   6548
That imparfitly here knewe,
And ek lyvede.
" Ye men knowe clerkes,
That han corsed the tyme   [moore
That evere thei kouthe or knewe
Than *Credo in Deum patrem;*
And principally hir pater-noster
Many a persone hath wisshed.
" I se ensamples myself,
And so may manye othere,
That servauntz that serven lordes
Selde fallen in arerage,
And tho that kepen the lordes catel,
Clerkes and reves.
" Right so lewed men,
And of litel knowyng,
Selden falle thei so foule
And so fer in synne,
As clerkes of holy chirche
That kepen Cristes tresor,
The which is mannes soule to save,
As God seith in the Gospel:
Ite vos in vineam meam."   6571

Passus Undecimus.

THANNE Scripture scorned
And a skile tolde,   [me,
And lakked me in Latyn,
And light by me she sette,
And seide "*Multi multa sciunt*
Et scipsos nesciunt."
  Tho wepte I for wo
And wrathe of hir speche ;
And in a wynkynge wrathe
Weex I a-slepe.
A merveillous metels
Mette me thanne,   6583
That I was ravysshed right there,
And Fortune me fette,
And into the lond of longynge
Allone she me broughte,   [erthe
And in a mirour that highte middel-
She made me to biholde.
"Sone," she seide to me,
"Here myghtow se wondres,
And knowe that thow coveitest,
And come therto, peraunter."
  Thanne hadde Fortune folwynge
Two faire damyseles ;   [hire

Concupiscentia-carnis   6596
Men called the elder mayde,
And Coveitise-of-eighes
Y-called was that oother.
Pride-of-parfit-lyvynge
Pursued hem bothe,
And bad me for my contenaunce
Acounten Clergie lighte.
   Concupiscentia-carnis
Colled me aboute the nekke,
And seide, "Thow art yong and
And hast yeres y-nowe   [yeepe,
For to lyve longe,
And ladies to lovye;
And in this mirour thow myght se
Myghtes ful manye,
That leden thee wole to likynge
Al thi lif tyme."
   The secounde seide the same,
"I shal sewe thi wille;
Til thow be a lord and have lond,
Leten thee I nelle,
That I ne shal folwe thi felawshipe,
If Fortune it like."
"He shal fynde me his frend,"
Quod Fortune therafter;
"The freke that folwede my wille
Failled nevere blisse."   [Elde,
   Thanne was ther oon that highte
That hevy was of chere;   [thee,
"Man," quod he, "if I mete with
By Marie of hevene!
Thow shalt fynde Fortune thee faille
At thi mooste nede,   6629

And *Concupiscentia-carnis*   6630
Clene thee forsake.
Bittrely shaltow banne thanne
Bothe dayes and nyghtes
Coveitise-of-eighe,
That evere thow hir knewe,
And Pride-of-parfit-lyvynge
To muche peril thee brynge."
   "Ye, recche thee nevere," quod
      Rechelesnesse,
Stood forthe in raggede clothes,
"Folwe forth that Fortune wole, 6640
Thow hast wel fer til Elde;
A man may stoupe tyme y-nogh,
Whan he shal tyne the crowne.
   "*Homo proponit* quod a poete,
And Plato he highte,
And *Deus disponit* quod he,
Lat God doon his wille.
If Truthe wol witnesse it be wel do
Fortune to folwe,
Concupiscentia-carnis,
Ne Coveitise-of-eighes,   6651
Ne shal noght greve thee gretly,
Ne bigile, but if thow wolt thiselve."
   "Ye, fare wel Phippe and Faun-
And forth gan me drawe, [teltee,"
Til *Concupiscentia-carnis*
Acorded alle my werkes.
   "Alas! eighe," quod Elde
And Holynesse bothe,   [nesse,
That wit shal torne to wrecched-
For wil to have his likyng."
   Coveitise-of-eighes   6662

Conforted me anoon after, 6663
And folwed me fourty wynter
And a fifte moore,
That of Do-wel ne Do-bet
Ne deyntee me thoughte.
I hadde no likyng, leve me if thee list,
Of hem ought to knowe.
Coveitise-of-eighes 6674
Com ofter in mynde
Than Do-wel or Do-bet,
Among my dedes alle.
  Coveitise-of-eighes 6674
Conforted me ofte,
And seide, "Have no conscience
How thow come to goode.
Go confesse thee to som frere,
And shewe hym thi synnes ;
For whiles Fortune is thi frend
Freres wol thee lovye,
And fecche thee to hir fraternitee,
And for the biseke
To hir priour provincial
A pardon for to have, 6685
And preien for thee pol by pol,
If thow be *pecuniosus.*"
Sed pœna pecuniaria non sufficit pro
    spiritualibus delictis.
  By wissynge of this wenche I
      wroughte,
Hir wordes were so swete,
Til I for-yat youthe,
And yarn into elde.
  And thanne was Fortune my foo,
For al hir faire speche ; 6695

And poverte pursued me,   6696
And putte me lowe.
    And tho fond I the frere a-fered,
And flittynge bothe
Ayeins oure firste for-warde ;
For I seide I nolde
Be buried at hire hous,
But at my parisshe chirche.
For I herde ones
How Conscience it tolde,
That there a man were cristned
Be kynde he sholde be buryed ;
Or where he were parisshen,
Right there he sholde be graven.
And for I seide thus to freres,
A fool thei me helden,
And loved me the lasse
For my lele speche.
    Ac yet I cryde on my confessour,
That heeld hymself so konnyng ;
" By my feith ! frere," quod I,
" Ye faren lik thise woweris
That wedde none widwes   6718
But for to welden hir goodes.
Right so, by the roode !
Roughte ye nevere
Where my body were buryed,
By so ye hadde my silver.
    "Ich have muche merveille of yow,
And so hath many another,
Whi youre covent coveiteth
To confesse and to burye,
Rather than to baptize barnes
That ben catecumelynges.   6729

Baptizynge and buryinge   6730
Bothe beth ful nedefulle;
Ac muche moore meritorie,
Me thynketh it is to baptize.
For a baptized man may,
As thise maistres telleth,
Thorugh contricion come
To the heighe hevene.
Sola contritio, etc.
Ac barn withouten bapteme
May noght so be saved.
Nisi quis renatus fuerit.   6741
Loke ye, lettred men,
Wheither I lye or do noght."
And Lewté loked on me,
And I loured after.   [Lewtee,
  "Wherfore lourestow?"   quod
And loked on me harde.
  "If I dorste," quod I, "amonges
This metels avowe!"   [men
   "Yis, by Peter and by Poul!"
    quod he,
And took hem bothe to witnesse.
Non oderis fratres secrete in corde
   tuo, sed publice argue illos."
  "They wole aleggen also," quod I,
"And by the Gospel preven:
Nolite judicare quemquam."
   "And wherof serveth lawe?"
    quod Lewtee,
"If no lif undertoke it,
Falsnesse ne faiterie,
For som what the apostle seide,
Non oderis fratrem.   6761

And in the Sauter also   6762
Seith David the prophete,
Existimasti inique quod ero tui
     similis, etc.
  "It is *licitum* for lewed men
To sigge the sothe,
If hem liketh and lest,
Ech a lawe it graunteth ;
Excepte persons and preestes,
And prelates of holy chirche,
It falleth noght for that folk
No tales to telle,   6773
Though the tale be trewe,
And it touche synne.
  " Thyng that al the world woot,
Wherfore sholdestow spare
To reden it in retorik
To a-rate dedly synne ?
Ac be nevere moore the firste
Defaute to blame ;   [first,
Though thow se yvel, seye it noght
Be sory it nere amended.
No thyng that is pryvé,   6784
Publice thow it nevere ;
Neither for love preise it noght,
Ne lakke it for envye.
Parum lauda, vitupera parcius."
  " He seith sooth," quod Scripture
     tho,
And skipte an heigh, and preched.
Ac the matere that she meved,
If lewed men it knewe,
The lasse, as I leve,
Lovyen it thei wolde.   6794

This was hir teme and hir text,
I took ful good hede;
Multi to a mangerie
And to the mete were sompned;
And whan the peple was plener
    comen,
The porter unpynned the yate,
And plukked in *Pauci* pryveliche,
And leet the remenaunt go rome.
    Al for tene of hir text
Trembled myn herte;
And in a weer gan I wexe,   6805
And with myself to dispute
Wheither I were chosen or noght
    chosen.
On holi chirche I thoughte,
That under-fonged me atte font
For oon of Goddes chosene.
For Crist cleped us alle,
Come if we wolde,
Sarzens and scismatikes,
And so he dide the Jewes.
O vos omnes sitientes, venite, etc.
And bad hem souke for synne
Safly at his breste,
And drynke boote for bale,
Brouke it who so myghte.
    "Thanne may alle cristene come,"
      quod I,
" And cleyme there entree
By the blood that he boughte us
And thorugh bapteme after. [with
Qui crediderit et baptizatus fuerit,
    etc.   6826

For though a cristen man coveited
His cristendom to reneye,
Rightfully to reneye
No reson it wolde.
    " For may no cherl chartre make,
Ne his catel selle,
Withouten leve of his lord ;
No lawe wol it graunte.
Ac he may renne in arerage,
And rome so fro home,
And as a reneyed caytif
Recchelesly rennen aboute.   6838
And Reson shal rekene with hym,
And casten hym in arerage,
And putten hym after in a prison
In purgatorie to brenne,
For hise arerages rewarden hym there
To the day of dome ;
But if Contricion wol come,
And crye, by his lyve,
Mercy for hise mysdedes,
With mouthe and with herte,"
    " That is sooth," seide Scripture ;
" May no synne lette
Mercy al to amende,
And mekenesse hir folwe.
For thei beth, as oure bokes telleth,
Above Goddes werkes."
Misericordia ejus super omnia opera
        ejus.
    " Ye, baw for bokes," quod oon
Was broken out of helle,
Highte Trojanus, hadde ben a trewe
Took witnesse at a pope, [knyght,

How he was ded and dampned 6861
To dwellen in pyne,
For an uncristene creature ;
" Clerkes wite the sothe,
That al the clergie under Crist
Ne myghte me cracche fro helle,
But oonliche love and leautee,
And my laweful domes.
    " Gregorie wiste this wel,
And wilned to my soule
Savacion for soothnesse
That he seigh in my werkes ;   6872
And after that he wepte,
And wilned me were graunted
Grace; withouten any bene biddyng
His boone was under-fongen,
And I saved, as ye see,
Withouten syngynge of masses.
By love and by lernyng
Of my lyvynge, in truthe,
Broughte me fro bitter peyne
Ther no biddyng myghte."
    Lo ! ye lordes, what leautee dide
By an emperour of Rome,
That was an uncristene creature,
As clerkes fyndeth in bokes.
Nought thorugh preiere of a pope,
But for his pure truthe,
Was that Sarsen saved.
As seint Gregorie bereth witnesse.
    Wel oughte ye, lordes, that lawes kepe,
This lesson to have in mynde,
And on Trojanus truthe to thenke,

And do truthe to the peple.   6894
" Lawe, withouten love," quod Tro-
" Ley ther a bene,   [janus,
Or any science under sonne,
The sevene artz and alle,
But thei ben lerned for oure Lordes
Lost is al the tyme ;"   [love,
For no cause to cacche silver therby,
Ne to be called a maister,
But al for love of oure Lord,
And the bet to love the peple,
For seint Johan seide it,   6905
And sothe arn hise wordes.
Qui non diligit, manet in morte.
Who so loveth noght, leve me,
He lyveth in deep deyinge ;
And that alle manere men,
Enemyes and frendes,
Love hir eyther oother,
And leve hem, as hemselve,
Who so leveth noght, he loveth
God woot the sothe !   [noght,
Crist comaundeth ech a creature
To conformen hym to lovye,
And sovereynly the povere peple,
And hir enemyes after.
For hem that haten us
Is oure merite to lovye,
And povere peple to plese,
Hir preieres maye us helpe.
And oure joye and oure heele
Jhesu Crist of hevene
In a povere mannes apparaille
Pursued us evere ;   6927

And loketh on us in hir liknesse,
And that with lovely chere,
To knowen us by oure kynde herte
And castynge of oure eighen,
Wheither we love the lordes here
Bifore the Lord of blisse ;
And exciteth us by the Euvangelie
That whan we maken festes,
We sholde noght clepe oure kyn
Ne none kynnes riche.   [therto,
Cum facitis convivia, nolite invitare
        amicos.   6939
" Ac calleth the carefulle therto,
The croked and the povere.
For youre frendes wol feden yow,
And fonde yow to quyte   [gifte ;
Youre festynge and youre faire
Ech frend quyteth so oother.
  " Ac for the povere I shal paie,
And pure wel quyte hir travaille,
That gyveth hem mete or moneie,
Or loveth hem for my sake."
For the beste ben som riche,   6950
And some beggeres and povere.
For alle are we Cristes creatures,
And of his cofres riche,
And bretheren as of oo blood,
As wel beggeres as erles.
For on Calvarie of Cristes blood
Cristendom gan sprynge,
And blody bretheren we bicomen
Of o body y-wonne,   [there
As *quasi modo geniti,*
And gentil-men echone ;   6961

No beggere ne boye amonges us,
But if it synne made.
Qui facit peccatum, servus est pec-
    cati.
    " In the olde lawe,
As holy lettre telleth,
Mennes sones
Men callen us echone,
Of Adames issue and Eve,
Ay til God man deide ;
And after his resurexcion
Redemptor was his name, [y-brought,
And we hise bretheren thorugh hym
Bothe riche and povere.   [ren,
    " For-thi love we as leve brethe-
And ech man laughe of oother ;
And of that ech man may forbere
Amende there it nedeth ;
And every man helpe oother,
For hennes shul we alle.
Alter alterius onera portate.
    " And be we noght un-kynde of
        oure catel,
Ne of oure konnyng neither.   6984
For woot no man how neigh it is
To ben y-nome fro bothe.
For-thi lakke no lif oother,
Though he moore Latyn knowe ;
Ne under-nyme noght foule ;
For is noon withoute defaute.
For what evere clerkes carpe
Of cristendom or ellis,
Crist to a commune womman seide,
In commune at a feste,   6994

That *fides sua* sholde saven hire,
And salven hire of synnes.
  "Thanne is bileve a lele help,
Above logyk or lawe.
Of logyk or of lawe
In *Legenda Sanctorum*
Is litel alowaunce maad,
But if bileve hem helpe.
For it is over longe er logyk
Any lesson assoille;
And lawe is looth to lovye,
But if he lacche silver.   7006
Bothe logyk and lawe,
That loveth noght to lye,
I conseille alle cristene
Clyve noght theron to soore;
For some wordes I fynde writen,
That were of feithes techyng,
That saved synful men,
As seint Johan bereth witnesse.
Eadem mensura qua mensi fueritis,
    remetietur vobis.
  "For-thi lerne we the lawe of
As oure Lord taughte,   [love,
And as seint Gregorie seide
For mannes soule helthe:
Melius est scrutari scelera nostra,
    quam naturas rerum.
  "Why I meve this matere,
Is moost for the povere;
For in hir liknesse oure Lord
Ofte hath ben y-knowe.
Witnesse in the Pask wyke
Whan he yede to Emaüs;   7028

Cleophas ne knew hym noght   7029
That he Crist were,
For his povere apparaille,
And pilgrymes wedes,
Til he blessede and brak
The breed that thei eten ;
So bi hise werkes thei wisten
That he was Jhesus,
Ac by clothyng thei knewe hym
Ne by carpynge of tunge.   [noght,
And al was in ensample
To us synfulle here,   7040
That we sholde be lowe
And loveliche of speche,   [proudly,
And   apparaille   us   noght   over
For pilgrymes are we alle.

   "And in the apparaille of a povere
And pilgrymes liknesse,   [man,
Many tyme God hath ben met
Among nedy peple,
Ther nevere segge hym seigh
In secte of the riche.

   " Seint Johan and othere seintes
Were seyen in poore clothyng,
And as povere pilgrymes
Preyed mennes goodes.   [lighte,

   " Jhesu Crist on a Jewes doghter
Gentil womman though she were,
Was a pure povere maide,
And to a povere man y-wedded.

   " Martha on Marie Maudeleyne
An huge pleynt made,
And to oure Saveour self
Seide thise wordes :   7062

Domine, non est tibi curæ quod
soror mea reliquit me solam
ministrare.
"And hastily God answerde,
And eitheres wille folwed,
Bothe Marthaes and Maries,
As Mathew bereth witnesse ;
Ac poverte God putte bifore,
And preised that the bettre.
Maria optimam partem elegit, quæ
non, etc.
"And alle the wise that evere were,
By aught I kan aspye,
Preiseden poverte for best lif,
If pacience it folwed,
And bothe bettre and blesseder
By many fold than richesse.
For though it be sour to suffre,
Therafter cometh swete ;
As on a walnote withoute
Is a bitter barke,
And after that bitter bark,
Be the shelle aweye,   7085
Is a kernel of confort
Kynde to restore.
"So is after poverte or penaunce
Paciently y-take ;
For it maketh a man to have mynde
In God, and a gret wille
To wepe and to wel bidde,
Wherof wexeth mercy,
Of which Crist is a kernelle
To conforte the soule.
And wel sikerer he slepeth,   7096

The man that is povere,   7097
And lasse he dredeth deeth,
And in derke to ben y-robbed,
Than he that is right riche,
Reson bereth witnesse.
Pauper ego ludo, dum tu dives me-
  ditaris.
  " Al though Salomon seide,
As folk seeth in the Bible,
Divitias nec paupertates, etc.
Wiser than Salomon was
Bereth witnesse and taughte   7108
That parfit poverte was
No possession to have,
And lif moost likynge to God,
As Luc bereth witnesse :
Si vis perfectus esse, vade et vende.
  " And is to mene to men
That on this moolde lyven,
Who so wole be pure parfit
Moot possession forsake,
Or selle it, as seith the Book,
And the silver dele
To beggeris that goon and begge
And bidden good for Goddes love.
For failed nevere man mete
That myghtful God serveth,
As David seith in the Sauter
To swiche that ben in wille
To serve God goodliche,
Ne greveth hym no penaunce :
Nihil inpossibile volenti.
Ne lakketh nevere liflode,
Lynnen ne wollen.   7130

*Inquirentes autem Dominum non
minuentur omni bono.*
" If preestes weren parifite,
Thei wolde ne silver take
For masses ne for matyns,
Noght hir mete of usureres,
Ne neither kirtel ne cote,
Theigh thei for cold sholde deye,
And thei hir devoir dide,
As David seith in the Sauter :
*Judica me, Deus, et decerne causam
meam.*   7142
" *Spera-in-Deo* speketh of preestes
That have no spendyng silver,
That if thei travaille truweliche
And truste in God almyghty,
Hem sholde lakke no liflode,
Neyther lynnen ne wollen.
And the title that ye take ordres by
Telleth ye ben avaunced;   [silver
Thanne nedeth yow noght to take
For masses that ye syngen.
For he that took yow youre title,
Sholde take yow youre wages,
Or the bisshop that blessed yow,
If that ye ben worthi.   [knyght,
" For made nevere kyng no
But he hadde catel to spende
As bifel for a knyght,
Or foond hym for his strengthe.
It is a careful knyght,
And of a caytif kynges makyng,
That hath no lond ne lynage riche,
Ne good loos of hise handes.   7164

" The same I segge, for sothe,
By alle swiche preestes
That han neither konnynge ne kyn,
But a crowne one,
And a title, a tale of noght,
To his liflode at his meschief.
He hath moore bileve, as I leve,
To lacche through his croune
Cure, than for konnyng,
Or knowen for clene berynge.
I have wonder for why
And wherefore the bisshope   7170
Maketh swiche preestes,
That lewed men bitrayen.
    " A chartre is chalangeable
Bifore a chief justice ;
If fals Latyn be in the lettre,
The lawe it impugneth,
Or peynted parentrelynarie,
Or percelles over-skipped ;
The gome that gloseth so chartres
For a goky is holden.
    " So is it a goky, by God !   7187
That in his gospel failleth,
Or in masse or in matyns
Maketh any defaut.
*Qui offendit in uno, in omnibus est
      reus.*
    " And also in the Sauter
Seith David to over-skipperis,
*Psallite Deo nostro, psallite, quo-
      niam rex terræ Deus Israel,
      psallite sapienter.*
    " The bisshop shal be blamed

Bifore God, as I leve,   [knyghtes
That crouneth swiche Goddes
That konneth noght *sapienter*
Synge, ne psalmes rede,
Ne seye a masse of the day.
And never neither is blame-lees
The bisshope ne the chapeleyn ;
For hir either is endited,
And that is, *ignorantia*
Non excusat episcopos
Nec idiotes preestes.

   " This lokynge on lewed preestes
Hath doon me lepe from poverte,
The which I preise ther pacience is
Moore perfit than richesse."

A C muche moore in metynge
     thus
With me gan oon dispute ;
And slepynge I seigh al this.
And sithen cam Kynde,
And nempned me by my name,
And bad me nymen hede,   7219
And thorugh the wondres of this
Wit for to take.   [world
And on a mountaigne that myddel-
Highte, as me thoughte,   [erthe
I was fet forth
By ensamples to knowe
Thorugh ech a creature and kynde
My creatour to lovye.
   I seigh the sonne and the see,
And the sond after ;
And where that briddes and beestes

By hir makes yeden ;   7231
Wilde wormes in wodes,
And wonderful foweles
With fleckede fetheres
And of fele colours.
　　Man and his make
I myghte bothe biholde ;
Poverte and plentee ;
Bothe pees and werre ;
Blisse and bale bothe
I seigh al at ones ;
And how men token mede,   7242
And mercy refused.
　　Reson I seigh soothly
Sewen alle beestes,
In etynge, in drynkynge,
And in engendrynge of kynde ;
And after cours of concepcion,
Noon took kepe of oother   [tyme,
As whan thei hadde ryde in rotey
Anoon right therafter
Males drowen hem to males
A-morwenynges by hemselve,   7253
And in evenynges also
The males ben fro femelles.
Ther ne was cow ne cow-kynde
That conceyved hadde,
That wolde belwe after boles,
Ne boor after sowe ;
Bothe hors and houndes,
And alle othere beestes,
Medled noght with hir makes
That with fole were.
　　Briddes I biheld   7264

That in buskes made nestes,   7265
Hadde nevere wye wit
To werche the leeste.
I hadde wonder at whom
And wher the pye lerned
To legge the stikkes
In whiche she leyeth and bredeth.
Ther nys wrighte, as I wene,
Sholde werche hir nestes to paye ;
If any mason made a molde therto,
Muche wonder it were.

    Ac yet me merveilled moore,
How many othere briddes
Hidden and hileden
Hir egges ful derne
In mareys and moores,
For men sholde hem noght fynde ;
And hidden hir egges,
Whan thei therfro wente,
For fere of othere foweles,
And for wilde beestes.

    And some troden hir makes,
And on trees bredden,   7287
And broughten forth hir briddes so
Al above the grounde ;
And some briddes at the bile
Thorugh brethyng conceyved ;
And some caukede ; and took kepe
How pecokkes bredden.
Muche merveilled me
What maister hem made,
And who taughte hem on trees
To tymbre so heighe,
Ther neither burn ne beest   7298

May hir briddes rechen.   7299
    And sithen I loked upon the see,
And so forth upon the sterres ;
Manye selkouthes I seigh,
Ben noght to seye nouthe.
    I seigh floures in the fryth,
And hir faire colours ;
And how among the grene gras
Growed so manye hewes,
And some soure and some swete,
Selkouth me thoughte ;
Of hir kynde and hir colour   7310
To carpe it were to longe.
    Ac that moost meved me
And my mood chaunged,
That Reson rewarded
And ruled alle beestes,
Save man and his make ;
Many tyme and ofte
No reson hem folwede.
And thanne I rebukede
Reson, and right
Til hymselven I seyde :   7321
" I have wonder of thee," quod I,
" That witty art holden,   [make,
Why thow ne sewest man and his
That no mysfeet hem folwe."
    And Reson a-rated me,
And seide, " Recche thee nevere ;
Why I suffre or noght suffre,
Thiself hast noght to doone.
Amende thow it, if thow myght,
For my tyme is to abide.
Suffraunce is a soverayn vertue,

And a swift vengeance.   7333
Who suffrede moore than God?"
"No gome, as I leeve.   [quod he;
He myghte amende in a minute while
Al that mys-standeth;
Ac he suffreth for som mannes goode,
And so it is oure bettre,
The wise and the witty
Wroot thus in the Bible:
De re quæ te non molestat, noli
        certare.

    "For be a man fair or foul,   7344
It falleth noght for to lakke
The shap ne the shaft
That God shoop hymselve;
For al that he dide was wel y-do,
As holy writ witnesseth:
Et vidit Deus cuncta quæ fecerat, et
        erant valde bona.
    "And bad every creature
In his kynde encreesse;
Al to murthe with man,
That moste wo tholie   7355
In fondynge of the flessh,
And of the feend bothe.
For man was maad of swich a matere,
He may noght wel a-sterte
That ne som tyme hym bitit
To folwen his kynde.
Caton a-cordeth therwith,
Nemo sine crimine vivit."
    Tho caughte I colour anoon,
And comsed to ben ashamed,
And awaked therwith.   7366

Wo was me thanne,   7367
That I in metels ne myghte
Moore have y-knowen.
And thanne seide I to myself,
And childe that tyme,   [quod I,
"Now I woot what Do-wel is,
By deere God! as me thynketh."
   And as I caste up myne eighen,
Oon loked on me and asked
Of me, what thynge it were:
"Y-wis, sire," I seide,
"To se muche and suffre moore,
Certes," quod I, "is Do-wel."
   "Haddestow suffred," he seide,
"Slepynge tho thow were,
Thow sholdest have knowen that
    Clergie kan,
And contreved moore thorugh reson.
For Reson wolde have reherced thee
Right as Clergie seide.
Ac for thyn entre-metynge,
Here artow forsake.
Philosophus esses, si tacuisses   7388
   "Adam, whiles he spak noght,
Hadde paradis at wille;
Ac whan he mamelede aboute mete,
And entre-metede to knowe
The wisedom and the wit of God,
He was put fram blisse.
   "And right so ferde Reson bi thee;
Thow with thi rude speche
Lakkedest and losedest thyng
That longed the noght to doone.
Tho hadde he no likyng
For to lere the moore.   7400

"Pryde now and presumpcion 7401
Peraventure wol thee appele,
That Clergie thi compaignye
Kepeth noght to suwe.
Shal nevere chalangynge nechidynge
Chaste a man so soone,
As shal shame, and shenden hym,
And shape hym to amende.
For lat a dronken daffe
In a dyk falle,
Lat hym ligge, loke noght on hym,
Til hym liste aryse.   7412
For though Reson rebuked hym
It were but pure synne.   [thanne,
Ac whan nede nymeth hym up
For doute lest he sterve,
And shame shrapeth hise clothes,
And hise shynes wassheth.
Thanne woot the dronken daffe
Wherfore he is to blame."
    "Ye siggen sooth," quod I;
" Ich have y-seyen it ofte,
Ther smyt no thyng so smerte,
Ne smelleth so soure,
As shame, there he sheweth hym ;
For every man hym shonyeth.
Why ye wisse me thus," quod I,
" Was for I rebuked Reson."
    "Certes," quod he, "that is sooth ;"
And shoop hym for to walken.
And I aroos up right with that,
And folwed hym after,
And preyde hym of his curteisie
To telle me his name.   7434

"I AM Ymaginatif," quod he,
    " Ydel was I nevere,
Though I sitte by myself,
In siknesse nor in helthe.
    I have folwed thee, in feith!
Thise fyve and fourty wynter,
And manye tymes have meved thee
To thynke on thyn ende,
And how fele fernyeres are faren,
And so fewe to come ;
And of thi wilde wantownesse
Tho thow yong were,   7446
To amende it in thi middel age,
Lest myght the failled
In thyn olde elde,
That yvele kan suffre
Poverte or penaunce,
Or preyeres to bidde.
Si non in prima vigilia, nec in se-
    cunda, etc.
    "Amende thee, while thow myght ;
Thow hast ben warned ofte
With poustees of pestilences,
With poverte and with angres ;   7458

And with thise bittre baleises   7459
God beteth his deere children.
Quem diligo, castigo.
 " And David in the Sauter seith
Of swiche that loveth Jhesus :
Virga tua et baculus tuus ipsa me
    consolati sunt.   [thi staf,
 " Al though thow strike me with
With stikke or with yerde,
It is but murthe as for me,
To amende my soule.   [kynges,
And thow medlest thee with ma-
And myghtest go seye thi Sauter,
And bidde for hem that gyveth thee
For ther are bokes y-knowe [breed,
To telle men what Do-wel is,
Do-bet and Do-best bothe,
And prechours to preven what it is
Of many a peire freres."
 I seigh wel he seide me sooth ;
And som what me to excuse,
Seide Caton conforted me his sone,
That clerk though he were,   7481
To solacen hym som tyme,
As I do whan I make :
Interpone tuis interdum gaudia curis.
 " And of holy men I herde,"
" How thei outher while [quod I,
Pleyden the parfiter,
To ben in manye places,
Ac if ther were any wight
That wolde me telle
What were Do-wel and Do-bet 7492

And Do-best at the laste,   7493
Wolde I nevere do werk,
But wende to holi chirche,
And ther bidde my bedes,
But whan ich ete or slepe."
  "Poul in his pistle," quod he,
"Preveth what is Do-wel:
Fides, spes, caritas, et major horum,
    etc.
Feith, hope, and charité;
And alle ben goode,
And saven men sondry tymes; 7504
Ac noon so soone as charité.
For he dooth wel withouten doute,
That dooth as lewté techeth;
That is, if thow be man maryed,
Thi make thow lovye,
And lyve forth as lawe wole,
While ye lyven bothe.
  "Right so if thow be religious,
Ren thow nevere ferther
To Rome ne to Rochemador,
But as thi rule techeth;   7515
And hold thee under obedience,
That heigh wey is to hevene.
  "And if thow be maiden to marye,
And myght wel continue,
Seke thow nevere seint ferther
For no soule helthe.
For what made Lucifer
To lese the heighe hevene?
Or Salomon his sapience,
Or Sampson his strengthe?
Job the Jew his joye   7526

Ful deere a-boughte ; 7527
Aristotle and othere mo,
Ypocras and Virgile ;
Alisaundre, that al wan,
Elengliche ended.
Catel and kynde wit
Was combraunce to hem alle.
  "Felice hir fairnesse
Fel hire al to sclaundre ;
And Rosamounde right so,
Reufulliche to bileve,
The beauté of hir body 7538
In baddenesse she despended.
Of manye swiche I may rede,
Of men and of wommen,
That wise wordes wolde shewe,
And werche the contrarie.
Sunt homines nequam bene de virtute
    loquentes.
  "And riche renkes right so
Gaderen and sparen,
And tho men that thei moost haten
Mynistren it at the laste. 7549
And for thei suffren and see
So manye nedy folkes,
And love hem noght as oure Lord bit,
Thei lesen hir soules.
Date et dabitur vobis.
  "And richesse right so,
But if the roote be trewe.
Ac grace is a gras therof
Tho grevaunces to abate.
Ac grace ne groweth noght
But amonges lowe ; 7560

Pacience and poverte   7561
The place highte ther it groweth,
And in lele lyvynge men,
And in lif holy,
And thorugh the gifte of the Holy
As the Gospel telleth.   [Goost,
Spiritus ubi vult spirat.
    "Clergie and kynde wit
Cometh of sighte and techyng ;
As the book bereth witnesse
To burnes that kan rede.
Quod scimus loquimur, quod vidimus
        testamur.
    "Of *quod scimus* cometh clergie
And konnynge of hevene ;
And of *quod vidimus* cometh kynde
Of sighte of diverse peple.   [wit,
Ac grace is a gifte of God,
And of greet love spryngeth ;
Knew nevere clerk how it cometh
Ne kynde wit the weyes.   [forth,
Nescit aliquis unde venit, aut quo
        vadit, etc.   7583
    "Ac yet is clergie to comende,
And kynde wit bothe ;
And namely clergie, for Cristes love
That of clergie is roote.
For Moyses witnesseth that God
For to wisse the peple   [wroot
In the olde lawe, as the lettre telleth,
That was the lawe of Jewes,
That what womman were in avoutrye
Were she riche or poore,   [taken,
With stones men sholde hir strike,

And stone hire to dethe.   7595
  " A womman, as I fynde,
Was gilty of that dede.
Ac Crist of his curteisie
Thorugh clergie hir saved ;
And thorugh caractes that Crist
The Jewes knewe hemselve [wroot,
Giltier as a-fore God,
And gretter in synne,
Than the womman that there was,
And wenten awey for shame.
  " The clergie that there was,
Conforted the womman.
Holy kirke knoweth this,
That Cristes writyng saved hire.
So clergie is confort
To creatures that repenten,
And to mansede men
Meschief at hire ende.
  " For Goddes body myghte noght
Of breed, withouten clergie ; [ben
The which body is bothe
Boote to the rightfulle,   7617
And deeth and dampnacion
To hem that deyeth yvele,
As Cristes caracte confortede,
And bothe coupable shewed,
The womman that the Jewes
        broughte,
That Jhesus thoughte to save.
Polite judicare, et not judicabimini.
Right so Goddes body, bretheren,
But if it be worthili taken,
Dampneth us at the day of dome,

As the caractes dide the Jewes.
  "For-thi I counseille thee, for
      Cristes sake,
Clergie that thow lovye.
For kynde wit is of his kyn,
And neighe cosynes bothe
To oure Lord, leve me ;
For-thi love hem, I rede.
For bothe ben as mirours
To amenden oure defautes,
And lederes for lewed men
And for lettred bothe.   7638
  "For-thi lakke thow nevere logik,
Lawe ne hise custumes ;
Ne countreplede clerkes,
I counseille thee for evere.
For as a man may noght see,
That mysseth hise eighen ;
Na-moore kan no clerk,   [bokes.
But if he caughte it first thorugh
Al though men made bokes,
God was the maister,
And seint spirit the samplarie, 7649
And seide what men sholde write.
  "Right so ledeth lettrure
Lewed men to reson ;
And as a blynd man in bataille
Bereth wepne to fighte,
And hath noon hap with his ax
His enemy to hitte,
Na-moore kan a kynde witted man,
But clerkes hym teche,
Come for al his kynde wit
To cristendom, and be saved. 7660

Which is the cofre of Cristes tresor,
And clerkes kepe the keyes
To unloken it at hir likyng,
And to the lewed peple
Gyve mercy for hire mysdedes,
If men it wolde aske
Buxomliche and benigneliche,
And bidden it of Grace.
  "*Archa Dei* in the olde lawe
Levytes it kepten;
Hadde nevere lewed man leve
To leggen hond on that cheste,
But he were preest or preestes sone,
Patriark or prophete.
For clergie is kepere
Under Crist of hevene.
Was ther nevere no knyght,
But clergie hym made.
Ac kynde wit cometh
Of alle kynnes syghtes,
Of briddes and of beestes,
Of tastes of truthe and of deceites
  " Lyveris to-forn us
Useden to marke
For selkouthes that thei seighen,
Hir sones for to teche;
And helden it an heigh science
Hir wittes to knowe.
Ac thorugh hir science soothly
Was nevere no soule y-saved,
Ne broght by hir bokes
To blisse ne to joye;
For alle hir kynde knowynges
Come but of diverse sightes. 7694

"Patriarkes and prophetes   7695
Repreveden hir science,
And seiden hir wordes and hir wis-
Nas but a folye;   [domes
And to the clergie of Crist
Counted it but a trufle.
*Sapientia hujus mundi stultitia est
        apud Deum.*
"For the heighe Holy Goost
Hevene shal to-cleve,
And love shall lepen out after
Into the lowe erthe;   7706
And clennesse shal cacchen it,
And clerkes shullen it fynde.
Pastores loquebantur ad invicem.
"He speketh there of riche men
Ne of right witty,   [right noght,
Ne of lordes that were lewed men,
But of the hyeste lettred oute.
Ibant magi ab oriente.
"If any frere were founde there,
I gyve thee fyve shillynges;
Ne in none burgeises cote   7717
Was that barn born;
But in a burgeises place
Of Bethlem the beste.
*Sed non erat ei locus in diversorio, et
        pauper non habet diversorium.*
"To pastours and to poetes
Appered the aungel,
And bad hem go to Bethlem
Goddes burthe to honoure;
And songe a song of solas,
Gloria in excelsis Deo!   7728

" Clerkes knewen it wel,   7729
And comen with hir presentz,
And diden homage honurably
To hym that was almyghty.
" Why I have tolde al this,
I took ful good hede
How thow contrariedest Clergie
With crabbede wordes,
How that lewde men lightloker
Than lettrede were saved,
Than clerkes or kynde witted men
Of cristene peple ;   7740
And thow seidest sooth of somme,
Ac se in what manere.
" Tak two stronge men,
And in Themese cast hem,
And bothe naked as a nedle,
Her noon sikerer than oother ;
That oon hath konnynge and kan
Swymmen and dyven ;
That oother is lewed of that labour,
That lerned nevere swymme ;
Which trowestow of tho two   7751
That is in moost drede ?
He that nevere ne dyved,
Ne noght kan of swymmyng ?
Or the swymmere that is saaf
By so hymself like,
Ther his felawe fleteth forth
As the flood liketh,
And is in drede to drenche,
That nevere dide swymme ? "
" That swymme kan noght," I
" It semeth to my wittes." [seide,

"Right so," quod the renk.   7763
" Reson it sheweth,
That he that knoweth clergie
Kan sonner arise
Out of synne, and be saaf,
Though he synne ofte,
If hym liketh and lest,
Than any lewed leelly.
For if the clerk be konnynge,
He knoweth what is synne,   [sion
And how contricion withoute confes-
Conforteth the soule ;   7774
As thow seest in the Sauter,
In Salmes oon or tweyne,
How contricion is comended,
For it cacheth awey synne.
Beati quorum remissæ sunt iniqui-
     tates, et quorum tecta sunt, etc.
"And this conforteth ech a clerk,
And covereth hym fro wanhope.
In which flood the fend
Fondeth a man hardest.
Ther the lewed lith stille,   7785
And loketh after lente, [to shrifte,
And hath no contricion er he come
And thanne kan he litel telle,
But as his lores-man lereth hym
Bileveth and troweth ;   [preest,
And that is after person or parissh
The whiche ben peraventure
Unkonnynge to lere lewed men,
As Luc bereth witnesse :
Dum cæcus ducit cæcum, etc.
" Wo was hym marked   7796

That wade moot with the lewed !
Wel may the barn blesse that man
That hym to book sette,
That lyvynge after lettrure
Saveth hym lif and soule.
Dominus pars hereditatis meæ,
Is a murye verset,
That hath take fro Tybourne
Twenty stronge theves ;
Ther lewed theves ben lolled up,
Loke how thei be saved.

  "The thef that hadde grace of God
On Good-friday, as thow spekest,
Was for he yald hym creaunt to
      Crist on the cros,
And knewliched hym gilty,
And grace asked of God,
That to graunten it is redy
To hem that buxomliche biddeth it,
And ben in wille to amenden.
Ac though that theef hadde hevene,
He hadde noon heigh blisse,
As seint Johan and othere seintes
That deserved hadde bettre.

  "Right as som man yeve me mete,
And a-mydde the floor sette me,
And hadde mete moore than y-
      nough,
Ac noght so muche worshipe
As tho that seten at the syde table,
Or with the sovereynes of the halle ;
But sete as a beggere bord-lees
By myself on the grounde.
So it fareth by that felon

That a Good-friday was saved.   7829
He sit neither with seint Johan,
Symond ne Jude,
Ne with maydenes ne with martires,
Confessours ne wydewes ;
But by hymself as a soleyn,
And served on erthe.
For he that is ones a thef
Is evere moore in daunger,
And, as lawe liketh,
To lyve or to deye.
De peccato propitiato, noli esse sine
       metu.
And for to serven a seint
And swich a thef togideres,
It were neither reson ne right
To rewarde hem bothe y-liche.

  " And right as Trojanus the trewe
Dwelte noght depe in helle, [knyght
That oure Lord ne hadde hym lightly
So leve I the thef be in hevene. [out,
For he is in the loweste of hevene,
If oure bileve be trewe ;   7851
And wel loselly he lolleth there,
By the lawe of holy chirche.
Qui reddit unicuique juxta opera
       sua, etc.
  " And why that oon theef on the
Creaunt hym yald   [cros
Rather than that oother theef,
Though thow woldest appose,
Alle the clerkes under Crist
Ne kouthe the skile assoille.
Quare placuit, quia voluit.   7862

" And so I seye by thee   7863
That sekest after the whyes,
And a-resonedest Reson
A rebukynge as it were ;
And of the floures in the fryth,
And of hire faire hewes,
Wherof thei cacche hir colours
So clere and so brighte ;
And willest of briddes and of beestes,
And of hir bredyng, to knowe,
Why some be a-lough and some a-
Thi likyng it were ;   [loft,
And of the stones and of the sterres
Thow studiest, as I leve ;
How evere beest outher brid
Hath so breme wittes.

" Clergie ne kynde wit
Ne knew nevere the cause ;
Ac kynde knoweth the cause hym-
And no creature ellis.   [self,
He is the pies patron,
And putteth it in hir ere
There the thorn is thikkest   7885
To buylden and brede.
And kynde kenned the pecok
To cauken in swich a kynde ;
And kenned Adam
To knowe his pryvé membres,
And taughte hym and Eve
To helien hem with leves.

" Lewed men many tymes
Maistres thei apposen,
Why Adam ne hiled noght first
His mouth that eet the appul,   7896

Rather than his likame a-logh ;
Lewed asken thus clerkes.
   " Kynde knoweth whi he dide so,
Ac no clerk ellis,
Ac of briddes and of beestes
Men by olde tyme
Ensamples token and termes,
As telleth the poetes ;
And that the faireste fowel
Foulest engendreth,
And feblest fowel of flight is
That fleeth or swymmeth ;   7908
And that the pecok and the pehen
Proude riche men bitokneth ;
For the pecok, and men pursue hym,
May noght flee heighe,
For the trailynge of his tail
Overtaken is he soone,
And his flessh is foul flessh,
And his feet bothe,
And un-lovelich of ledene,
And looth for to here.
   " Right so the riche,   7919
If he his richesse kepe,
And deleth it noght til his deeth-day,
The tail of alle sorwe
Right so as the pennes of the pecok
Peyneth hym in his flight.
So is possession peyne
Of pens and of nobles,
To alle hem that it holdeth,
Til hir tail be plukked.   [thanne
   " And though the riche repente
And bi-rewe the tyme   7930

That evere he gadered so grete, 7931
And gaf therof so litel ;
Though he crye to Crist thanne
With kene wil, I leve,
His ledene be in oure Lordes ere
Like a pies chiteryng.
And whan his caroyne shal come
In cave to be buryed,
I leve it flawme ful foule
The fold al aboute,
And alle the othere ther it lith
Envenymeth thorugh his attre.
    " By the po feet is understande,
As I have lerned in Avynet,
Executours false frendes
That fulfille noght his wille
That was writen and thei witnesse
To werche right as it wolde.
Thus the poete preveth that the pecok
For hise fetheres is reverenced,
Right so is the riche
By reson of hise goodes.
    " The larke, that is a lasse fowel,
Is moore lovelich of ledene,
And wel a wey of wynge
Swifter than the pecok,
And of flessh by fele fold
Fatter and swetter ;
To lowe libbynge men
The larke is resembled.
    " Aristotle the grete clerk
Swiche tales he telleth.
Thus he likneth in his logik
The leeste fowel oute,   7964

And wheither he be saaf or noght
The sothe woot no clergie,   [saaf
Ne of Sortes ne of Salomon
No scripture kan telle.
Ac God is so good, I hope,
That siththe he gaf hem wittes
To wissen us weyes therwith
That wissen us to be saved,
And the bettre for hir bokes
To bidden we ben holden,
That God for his grace
Gyve hir soules reste.   7976
For lettred men were lewed men yet,
Ne were loore of hir bokes."

  "Alle thise clerkes," quod I tho,
"That in Crist leven,
Seyen in hir sermons
That neither Sarsens ne Jewes
Ne no creature of Cristes liknesse
Withouten cristendom worth saved."

  "*Contra*," quod Ymaginatif thoo,
And comsed for to loure ;
And seide "*Salvabitur*   7987
*Vix justus in die judicii.
Ergo salvabitur*," quod he,
And seide na-moore Latyn.

  "Trojanus was a trewe knyght,
And took nevere Cristendom,
And he is saaf, so seith the book,
And his soule in hevene.
For ther is fullynge of font,
And fullynge in blood shedyng,
And thorugh fir is fullyng,
And that is ferme bileve.   7998

Advenit ignis divinus non combu-
    rens, sed illuminans, etc.
  "Ac   Truthe   that   trespased
    nevere,
Ne traversed ayeins his lawe,
But lyveth as his lawe techeth,
And leveth ther be no bettre;
And if ther were, he wolde amende,
And in swich wille deieth,
Ne wolde nevere trewe god,
But truthe were allowed, [worth,
And wheither it be worth or noght
The bileve is gret of truthe,   8010
And an hope hangynge therinne
To have a mede for his truthe.
For *Deus dicitur quasi dans vitam*
    æternam suis, hoc est fidelibus.
    Et alibi: Si ambulavero in
    medio umbræ mortis.
  "The glose graunteth upon that vers
A greet mede to Truthe,
And wit and wisdom," quod that wye,
" Was som tyme tresor
To kepe with a commune,   8021
No catel was holde bettre,
And muche murthe and manhod; "
And right with that he vanysshed.

ND I awaked therwith   8025
Wit-lees ner-hande,
And as a freke that fre were
Forth gan I walke
In manere of a mendinaunt
Many a yer after,
And of this metyng many tyme
Muche thought I hadde.
    First how Fortune me failed
At my mooste nede ;
And how that Elde manaced me,
Myghte we evere mete ;   8036
And how that freres folwede
Folk that was riche,
And folk that was povere
At litel pris thei sette ;
And no corps in hir kirk-yerde
Nor in his kirk was buryed,
But quik he biquethe aught
To quyte with hir dettes ;
And how this Coveitise over-com
Clerkes and preestes ;
And how that lewed men ben lad,
But oure Lord hem helpe,   8048

Thorugh un-konnynge curatours,
To incurable peynes.
  And how that Ymaginatif
In dremels me tolde
Of Kynde and of his konnynge,
And how curteis he is to bestes,
And how lovynge he is to briddes
On londe and on watre.
Leneth he no lif
Lasse ne moore.
The creatures that crepen
Of kynde ben engendred.   8060
And sithen how Ymaginatif seide,
Vix salvabitur;
And whan he hadde seid so,
How sodeynliche he passed.
  I lay doun longe in this thoght,
And at the laste I slepte.
And as Crist wolde, ther com Con-
To conforte me that tyme, [science
And bad me come to his court,
With Clergie sholde I dyne;
And for Conscience of Clergie spak,
I com wel the rather.
And there I seigh a maister,
What man he was I nyste,
That lowe louted
And loveliche to Scripture.
  Conscience knew hym wel,
And welcomed hym faire.
Thei wesshen and wipeden,
And wenten to the dyner.
And Pacience in the paleis stood
In pilgrymes clothes,   8082

And preyde mete *par charité*   8083
For a povere heremyte.
  Conscience called hym in,
And curteisliche seide,
" Welcome ! wye ; go and wasshe ;
Thow shalt sitte soone."
  This maister was maad sitte,
As for the mooste worthi.
And thanne Clergie and Conscience
And Pacience cam after.
  Pacience and I
Were put to be macches,   8094
And seten bi oureselve
At the side borde.
  Conscience called after mete ;
And thanne cam Scripture,
And served hem thus soone
Of soundry metes manye,
Of Austyn, of Ambrose,
And of the foure Euvangelistes,
Edentis et bibentis quæ apud eos
    sunt.
  Ac this maister nor his man   8105
No maner flesshe eten ;
Ac thei eten mete of moore cost,
Mortrews and potages
Of that men mys-wonne
Thei made hem wel at ese.
Ac hir sauce was over sour,
And unsavourly grounde
In a morter *post mortem*
Of many a bitter peyne,
But if thei synge for tho soules,
And wepe salte teris.   8116

*Vos qui peccata hominum comeditis,
nisi pro eis lacrimas et ora-
tiones effunderitis, ea quæ in
deliciis comeditis, in tormentis
evometis.*

Conscience ful curteisly tho
Comaunded Scripture
Bifore Pacience breed to brynge
And me that was his macche.
He sette a sour loof to-forn us,
And seide, "*agite pœnitentiam.*"
"As longe," quod I, "as I lyve,
And lycame may dure."
"Here is propre service," quod
    Pacience,
"Ther fareth no prince bettre,"
    And thanne he broughte us forth
    a mees of oother mete,
Of *Miserere mei, Deus,*   [*quorum,*
And he broughte us of *Beati*
Of *Beatus-virres* makyng.
Et quorum tecta sunt peccata in a
    disshe,   [*tibi.*
Of derne shrifte *Dixi et confitebor*
"Bryng Pacience som pitaunce,"
Pryveliche quod Conscience.
    And thanne hadde Pacience a
    pitaunce.
*Pro hac orabit ad te omnis sanctus
    in tempore oportuno.*
And Conscience conforted us,
And carped us murye tales.
*Cor contritum et humiliatum Deus
    non despicies.*

Pacience was proud   8147
Of that propre service,
And made hym murthe with his
Ac I mornede evere,   [mete ;
For this doctour on the heighe dees
Drank wyn so faste.
Væ vobis qui potentes estis ad bi-
    bendum vinum !
He eet manye sondry metes,
Mortrews and puddynges,
Wombe-cloutes and wilde brawen,
And egges y-fryed with grece.
     Thanne seide I to myself so
Pacience it herde,
" It is noght foure dayes that this
Bifore the deen of Poules   [freke
Preched of penaunces
That Poul the apostle suffrede,
In fame et frigore
And flappes of scourges."
Ter cæsus sum, et a Judeis quinquies
        quadragenas, etc.
     Ac o word thei over-huppen
At ech a tyme that thei preche,
That Poul in his Pistle
To al the peple tolde :
Periculum est in falsis fratribus.
     Holi writ bit men be war,
I wol noght write it here
In Englisshe, on aventure
It sholde be reherced to ofte,
And greve therwith goode men,
Ac gramariens shul redde.
Unusquisque a fratre se custodiat,

*quia, ut dicitur, periculum est
in falsis fratribus.*
  Ac I wiste nevere freke that as a
    frere yede
Bifore men on Euglisshe
Taken it for his teme,
And telle it withouten glosyng.
They prechen that penaunce is
Profitable to the soule,
And what meschief and *male ese*
Crist for man tholede.
  " Ac this Goddes gloton," quod I,
" With hise grete chekes,
Hath no pité on us povere,
He perfourneth yvele ;
That he precheth he preveth noght,"
To Pacience I tolde,
And wisshed ful witterly,
With wille ful egre,
That disshes and doublers
Bifore this ilke doctour
Were molten leed in his mawe,
And Mahoun amyddes.   8202
" I shal jangle to this jurdan
With his juste wombe,
To telle me what penaunce is,
Of which he preched rather."
  Pacience   perceyved   what   I
    thoughte,
And wynked on me to be stille,
And seide, " Thow shalt see thus
    soone,
Whan he may na-moore,
He shal have a penaunce in his
    paunche,   8211

And puffe at ech a worde ;   8212
And thanne shullen his guttes go-
And he shal galpen after.   [thele,
For now he hath dronken so depe,
He wole devyne soone,
And preven it by hir Pocalips
And passion of seint Avereys,
That neither bacon ne brauu,
Blancmanger ne mortrews,
Is neither fissh nor flesshe,
But fode for a penaunt   [Trinité,
And thanne shal he testifie of the
And take his felawe to witnesse,
What he fond in a frayel,
After a freres lyvyng ;
And but he first lyve be lesyng,
Leve me nevere after.
And thanne is tyme to take,
And to appose this doctour
Of Do-wel and Do-bet,
And if Do-wel be any penaunce."

    And I sat stille, as Pacience seide,
And thus soone this doctour,   8234
As rody as a rose,
Rubbede hise chekes,
Coughed and carped ;
And Conscience hym herde,
And tolde hym of a Trinité,
And toward us he loked. [quod I,
  " What is Do-wel, sire doctour?"
" Is it any penaunce ?"
  " Do-wel," quod this doctour,
And took the cuppe and drank,
" Is do noon yvel to thyn even-
    cristen   8245

Nought by thi power."   [quod I,
  "By this day! sire doctour,"
"Thanne be ye noght in Do-wel;
For ye han harmed us two,
In that ye eten the puddyng,
Mortrews and oother mete,
And we no morsel hadde.
And if ye fare so in youre fermerye,
Ferly me thynketh,
But cheeste be ther charité sholde be.
And yonge children dorste pleyne,
I wolde permute my penaunce with
      youre,   8257
For I am in point to Do-wel."
  Thanne Conscience curteisly
A countenaunce made,
And preynte upon Pacience
To preie me to be stille;
And seide hymself, " Sire doctour,
And it be youre wille,
What is Do-wel and Do-bet,
Ye dyvynours knoweth."
  " Do-wel," quod this doctour,
" Do as clerkes techeth;
And Do-bet is he that techeth,
And travailleth to teche othere;
And Do-best doth hymself so,
As he seith and precheth."
Qui facit et docuerit, magnus voca-
      bitur in regno cœlorum.
  "Now thow, Clergie," quod Con-
" Carpest what is Do-wel. [science,
I have sevene sones," he seide,
" Serven in a castel,   8278

Ther the lord of lif wonyeth,   8279
To leren what is Do-wel ;
Til I se tho sevene
And myself acorde,
I am un-hardy," quod he,
"To any wight to preven it.
For oon Piers the Plowman
Hath impugned us alle,
And set alle sciences at a sope,
Save love one ;
And no text ne taketh
To mayntene his cause,   8290
But *Dilige Deum*,
And *Domine quis habitabit.*
And seith that Do-wel and Do-bet
Arn two infinités,
Whiche infinités, with a feith !
Fynden out Do-best,
Which shal save mannes soule ;
Thus seith Piers the Plowman."

  " I kan noght heron," quod Con-
" Ac I knowe wel Piers ; [science,
He wol noght ayein holy writ spoken,
I dar wel undertake.
Thanne passe we over til Piers come,
And preve this in dede.
Pacience hath be in many place,
And peraunter mouthed
That no clerk ne kan,
As Crist bereth witnesse :
Patientes vincunt, etc."   [tho,

  "Ac youre preiere," quod Pacience
" So no man displese hym.
Disce," quo he, "*Doce*,   8312

Dilige inimicos.　　　　　　8313
Disce, and Do-wel;
Doce, and Do-bet;
Dilige, and Do-best;
Thus taughte me ones
A lemman that I lovede,
Love was hir name:　　[quod she,
" With wordes and with werkes,"
" And wil of thyn herte,
Thow love leelly thi soule
Al thi lif tyme,
And so thow lere the to lovye,
For oure Lordes love of hevene,
Thyn enemy in alle wise
Evene forth with thiselve.
Cast coles on his heed
Of alle kynde speche,
Bothe with werkes and with wordes
Fonde his love to wynne;
And leye on him thus with love,
Til he laughe on the.
And but he bowe for this betyng,
Blynd mote he worthe.　　　8335
　　"Ac for to fare thus with thi frend,
Folie it were.
For he that loveth thee leelly,
Litel of thyne coveiteth.
Kynde love coveiteth noght
No catel but speche.
With halfe a laumpe lyne,
In Latyn, *Ex vi transitionis,*
I bere therinne aboute
Faste y-bounde Do-wel,
In a signe of the Saterday　　8346

That sette first the kalender,   8347
And al the wit of the Wodnesday
Of the nexte wike after,
The myddel of the moone,
As the nyght of bothe,
And herwith am I welcome
Ther I have it with me,
  "Undo it, lat this doctour deme
If Do-wel be therinne.
For, by hym that me made!
Myghte nevere poverte
Misese ne meschief,   8353
Ne no man with his tonge,
Coold ne care,
Ne compaignye of theves,
Ne neither hete ne hayl,
Ne noon helle pouke,
Ne fuyr ne flood,
Ne feere of thyn enemy,
Tene thee any tyme,
And thow take it with the.
Caritas nihil timet, etc."
  "It is but a dido," quod this doc-
"A disours tale;   [tour,
Al the wit of this world,
And wight mennes strengthe,
Kan noght conformen a pees
Bitwene and hise enemys,
Ne bitwene two cristene kynges
Kan no wight pees make
Profitable to either peple;"
And putte the table fro hym,
And took Clergie and Conscience
To conseil, as it were,   8360

That Pacience thow most passe,
For pilgrymes konne wel lye."
  Ac Conscience carped loude,
And curteisliche seide,
"Frendes, fareth wel ;"
And faire spak to Clergie,
"For I wol go with this gome,
If God wol yeve me grace,
And be pilgrym with Pacience,
Til I have preved moore."
  "What !" quod Clergie to Con-
"Ar ye coveitous nouthe [science,
After yeres-geves, or giftes,
Or yernen to rede redels ?
I shal brynge yow a Bible,
A book of the olde lawe,
And lere yow, if yow like,
The leeste point to knowe,
That Pacience the pilgrym
Parfitly knew nevere."   [science
  "Nay, by Crist !" quod Con-
To Clergie, "God thee for-yelde ;
For al that Pacience me profreth
Proud am I litel.
Ac the wil of the wye,
And the wil of folk here,
Hath meved my mood
To moorne for my synnes.
The goode wil of a wight
Was nevere bought to the fulle.
For ther nys no tresour, for sothe,
To a trewe wille.
  "Hadde   noght   Maudeleyne
For a box of salve,   [moore

Than Zacheus for he seide   8415
Dimidium   bonorum   meorum   do
    pauperibus?
And the poore widewe
For a peire of mytes,
Than alle tho that offrede
Into *gazophilacium?*"
    Thus curteisliche Conscience
Congeyed first the frere,
And sithen softeliche he seide
In Clergies ere,
" Me were levere, by oure Lord !
And I lyve sholde,
Have pacience perfitliche,
Than half thi pak of bokes."
    Clergie of Conscience
No congie wolde take,
But seide ful sobreliche,
" Thow shalt se the tyme
Whan thow art wery of-walked,
Wille me to counseille."
    "That is sooth," quod Con-
" So me God helpe !   [science,
If Pacience be oure partyng felawe,
And pryvé with us bothe,
Ther nys wo in this world
That we ne sholde amende,
And conformen kynges to pees,
And alle kynnes londes ;
Sarsens and Surré,
And so forth alle the Jewes,
Turne into the trewe feith,
And intil oon bileve."
    " That is sooth," quod Clergie,

" I se what thow menest ; 8449
I shal dwelle as I do,
My devoir to shewe,
And confermen fauntekyns,
And oother folk y-lered,
Til Pacience have preved thee,
And parfit thee maked."
  Conscience tho with Pacience
Pilgrymes as it were. [passed,
Thanne hadde Pacience, as pil-
In his poke vitailles, [grymes han,
Sobretee and symple speche, 8460
And soothfast bileve,
To conforte hym and Conscience,
If thei come in place
There un-kyndenesse and coveitise is,
Hungry contrees bothe.
  And as the wente by the weye,
Of Do-wel thei carped ;
Thei mette with a mynstral,
As me tho thoughte.
Pacience apposed hym first.
And preyde he sholde hem telle
To Conscience what craft he kouthe,
And to what contree he wolde.
  " I am a mynstrall," quod that
" My name is *Activa-vita ;* [man,
Al ydelnesse ich hatie,
For of actif is my name ;
A wafrer, wol ye wite,
And serve manye lordes,
And fewe robes I fonge,
Or furrede gownes.
Couthe I lye to do men laughe,

Thanne lacchen I sholde   8483
Outher mantel or moneie
Amonges lordes or mynstrals.
Ac for I kan neither taboure ne
Ne telle no gestes,   [trompe,
Farten ne fithelen
At festes, ne harpen,
Jape ne jogele,
Ne gentilliche pipe,
Ne neither saille ne saute,
Ne synge with the gyterne,
I have no goode giftes   8494
Of thise grete lordes.
For no breed that I brynge forth,
Save a benyson on the Sonday
Whan the preest preieth the peple
Hir pater-noster to bidde
For Piers the Plowman,
And that hym profit waiten ;
And that am I actif,
That ydelnesse hatie ;
For alle trewe travaillours
And tiliers of the erthe,   8505
Fro Mighelmesse to Mighelmesse
I fynde hem with my wafres.
  " Beggeris and bidderis
Of my breed craven,
Faitours and freres,
And folk with brode crounes.
I fynde payn for the pope,
And provendre for his palfrey ;
And I hadde nevere of hym,
Have God my trouthe !
Neither provendre ne personage

Yet of popes gifte,   8517
Save a pardon with a peis of leed
And two polles amyddes.
Hadde ich a clerc that couthe write,
I wolde caste hym a bille,
That he sente me under his seel
A salve for the pestilence,
And that his blessynge and hise
Bocches myghte destruye.   [bulles
In nomine meo dæmonia ejicient, et
    super ægros manus imponent, et
    bene habebunt.   8528
  "And thanne wolde I be prest to
Paast for to make,   [the peple
And buxom and busy
Aboute breed and drynke
For hym and for alle hise,
Founde I that his pardon
Mighte lechen a man,
As I bileve it sholde.
For sith he hath the power
That Peter hymself hadde,
He hath the pot with the salve,
Soothly as me thynketh.
Argentum et aurum non est mihi;
    quod autem habeo tibi do: in
    nomine Domini surge et am-
    bula.
  "Ac if myght of myracle hym faille,
It is for men ben noght worthi
To have the grace of God,
And no gilt of pope.
For may no blessynge doon us boote,
But if we wile amende,   8530

Ne mannes masse make pees   8551
Among cristene peple,
Til pride be pureliche for-do,
And thorugh payn defaute.
For er I have breed of mele,
Oft moot I swete ;   [y-nough,
And er the commune have corn
Many a cold morwenyng.
So er my wafres be y-wroght,
Muche wo I tholye.
   " At Londone, I leve,
Liketh wel my wafres ;   8562
And louren whan thei lakken hem.
It is noght long y-passed,
There was a careful commune,
Whan no cart com to towne
With breed fro Stratforde ;
Tho gonnen beggeris wepe,
And werkmen were agast a lite ;
This wole be thought longe.
In the date of oure Drighte,
In a drye Aprille,
A thousand and thre hundred   8573
Twies twenty and ten,
My wafres there were gesene
Whan Chichestre was maire."
   I took good kepe, by Crist !
And Conscience bothe,
Of Haukyn the actif man,
And how he was y-clothed.
He hadde a cote of Cristendom,
As holy kirke bileveth ;
Ac it was moled in many places
With manye sondry plottes ;   8584

Of pride here a plot,   8585
And there a plot of unbuxome speche,
Of scornyng and of scoffyng,
And of unskilful berynge,
As in apparaill and in porte
Proud amonges the peple,
Oother wise than he hym hath
With herte or sighte shewynge,
Hym willyng that alle men wende
He were that he is noght.
For-why he bosteth and braggeth
With manye bolde othes,   8596
And inobedient to ben undernome
Of any lif lyvynge;
And noon so singuler by hymself,
Ne so pomp holy,
Y-habited as an heremyte,
An ordre by hymselve,
Religion saunz rule
Or resonable obedience,
Lakkynge lettrede men
And lewed men bothe
In likynge of lele lif,   8607
And a liere in soule,
With inwit and with outwit
Ymagynen and studie,
As best for his body be
To have a badde name,
And entremetten hym over al
Ther he hath noght to doone,
Willynge that men wende
His wit were the beste.   [gomes,
And if he gyveth ought to povere
Telle what he deleth,   8618

Povere of possession in purs   8619
And in cofre bothe.
And as a lyoun on to loke,
And lordlich of speche,
Boldest of beggeris,
A bostere that noght hath,
In towne and in tavernes
Tales to telle,   [seigh,
And segge thyng that he nevere
And for sothe sweren it,
Of dedes that he nevere dide
Demen and bosten   8630
And of werkes that he wel dide
Witnesse, and siggen—
"Lo! if ye leve me noght,
Or that I lye wenen,
Asketh at hym or at hym,
And he yow kan telle
What I suffrede and seigh
And som tymes hadde,
And what I kouthe and knew,
And what kyn I com of."
Al he wolde that men wiste   8641
Of werkes and of wordes
Which myghte plese the peple,
And preisen hymselve.
Si hominibus placerem, Christi
    servus non essem.   Et alibi:
    Nemo potest duobus dominis
    servire.

    " By Crist!" quod Conscience tho,
" Thi beste cote, Haukyn,
Hath manye moles and spottes,
It moste ben y-wasshe."   8652

"Ye, who so toke hede," quod
"Bihynde and bifore,   [Haukyn,
What on bak and what on body half,
And by the two sydes,
Men sholde fynde manye frounces,
And manye foule plottes."
    And he torned hym as tyd,
And thanne took I hede,
It was fouler bi fele fold
Than it first semed.
It was bi-dropped with wrathe
And wikkede wille,   SGG4
With envye and yvel speche,
Entisynge to fighte,
Liynge and laughynge,
And leve tonge to chide,
Al that he wiste wikked
By any wight tellen it,
And blame men bihynde hir bak,
And bidden hem meschaunce,
And that he wiste by Wille
Tellen it Watte,
And that Watte wiste   S675
Wille wiste it after,
And make of frendes foes
Thorugh a fals tonge,
Or with myght or with mouth,
Or thorugh mennes strengthe
Avenge me fele tymes,
Other frete myselve
Withinne as a shepsteres shere,
Y-sherewed man and cursed.
*Cujus maledictione os plenum est
    et amaritudine, sub lingua ejus*

labor et dolor. Et alibi : Filii
hominum, dentes eorum arma
et sagittæ, et lingua eorum
gladius acutus.
"Ther is no lif that me loveth
Lastynge any while ;
For tales that I telle,
No man trusteth to me.
And whan I may noght have the
Swich malencolie I take, [maistrie,
That I cacche the crampe,
And the cardiacle som tyme,   8698
Or an ague in swich an angre,
And som tyme a fevere
That taketh me al a twelve monthe,
Til that I despise
Lechecraft of oure Lord,
And leve on a wicche,
And seye that no clerc ne kan,
Ne Crist, as I leve,
To the soutere of Southwerk,
Or of Shordyche dame Emme ;
And seye that no Goddes word
Gaf me nevere boote,
But thorugh a charme hadde I
And my chief heele."   [chaunce
   I waitede wisloker,
And thanne was it soilled
With likynge of lecherie,
As by lokynge of his eighe.
For ech a maide that he mette
He made hire a signe
Semynge to synne-warde,
And some tyme he gan taste   8720

Aboute the mouth, or bynethe 8721
Bigynneth to grope,
Til eitheres wille wexeth kene,
And to the werke yeden,
As wel in fastyngdayes and Fridaies
As forboden nyghtes,
And as wel in Lente as out of Lente,
Alle tymes y-liche.
Swiche werkes with hem
Were nevere out of seson,
Til thei myghte na-moore ;
And thanne murye tales,   8732
And how that lecchours lovye
Laughen and japen,
And of hir harlotrye and horedom
In hir elde tellen.
   Thanne Pacience perceyved
Of pointes of this cote,
That were colomy thorugh coveitise
And unkynde desiryng ;
Moore to good than to God
The gome his love caste,
And ymagynede how   8743
He it myghte have
With false mesures and met,
And with fals witnesse ;
Lened for love of the wed,
And looth to do truthe ;
And awaited thorugh which
Wey to bigile,
And menged his marchaundise,
And made a good moustre ;
" The worste withinne was,
A greet wit I let it,   8754

And if my neghebore hadde any
Or any beest ellis,   [hyne.
Moore profitable than myn,
Manye sleightes I made
How I myghte have it,
Al my wit I caste.
And but I it hadde by oother wey,
At the laste I stale it;
Or priveliche his purs shook,
And unpikede hise lokes;
Or by nyghte or by daye
Aboute was ich evere,   8766
Thorugh gile to gaderen
The good that ich have.
    "If I yede to the plowgh,
I pynched so narwe,
That a foot lond or a forow
Fecchen I wolde
Of my nexte neghebore,
And nymen of his erthe.
And if I repe, over-reche,
Of yaf hem reed that ropen
To seise to me with hir sikel   8777
That I ne sew nevere.
    "And who so borwed of me,
A-boughte the tyme
With presentes prively,
Or paide som certeyn;
So he wolde or noght wolde,
Wynnen I wolde,
And bothe to kith and to kyn
Unkynde of that ich hadde.
    "And who so cheped my chaffare,
Chiden I wolde,   8788

But he profrede to paic   8789
A peny or tweyne
Moore than it was worth;
And yet wolde I swere
That it coste me muche moore,
And swoor manye othes.
  "On holy daies at holy chirche
Whan ich herde masse,
Hadde I nevere wille, woot God,
Witterly to biseche
Mercy for my mysdedes,
That I ne moorned moore   8800
Nor losse of good, leve me,
Than for my likames giltes.
As if I hadde dedly synne doon,
I dredde noght that so soore,
As when I lened, and leved it lost,
Or longe er it were paied.
So if I kidde any kyndenesse
Myn even cristen to helpe,
Upon a cruwel coveitise
Myn herte gan hange.
  "And if I sente over see   8811
My servauntz to Brugges,
Or into Pruce-lond my prentis,
My profit to waiten,
To marchaunden with moneie,
And maken hire eschaunges,
Mighte nevere me conforte.
In the mene while
Neither masse ne matynes,
No none maner sightes;
Ne nevere penaunce perfournede,
Ne pater-noster seide,   8822

That my mynde ne was moore 8823
On my good in a doute,
Than in the grace of God,
And hise grete helpes.
Ubi thesaurus tuus, ibi et cor tuum.
  "Whiche ben the braunches
That bryngen a man to sleuthe?
He that moorneth noght for hise
Ne maketh no sorwe,   [mysdedes,
And penaunce that the preest en-
Perfourneth yvele,   [joyneth
Dooth noon almesse,   8834
Dred hym of no synne,
Lyveth ayein the bileve,
And no lawe holdeth,
Ech day is holy day with hym,
Or an heigh ferye;
And, if he aught wole here,
It is an harlotes tonge.
Whan men carpen of Crist,
Or of clennesse of soules,
He wexeth wroth and wol noght here
But wordes of murthe;   8845
Penaunce of povere men,
And the passion of seintes,
He hateth to here therof,
And alle that it telleth.
Thise ben the braunches, beth war,
That bryngen a man to wanhope.
  "Ye lordes and ladies,
And legates of holy chirche,
That fedeth fooles sages,
Flatereris and lieris,
And han likynge to lithen hem

To do yow to laughe, 8857
Vœ vobis qui ridetis, etc.
And gyveth hem mete and mede,
And povere men refuse ;
In youre deeth deyinge,
I drede me ful soore
Lest tho thre manner men
To muche sorwe yow brynge.
Consentientes et agentes pari pœna
        punientur.
  "Patriarkes and prophetes,
And prechours of Goddes wordes,
Saven thorugh hir sermons
Mannes soule fro helle.
Right so flatereris and fooles
Arn the fendes disciples
To entice men thorugh hir tales
To synne and to harlotrie.
Ac clerkes, that knowen holy writ,
Sholde kenne lordes
What David seith of swiche men,
As the Sauter telleth.
Non habitabit in medio domus meœ,
        qui facit superbiam, et qui
        loquitur iniqua.
  "Sholde noon harlot have au-
In halle nor in chambre,   [dience
Ther wise men were,
Witnesseth Goddes wordes,
Ne no mys-proud man
Amonges lordes ben allowed.
  "Ac flaterers and fooles
Thorugh hir foule wordes
Leden tho that loven hem   8890

To Luciferis feste,   1698
With *Turpiloquio,* a lady of sorwe,
And Luciferis fithele."
Thus Haukyn the actif man
Hadde y-soiled his cote,
Til Conscience acouped hym therof
In a curteis manere,
Why he ne hadde whasshen it,
Or wiped it with a brusshe.   1699